Blood is Thicker than Money

Magnolia Bluff Crime Chronicles, Book 38

Joe Congel

Blood is Thicker than Money: Magnolia Bluff Crime Chronicles

Copyright © 2025 Joseph A Congel

All rights reserved. No part of this book may be reproduced, stored in a retrieval program, or transmitted by any form or by any means, electronic or mechanical, including photocopying, recording, or conveyed via the internet or a website or otherwise except as may be expressly permitted by the applicable copyright statutes or in writing by the author and publisher.

The name of the town, the name of any business within Magnolia Bluff, and the names of all characters are the sole property of the Underground Authors. To utilize any of the aforesaid names, places, characters, an author must be an active member of the Underground Authors.

Book Cover Design:
Crispian Thurlborn
WYLDWOOD BOOKS
Bespoke Book Designs and Services
Wyldwoodpress.com - info@wyldwoodpress.com

Blood is Thicker than Money is a work of fiction. Names, characters, places, and incidents are either the product of the author's imagination or are used fictitiously. Any resemblance to actual persons, living or dead, or events is entirely incidental.

For Rita & Frank... as always

CHAPTER ONE

Brandon Turner sat on the end of his dock, staring out over the lake. His feet dangled down in front of him, his toes breaking the water's smooth surface. Leaning back, he cast the line from his fishing pole about twenty feet out into the lake and slowly cranked back the reel. He positioned his finger under the line so he could feel anything that might tug on the chunk of bait he'd attached to the hook.

It was a gorgeous Tuesday morning in mid-July. He could already feel the hot Texas sun heating up the top of his head.

Jason glanced over from where he was sitting and grinned. "You know, Brandon, you should rub a little of mom's suntan lotion into your scalp. Might prevent the direct beam of the sun from drying it out and setting your hair on fire. Nobody wants to smell that."

Turner raised his brow at the young man. "How about you just concentrate on getting your line in the water and never mind about me?"

Jason shrugged and snorted out a laugh. "Just sayin'."

"He makes a good point, hon," Joyce chimed in while stretching herself out on a lounge chair.

Turner cranked his body around just in time to catch the slight smile on her face. He took the opportunity to admire her tan. She was lying on her back, wearing a yellow two-piece that accentuated the gleaming bronze shade of her skin. The oversized dark sunglasses hugged her eyes, giving her face a movie star quality. *What an attractive woman,* he thought. *How did I get so lucky?*

Joyce leaned over and grabbed her beer off the towel lying on the dock beside her. She took a sip, exchanged the bottle for the towel, patted her brow, and leaned back out across the lounge. "This heat is brutal."

He shook his head at his girlfriend. "If the heat is so brutal, why are you lying there like a sacrificial offering to the Sun Gods?"

She sat up, flashed perfect white teeth, and gave him a wink. "I look good with a tan. And that takes sacrifice." She laid back down, adjusted her sunglasses, and without looking at him, added, "At least go put on a hat. You're gonna resemble a cooked lobster soon."

Turner pulled his feet from the water and stood up. "Fine, you win," he said as he marched up to the cabin. He looked back at Jason and said, "I wanna see you reeling in a nice big bass when I get back."

Max was sprawled out on the cool kitchen floor when he walked through the sliding glass door. "So, this is where you've been hiding," he said with a grin.

Turner had installed a glass panel with a built-in doggie door on the side of the slider. It decreased how far he could open the door, but it was worth it to give his buddy a little more freedom to go in and out on his own.

He grabbed a ball cap off the hook by the door and slid it on to his head. Before heading back outside, he looked down at his dog and said, "C'mon, Max, join us." He watched as the big Labrador stood, then stretched his front paws out in front of him before moving toward the door. When he'd finished with his routine, he lumbered past Turner and trotted off down the hill toward the dock.

Turner followed Max until the dog veered off into the

taller grass over by the side yard. "Enjoy yourself, boy," he called after his buddy.

Turner had just picked up his fishing pole and settled himself back in position on the dock when he heard a commotion behind him. He and Jason swung around while Joyce sat up, their eyes focused on the grassy upward slope toward the cabin. A young man was kneeling down next to Max and petting him on the head. Turner felt surprised as he watched his dog allow the stranger to get that close to him... until he realized he recognized the boy.

He'd met Ronnie Spatch when he questioned him during a murder investigation two years ago. Turner hadn't been in Magnolia Bluff two days when he found himself mixed up in a drug case that polarized his new hometown. A drug dealer was targeting high school kids, getting them hooked on heroin. If that wasn't bad enough, the kids began dying because the scumbag dealer was selling them heroin bags laced with fentanyl, a deadly combination. Ronnie was never a suspect. He just had the unfortunate luck to be working for one of the victims.

Ronnie waved when he glanced up from playing with Max and realized there were three sets of eyeballs staring at him. Turner couldn't imagine what the young man was doing at his home.

Jason looked over at Turner. "Who's that guy?"

"Someone I interviewed during that drug case that happened at your school a couple of years ago."

Joyce stood up and tied a towel around her waist and walked over to where Turner and Jason stood. "That's Ronnie Spatch," she said. "What's he doing here?"

"I have no idea," Turner replied. "Let's go find out."

He casually walked up the lawn with Joyce and Jason in tow. They stopped about halfway between the dock and the cabin and waited for Ronnie to make his way down to where they stood.

The young man hooked his left thumb in the belt loop of his jeans and extended his right arm at Turner. "Hey, Mr. Turner," he said. "It's been a spell, and you probably don't 'member me. I'm Ronnie Spatch. We met when my boss got himself kilt a few years back."

Turner shook the young man's hand and nodded. "I remember. And you're right. It's been a while. What brings you to my place?"

Ronnie put both hands in his pockets, sighed, and stared at the ground. He didn't say a word.

Turner spun toward Joyce, then back at the young man in front of him. "Ronnie? Are you okay?"

"No, sir. I'm not," he said, finally lifting his head. Turner could see his eyes were wet. "Somebody kilt my daddy."

Turner glanced over at Jason. "How about if you go take Max for a walk?"

Jason lowered his brows at Turner but walked away without saying a word. Turner looked back over at Ronnie. "Let's go sit on the patio where it's more comfortable and you can fill me in."

They walked the rest of the way to the cabin and took a seat around the patio table. Joyce gave the two men a forced smile. "I think there's a pitcher of iced tea in the refrigerator. Would you like a glass, Ronnie?"

"Iced tea would be fine, ma'am," he said without looking at her.

As soon as Joyce walked through the sliding door into the kitchen, Turner said, "I'm sorry about your father.

Why don't you tell me what happened?"

"That's the thing, Mr. Turner. I don't rightly *know* what happened."

Turner nodded at the boy. He thought back to when he'd questioned him that first time. He was going to have to take this slow if he wanted to get any answers. "You said someone killed your father. Do you know who or how your father died?"

Ronnie Spatch shook his head. "Nope. I don't know who kilt him," he said. "All I know is I found my daddy layin' b'side his tractor with a knife stickin' outta his belly." He began to tear up again. "There was blood everywhere. Blood stained on the tractor seat. Blood smeared all the way down the side of the tractor and blood all over the ground where my daddy laid dead. Why would somebody do that to him? He never done no harm to no one."

Turner hoped his face didn't betray the shock he felt for such a brutal killing. The way Ronnie described the scene, it sounded too personal to be a random murder. He'd met Ronnie senior and agreed with his son. The man kept to himself and didn't appear to be capable of pissing someone off to that extent. "What did the police say?"

Ronnie snorted out his reply. "The police? Chief Jager said his hands is full. Both his investigators are away on some special assignment or somethin'. And that new investigator of his is tryin' to suggest that maybe my daddy's death was some kind of farmin' accident." He shook his head. "I mean, what the hell? You ever hear of a 'farmin' accident' where the farmer ends up bleeding to death from a knife stuck in his belly? I shore as hell ain't."

Turner stared at the kid in disbelief. He knew that Sovern and GJ were away on special assignment, but surely they must have someone capable of running an investigation? He'd heard the chief brought in a guy who used to work with Nick Vandegan in Austin, but he hadn't had an opportunity to meet him yet.

He also thought Ronnie must have misunderstood about the cops thinking his father's murder was a farming accident. Even the Magnolia Bluff police can't be so naïve to think that anything other than a horrific murder took place at the Spatch farm. Unless Ronnie doesn't have all his facts straight.

"Ronnie," he began, "are you sure about what you saw when you found your father? Seeing him lying there the way you did must've been traumatic. It could've clouded what may have actually taken place."

"I know what I saw, Mr. Turner," he replied through gritted teeth. "My daddy was murdered, and I'd like you to hep me prove it."

The glass door slid back, and Joyce stepped onto the patio carrying a tray with three glasses and a pitcher of iced tea. She filled two of the glasses and set them on the table in front of Turner and their guest. She poured another for herself. "I'm sorry to hear about your daddy, Ronnie. He was a good man." She looked over at Turner and added. "I'll let you two finish up your business. I'll be down by the lake."

Ronnie took a swig of his tea. "This is good, ma'am," he said. "And I appreciate what you said about my daddy. Thank you."

She nodded at the boy, turned and headed to the dock.

Turner stared at his girlfriend as she walked down the hill.

"Might pretty lady ya got there, Mr. Turner," Ronnie said. "Smart too."

Turner nodded, then tore his eyes away from Joyce and looked at Ronnie. "I'm not sure what you want me to do," he said. "I'm sure the police have an investigation under way."

"I'm not so shore about that," Ronnie replied. "I hadn't heard from nobody in over a week. And when I call on the chief, he just says they're workin' on it. I need your hep. If it's about the money, I don't have a lot, but I can pay you what I got. Please, Mr. Turner."

Ronnie's answer didn't surprise him. A lot had changed since the last time he helped work on an investigation with the police. With Sovern and GJ away and not knowing much about the new sergeant investigator from Austin, Turner had been out of the loop regarding police business. Not to mention the new captain, Davis Briggs, made it clear he didn't need his help and didn't want his help. And ever since Briggs came on board, the chief has let him run the show.

That was fine with Turner. He'd finally been able to enjoy his retirement. Although he knew others in town felt like an already inept police force had gotten worse lately, the changes had actually been good for Turner's peace and serenity. He didn't mind that Captain Briggs frowned on anyone on his team asking for his help whenever the department hit a roadblock.

The last several months had given him what he came to Magnolia Bluff for—fishing, fishing, and more fishing. Since January, he'd only spoken with the chief the few times he'd seen him when he'd popped into the Really Good for coffee and a pastry to go during the morning hours.

Chief Jager was a regular part of a group of the town's folks who got together daily to sip coffee and gossip early in the morning at the coffee shop.

Turner looked across the table at the young man. He knew the kid was right. Tommy was stonewalling him. Maybe not on purpose. But it still amounted to the same thing. "I'll tell you what," he said. "I'll call the chief and see what I can find out for you. See if I can get you some much needed answers."

"Thank you," replied a relieved Ronnie. "I knew hiring you was the right move."

"You're not hiring me," Turner clarified. "I'm not a private eye for hire. I'm a retired cop that might be able to get Tommy to open up." He winked at the kid. "Besides, he owes me a favor or two."

Ronnie Spatch stood up and reached across the table. Turner followed suit and clasped the young man's hand. "No promises," he said. "Give me a day or two. I'll make a call and let you know what I find out."

"Thank you," Ronnie said as he vigorously shook Turner's hand. "I've taken up enough of your time. I'll leave you be." He stepped around the table and walked off the patio, disappearing around the corner of the cabin. A minute later, Turner heard a vehicle fire up, followed by the crunching of gravel as it headed back up the long driveway.

Once the sound of Ronnie's truck faded, Turner walked back down to the dock. Jason had joined his mother, and Max was lying on his side, trying to stay cool in the grass.

"That poor boy," said Joyce as Turner sat down beside her on the lounge chair. "First, he loses his mother to cancer when he was only twelve years old. And now his father is a victim of murder..." She let her voice trail off.

"Yeah, and Ronnie can't get a straight answer since

some kind of special assignment has taken half the police force away. And from what I've heard, they're not expected back anytime soon," he said, while shaking his head. "I don't think Tommy has the manpower to give to a murder investigation. At least not the *right* manpower."

Joyce rolled her eyes. "I think that's a bit of an exaggeration. From what I've heard, Davis Briggs runs a pretty tight ship. You know it's just Reece and Georgia Jean that are gone and *not* half the force. And you're also aware they brought in another sergeant investigator to fill the void. So not as dire a picture as you're painting."

"Yeah, well, it might as well be. I don't really know anything about Briggs or how competent this new investigator is. Like him or not, we all knew what we had with Sovern. At least he's run a murder investigation before. No idea about the new guy."

"Nick's a competent officer and he recommended the new investigator. I'm sure he wouldn't have done that if he wasn't capable of doing the job."

"You're right. Nick is an excellent officer. But he's not a detective investigator. And that's a different breed of cop. Does he really know his friend's track record on murder cases? Sovern's like a dog with a bone. He's rough around the edges, but he's somewhat competent."

Joyce smiled at Turner. "Aw, do you miss your little friend?"

"I don't," he said. "But I do think with the number of murders that happen in Magnolia Bluff every year, the rest of this town will miss him."

"Maybe it's time then."

Turner gave Joyce an inquisitive look. "Time for what?"

"To hang out your shingle."

"You mean private eye?"

"I know you've been thinking about it," she said. "With Reece and GJ being gone, you no longer have an excuse not to do it. And God knows this town could certainly use a guy like you. Think of it as an alternative for folks who don't exactly trust our police department to get the job done. You know, like how Harry's loan business is an alternative for the people who don't trust Mary Lou Fight's husband, Gunter, is working in their best interest at the bank when they need a loan."

Turner nodded. "You're right. It has crossed my mind once or twice."

"And I know you've looked into the requirements for registering as a PI in Texas. I overheard you on the phone with the Department of Public Safety's private security bureau last week."

"Okay, you got me," he said. "But I wouldn't be an alternative to the police. Eventually, I would still need to turn over information and they would still have to make the arrest."

"Which is exactly what was going on every time Reece or Tommy came to you and asked for help. Only this way you'll get paid for it and you can investigate by your rules and not theirs."

Turner sat there on the lounge chair and thought about that. Finally, he said, "Not this time."

She gave him a sideways glance. "Not this time? So, you don't think the time is right?" She shook her head. "Let me reiterate—"

"Let me finish what I was saying," he said, cutting her off. "Not this time. I won't get paid this time. I can't take money from Ronnie Spatch. It wouldn't feel right." He took in a deep breath and smiled. "My first case as a private investigator will be *pro bono*. I'll give Ronnie a call in the morning. I'll let him know I've decided to take him on as my first client as a PI and investigate his father's murder. Then I'll give Tommy a call and fill him in, so he won't feel blindsided."

Joyce returned his smile. "Now that's the man I know and love."

CHAPTER TWO

After getting off the phone with Ronnie Spatch, Turner took the drive over to the precinct rather than calling Tommy. He figured he could talk to the chief about Ronnie's dad and maybe learn a little about the new sergeant investigator.

He swung by the Bluff Bakery and picked up a dozen assorted donuts on the way. Not so much as a bribe, but more of a friendly offering, since he planned on picking Tommy's brain about the Spatch case.

Even though the chief told him many times that if he ever needed a favor, he could just ask, things had changed. For one, the department hadn't asked for his help in quite some time. And he was well aware that Davis Briggs was responsible for that.

Turner scrunched his brows. Why did he even care? He had done his time as a cop. When he retired and moved to Magnolia Bluff, it was never his idea or intention to get mixed up in any kind of small-town police investigation in the first place.

He'd left it all back in New York City. Or at least he thought he had. But for some odd reason, not being asked to consult or help in any other way with the occasional investigation grated on him. He hated to admit it, but he missed the action.

He'd had his reasons for retiring when he did, but now, a couple of years into it, Turner realized he still had a lot to give. Part of the reason he'd been contemplating the idea of becoming a PI.

He pulled around the back of the town hall building and parked in the rear lot next to where the police station was located. After hopping out of his pickup, he reached across the seat and grabbed the box of doughy treats and headed inside.

Gloria looked up from her computer and smiled as he came through the door. "Hello, stranger. My gosh, it's been a while. What brings you in this morning?" Her tongue traced around the outside of her lips. "Mmm, and with a box of yummy donuts."

She leaned toward him and opened the box while he was still holding onto it. He watched her as she scanned the contents. Then suddenly, her eyes snapped up at him. "Are you okay?" he said as he saw a concerned look appear across her face.

"It just occurred to me I should be asking you that question," she said. "Is everything all right? You're not here to report a crime, are you?"

Turner walked around the desk and gave her a quick side hug. "It's good to see you, Gloria," he said. "And no, I'm not here to report a crime. I was hoping I could speak with Tommy for a few minutes. Is he around?"

"He's in his office. I'll let him know you're here."

"Not necessary," he said, flashing a smile. "I know the way. I'll surprise him."

"Might not be the best idea to just pop in. He's got Captain Briggs in with him. Better let me call him." She pushed a button on the phone sitting on her desk and waited.

A few seconds later, Turner heard the chief's voice crackle through the speaker. "What is it, Gloria?"

Her eyes glanced up at Turner as she said, "Brandon is here. He needs to talk to you."

"Tell him I'll be there in a minute," came the irritated voice from the speaker.

Turner laid the box of donuts on the desk and then sat on the corner facing Gloria. "Tommy sounds a little stressed," he said, then leaned in closer. "What're he and Briggs talking about?"

She picked a white sugar dusted treat from the box and cooed. "Ooh, these are my favorites." After swallowing a bite of the confection, she said, "I believe they're discussing the third shift roster. The captain wants to move Hans to the night shift, and Tommy is bucking the change. Briggs is up in arms since he'd already posted the shift change without consulting with Tommy."

"Let me guess," said Turner. "Briggs feels if Tommy makes him put Hans back on the early shift, it will undermine his authority with the team."

She pointed her half-eaten donut at Turner. "Precisely." She shrugged. "Briggs might have a point. I mean, Tommy did put him in charge of the troops. Seems like scheduling should be his call."

"How does Hans feel about being moved to third shift?"

"You know Hans," she said. "Doesn't seem to bother him."

Turner nodded. "Well, Tommy must have a reason for not wanting him on overnights."

"Maybe. But you'll have to ask him yourself. He doesn't share with me."

Turner lifted himself off the corner of the desk as Tommy and Captain Briggs walked out from the hallway that led down to the chief's office.

Briggs glanced over at Turner and let out a grunt.

Turner, trying to be cordial, nodded slightly and said, "Captain Briggs, good to see you."

"Turner," barked Briggs with a curt nod as he hurried past him.

"Don't mind him, Brandon," Tommy said. "He acts that way around everybody."

"No issue," replied Turner. "I understand guys like him. Dealt with plenty of his type when I was on the job in New York."

The chief grinned. "You mean overbearing? Believes he's right all the time? That type?"

"Exactly," smiled Turner. He looked at Tommy and then nodded at the box sitting on the desk. "You look stressed. I brought donuts."

Tommy lowered his eyes. "What're these supposed to be? Some kind of bribe?"

Turner could tell by the chief's tone that it'd already been a long day—and it wasn't even eleven AM yet. "Not a bribe, Chief. But I do need a favor."

Tommy slowly shook his head back and forth. "Fresh outta favors, Brandon. Sorry."

"Well, maybe not so much a favor as needing a little information. Can we talk in your office?"

Tommy's lips puffed as he blew out a sigh. "You're not leaving until I say yes, are you?"

Turner cocked his head slightly and grinned. "No. I'm not."

He followed the chief down to his office. Once they were situated, Tommy looked across his desk and said, "What's this all about?"

"Ronnie Spatch, Senior," replied Turner. "Junior came to see me at my home yesterday. He was pretty upset, Tommy. According to him, you're not taking his father's murder seriously."

"Did he really say that?"

"What he said is that the investigator you replaced Sovern with thinks senior wasn't murdered. Told Ronnie Junior that it was more likely some kind of farming accident." Turner sat back in his chair and folded his arms across his chest. "I've gotta agree with the kid—I've never heard of a farming accident where the corpse ends up with a bloody knife stuck in its stomach."

Tommy rolled his eyes. "First of all, I did not *replace* Reece," he said. "Sergeant Investigator Palmer Kraus is here on a transfer from Austin until Reece and Georgia Jean return. And that's not what he told Ronnie." He shook his head. "His daddy was murdered. And it wasn't pleasant either. Palmer promised to do everything he could to find out what happened to his father. He assured the kid he follows all his investigations to the end, even the ones that turn out to be farmin' accidents. He never implied Ronnie Senior's death was a farmin' accident."

"Maybe just a poor choice of words on his part. Perhaps you should remind the new sergeant investigator that this isn't Austin. What he says is as important as how he says it. His words matter. Easy for small-town people like Ronnie to misunderstand the meaning."

"I don't know if that's a fair assessment," replied Tommy. "We both know Ronnie is different. A little slower between the ears. Most folks in Magnolia Bluff wouldn't have misunderstood the meaning."

"Something Sergeant Kraus should've recognized. If he had, maybe he'd a been a bit more careful with his phrasing, so there would've been no possibility of causing unneeded stress for a guy like young Ronnie."

Tommy threw up his hands and surrendered. "Okay,

okay. I'll take it under advisement and have a talk with him."

"One more thing," Turner said, pushing on. "He told me that every time he calls you for an update, all you say is you're working on it."

"We are working on it," the chief replied. "What am I supposed to say? We don't have any suspects yet. Heck, we don't even have a credible lead yet. You know how things go during an investigation. Sometimes there's nothing else I can say."

"Well, Ronnie thinks you're stonewalling him. He thinks you're too busy with other things to give his father's murder the attention it deserves. He's also worried that Kraus might not be the best cop to put on this case." Turner paused and took a breath before continuing. "I can't believe I'm saying this, but I know Sovern would be all over this investigation. Is Kraus as good an investigator as Sovern?"

"He comes highly recommended."

"So I've heard," replied Turner. "But is he up to the task? Will he dig to the point of annoyance the way Sovern would?"

"We've got this," an exhausted Tommy said. "I have faith in Captain Briggs and Sergeant Investigator Palmer Kraus to do a thorough and proper investigation that will result in us apprehending the person who took the life of Ronnie Spatch, Sr." He leveled his eyes at Turner. "Thank you for your concern, but we've got this. Go home. Enjoy your retirement. I thought that's what you wanted, anyway."

"I wish it was that easy," replied Turner. "I'll be looking into the murder myself, Tommy." He caught the surprised look on the chief's face. "Don't worry, I'll keep you in the loop and call you if an arrest needs to be made."

"What do you mean you'll be looking into it?" asked a perplexed Tommy. "I haven't asked for your help on this. And I know Captain Briggs didn't call you for help, either."

He looked at Tommy and smiled. "Oh, didn't I tell you? I've decided to open my own private investigation business and Ronnie's my first client. He hired me to find out who murdered his father. Now, what can you tell me about what happened?"

Tommy was speechless. He sat there, eyebrows scrunched, staring at Turner.

"Chief? Are you okay?"

"Uh… yeah," Tommy replied. "You caught me off guard, that's all. So you're a PI now?"

"I know," Turner said. "I can't believe it myself. Especially after all the grief I gave you and Sovern about leaving me alone over the last couple of years."

"You did make us beg pretty hard," acknowledged Tommy. "And now you're gonna be a private eye." The chief grinned. "I knew you'd miss it. Guys like you, a cop in a big city all those years, just walks away and moves to a small town to retire… hard thing to do."

Turner nodded. "Harder than I thought it would be. Turns out I miss the action."

"You're welcome," Tommy grinned.

Turner gave him a curious look. "For what? I don't remember thanking you."

"For keeping you engaged in the action since you moved to Magnolia Bluff."

"Yeah, I guess I do have you and Sovern to blame for this. The funny thing is, though, as horrific as the circumstances of those investigations were, there's no denying the satisfaction I felt when we solved those murders. And since you haven't asked for my involvement in your cases for the last year or so, my life's become a bit boring. Turns out I need something more than fishing to occupy my time."

"What about Joyce and Jason?"

"Oh, they're great. Don't misunderstand, they fulfill me in every way. But Joyce has a job that keeps her busy, and Jason has school and baseball, not to mention he's been spending more time lately out on Hank and Ann's farm horseback riding with Camila."

Tommy raised an eyebrow and smiled. "Jason's sweet on that girl?"

"He's sixteen," replied Turner, returning his smile. "You remember what it was like when you were that age?"

They both nodded, lost in thought for a moment.

"Anyway," continued Turner, "I needed something more for me. Being a cop is all I know. But ever since Briggs joined your department, my phone stopped ringing. Which I thought was a good thing. But I guess it wasn't. And even though I had a certain amount of freedom when I was helping you and Sovern, I'm too old to play by the structured rules of a police department anymore. So opening up my own private eye business feels right."

"I get it. Truly, I do. I've been a little restless lately myself. Bringing Davis in has cut back my time in the field. Some days I just sit here at my desk. It drives me nuts."

Turner nodded. "So, what can you tell me about the murder?"

"Nothin' much to tell," said Tommy. He leaned over and lowered his voice. "To be honest, I'm glad Ronnie Junior came to you. Having another investigator looking into what happened to his daddy can't hurt. Truth be told, we got our hands full around here."

Turner stood up and nodded. "Thanks for not making this weird," he said.

"No problem. Just don't interfere with Palmer's investigation. I'll fill him and Captain Briggs in, so he doesn't jump all over you if he runs across you out in the field."

"I appreciate that. Thanks again." Turner left the chief sitting in his office as he walked down the hallway, said goodbye to Gloria, and went outside into the bright morning sunshine.

He climbed back up into his truck and started the engine. After taking a moment to inventory his thoughts, he nodded to himself. "Time to get to work," he said to no one as he shifted the vehicle into gear and drove away.

CHAPTER THREE

Turner pointed his truck in the direction of the Spatch farm. Ronnie lived on Muskrat Road, about a quarter mile past the Magnolia Bluff cemetery. He made a left turn and drove until he saw the weathered wagon wheel leaning against the oak tree in the front yard.

His lips turned upward as he thought back to when Lily gave him the directions to Ronnie's place two years ago. She'd told him to look for the big old wooden wagon wheel sitting up against the tree. She called it Texas farm yard art. He had to admit the wheel was the perfect touch and blended nicely with the tree it rested against.

He pulled into the gravel driveway and parked behind a small red pickup that had seen better days. He remained inside his truck for a minute, then got out and leaned against the front grill of the pickup. The buzzing of insects was the only sound that cut through the stillness as he observed the house.

It sat back a few yards from the tree and looked the same as it had the last time he'd been there. The same broken shutters surrounded the same dirty grille patterned windows, and the wraparound porch still desperately needed a fresh coat of paint.

Turner stepped onto the porch and rapped his knuckles on the wooden frame of the screen door. The interior front door was open, allowing the searing heat of the day to push its way through the screen and into the house. He could already feel the thickness of the inside air penetrating his clothing and sticking to his body before he ever walked through the entrance of the home.

He squinted through the screen, but it was too dark inside to see anything. After a few minutes, he rapped his knuckles on the door again and called out into the room. "Ronnie, are you in there? It's Brandon Turner. I just came from the police station."

No one came to the door. Turner tried pulling the handle, but the screen door didn't budge. He stepped back and assessed the front of the house. There were windows on either side of the door, so he walked across the porch looking for one that might give him a view into the home. All the windows had curtains that were drawn and made it impossible to see if anyone was inside.

Turner stepped from the porch and walked around to the rear of the property. The tractor was off to the right, sitting outside the barn. He assumed the tractor and the area remained untouched, since it was where Ronnie Senior was found. Although it struck him as odd that there wasn't any yellow crime scene tape up to ensure the scene stayed untouched. He wanted to investigate, since that's one of the reasons he was there, but needed to find Ronnie first.

He turned his attention to the back of the house. There was a wooden door with a small window on the left side. Further down to the right, there was a pair of painted heavy-duty steel cellar doors butted up against the house at a ninety-degree angle. A large, rusty hasp, secured with an equally large, rusty padlock, straddled the doors.

Turner grinned. He hadn't seen a pair of cellar doors like that since the pair on the backside of his grandparent's house back when he was a kid. Of course, the paint wasn't flaking off of his grandparent's doors.

Someone, most likely Senior, had laid a series of bricks into the ground that stretched between the two doors in rows that went out about ten feet from the foundation of the house. Sitting on the bricks, and the only thing giving away their purpose, was one lone, rusted, folding lawn chair opened up next to a makeshift table constructed out of three cinder blocks stacked one on top of the other. A crude, yet effective patio.

Turner walked over to the door on the left side and peered through the window. There was a green-colored refrigerator with an old style GE logo dating back to the nineteen-fifties sitting in the corner of the room. An old white gas stove sat next to the fridge. The door obviously led into the kitchen. He could also partly see into the room beyond the kitchen but not clearly enough to recognize if it was the living or the dining room.

He knocked on the wood frame and yelled out to Ronnie. No answer. He wiggled the doorknob, and the door swung inward, banging against a counter. Turner poked his head through and called for Ronnie again before stepping through the doorway.

There was an old Formica kitchen table with three chairs sitting in the middle of the room. The chairs were stained and coated with dust. They had cuts in the cushions, allowing straw laced cotton to pop through the small tears in the vinyl seats.

An old 1960s Polaroid Land camera sat on the table. Turner picked it up and examined it. He hadn't seen one since he was a boy. His mom was an amateur photographer and collected old cameras. She had an old Polaroid Land camera similar to the one he was holding.

He wondered if it worked. He aimed it at the stove and pressed the shutter release button on the top. The camera groaned and then spit out a glossy paper from the front. He laid it on the table and watched the image gradually appear.

He picked it up and studied the photo. "Yep," he said out loud. "Looks like a picture of the stove."

Turner marveled at the idea of being able to snap a photo and watch it develop right before your eyes. An innovative idea that had been beaten into submission over the years as newer technology emerged.

He put the camera and photo back on the table and continued his search.

He walked over and looked into the deeply discolored porcelain sink, and all the dirty dishes and silverware piled inside it. Flies buzzed around crusted food particles. Dried ketchup stuck to the plates, forks, and knives. The overbearing heat mixed with the putrid smells inside the home added to the depression he felt for how young Ronnie Spatch lived.

He remembered the last time he'd been in this kitchen. Same outdated appliances, same sink, and the same table and chairs where he sat and interrogated Ronnie Junior. The only thing missing back then was all the dust everywhere, the cluttered look of the countertops and the stack of dirty dishes overflowing from the sink.

Shaking his head, he thought to himself that Ronnie Senior would have his son's hide if he saw the condition this kitchen was in.

Turner stood under the archway between the kitchen and the living room and listened. It was quiet. Too quiet. The house sounded empty. Not the kind of empty from someone not being home, but the kind of empty felt inside of a house not being lived in.

A quick check through the rest of the rooms confirmed he was alone.

Where the hell was Ronnie? He knew the boy had to be somewhere on the property because the old pickup was parked in the driveway.

Turner went back outside and stood on the patio. Cupping his hand over his eyes to block out the sun, he surveyed the property behind the house.

The barn. It sat right behind the tractor. He strode across the back lawn toward the only other building on the property. He could see the timbered structure still had a few flakes of red paint here and there that were holding on for dear life. However, as he got closer, he noted the building was indeed old, but it appeared to be solid.

Before going inside, Turner walked around the tractor, noting as he passed that someone had scrubbed clean the seat and the steel sides of the antiquated farm machine.

No crime scene tape. And the blood, along with any possible trace evidence, had been washed away.

Odd, he thought. He would need to ask Tommy about that.

After using his cell phone to snap a couple pictures of the crime scene area, he pulled on one of the double-sided wooden doors and entered the barn.

Again, what immediately struck him was how quiet it was. No cows mooing or horses clomping around inside of a stall. Nothing but the constant buzzing sound of flies.

"Ronnie," he called out. "It's Brandon. Are you pitching some hay around in here somewhere?"

No answer. He used the flashlight on his phone to get a better look at his surroundings. He saw a workbench in the corner with an array of different tools spread out across the top. Near the bench, on the floor, was a box filled with rags and some old plastic bottles that seemed to contain cleaning supplies.

There were two metal saddle racks, each with a leather saddle draped across them in the corner opposite the work bench. And there was another farm vehicle of some sort parked in the middle of the floor. This one was huge. It had to be ten feet up from the ground just to reach the seat. Being a city boy, born and bred, he had no idea what he was looking at. But it didn't look like any kind of tractor he'd ever seen before.

His eyes followed the gleaming red metal as he circled around the back side of the monstrous machine. His foot bumped into something solid, which caused him to drop his phone.

Turning his focus away from the big red machine, his eyes followed the glow from the phone's flashlight as it washed over Ronnie Spatch, who was lying face down in a pool of blood on the dirt floor.

CHAPTER FOUR

Turner watched as the paramedic team lifted Ronnie onto a gurney and then up and inside the ambulance. Lights flashed, and the siren sounded as the vehicle left the Spatch farm, turned onto Muskrat Road, and rushed off to Burnet Medical Center.

The good news was that Ronnie Junior wasn't dead. Yet. The bad news was he needed surgery, which meant Turner would have to wait before he could get any answers from Ronnie about what happened in the barn. That is, if he survived the surgery.

Turner stood there watching the dry, smoky dust settle back onto the street where the ambulance tires hit the hot, sun-baked dirt that lined the side of Muskrat Road.

With a weary shake of his head, he stared at the heat shimmering off the cracked asphalt, his expression vacant. "Who did this to you, Ronnie?"

He turned away from the road and walked back toward the house. There was a man in a tailored gray pinstriped suit marching his way. Turner dropped his head and sighed. *Just what I need right now,* he thought. *This guy must be the new investigator.*

The man stopped directly in front of him. "Brandon Turner?" he said while reaching into his jacket pocket and pulling out a small notebook. "You're the one who called 911."

Turner took the man in for a minute before answering. "You have me at a loss," he said. "You seem to know who I am, but you haven't introduced yourself."

"Sergeant Investigator Palmer Kraus," he said, extending his hand. "The captain warned me about you."

Turner ignored the offer of a handshake. He folded his arms across his chest. "Warned you?"

Kraus pulled back his hand. "Yes," he replied. "Said you'd probably be a hard-ass right outta the gate." He smirked. "Guess he was right."

"I know what Briggs thinks of me," said Turner. "And you can let him know I have no intention of getting in anybody's way regarding this investigation. But you can also let him know I'm not going away either. Ronnie hired me to look into his father's death and I will be doing just that."

Palmer Kraus nodded. "That's good to hear, Turner. Because Captain Briggs and I don't share the same thoughts on this subject. At least not where you're concerned. The chief also talked to me about you, so I know your background as a twenty-three-year veteran of the New York City Police Department and what you've done to help keep your little community safe over the last couple of years. I don't consider you an outsider or a civilian." He leaned forward and grinned. "Or a villain."

A smile crossed Turner's lips. "Well, Sergeant," he said, extending the palm of his hand. "Then I guess I will shake your hand after all."

Kraus took a step forward and clasped Turner's outstretched hand. "I'm glad we got that over with," he said. A frown appeared. "Now, what the hell happened here?"

Turner shook his head. "I wish I knew. I came by to see Ronnie so I could fill him in on what Tommy and I talked about earlier at the station and found him lying on the barn floor. He was unconscious and covered in blood. There was a deep wound in his abdomen, most likely caused by a hunting knife. He was barely breathing." Turner took in a breath of his own before continuing. "I grabbed several rags out of a box I found in the barn and pressed down on the wound. I kept applying pressure until the paramedics arrived and took over. That's all I know."

The sergeant was jotting in his notebook. When he'd finished, he looked Turner in the eye and said, "Tell me what bothers you about this. From what Chief Jager said to me, I can trust your instincts. I'm sure you didn't walk directly to the barn when you got here. Tell me what you observed before you found Mr. Spatch inside the barn. And tell me what you *think* might've happened."

A slight grin escaped Turner's lips. He had to admit, he liked Kraus. "You're right, Sergeant. Several things bothered me," he said, then proceeded to tell the police investigator what he saw inside and outside the house leading up to when he found Ronnie inside the barn.

"I'm also wondering about the crime scene," he continued, wrapping up his observations. "There's no tape protecting the area and the tractor's been scrubbed clean of blood and any trace evidence. And there's no blood in the grass. It looks like it was hosed down. Is your team responsible?"

Kraus crinkled his brow. "No. We're not responsible for that," he said. "We left everything alone since we're still waiting for all the lab results to be processed back in Austin. Mr. Spatch knew he was not to touch or remove anything in the area sectioned off around the tractor."

"Ronnie may not have cleaned this up," Turner stated.

"Well, then who do you suggest may have removed

the tape and scrubbed the area?"

Turner thought for a moment before answering. Finally, he said, "It's possible that while Ronnie wasn't home, whoever killed Ronnie Senior came back and scrubbed the tractor and the surrounding area, trying to get rid of any evidence they think the police may have missed."

"And Mr. Spatch came home while they were here?"

"It's a theory," shrugged Turner.

"I suppose," replied the sergeant investigator. "A weak theory, but a theory nonetheless."

"Yeah," agreed Turner. "I'm not sure I buy it either. Hopefully, we can question Ronnie sooner than later and get some answers."

Kraus lowered his eyes. "You know he lost a lot of blood? There's no guarantee…"

"I know," Turner said, cutting off the sergeant. "But I can hope."

Ronnie was still in surgery when Turner arrived at the hospital. It had been almost two hours since the paramedics loaded the young man into the ambulance and left the Spatch farm. He'd called Joyce on the way over to fill her in on the situation with Ronnie. She wanted to meet him there, but he told her considering Ronnie was in surgery, there was no reason, and he would see her later.

Now he was pacing back and forth in the waiting area like a nervous father-to-be while on the phone with Chief Jager. He was trying to convince him to tell the desk nurse he was working with the police, so they would give him any updates on Ronnie's condition.

"Don't worry," he said. "I promise I won't tell Briggs

you helped me on this."

"I am not concerned with Captain Briggs," grunted out Tommy.

"Then why are you making this so hard? I told you I was working the Spatch murder."

"We don't know whether his father's murder connects to Ronnie's situation. Might be a whole 'nother case, Brandon."

"You're kidding, right?" he paused and took in a calming breath. Then, figuring he'd try a different approach, added, "By the way, Sergeant Kraus has a good head on his shoulders."

"Glad you two hit it off," said Tommy. "Your remarks about him were a little harsh earlier."

"I'll admit I judged him a bit hard without ever meeting him. But, based on what Ronnie told me, it didn't sound like he was all that invested in trying to catch a murderer. It felt to Ronnie like Kraus was dismissing him."

"Well, now you see that's not the case."

"You're right," said Turner. "And I appreciate you talking to Sergeant Kraus about me. I think it helped us get past the initial introductions."

"You're welcome. You know you've been an enormous asset to the MBPD and to me personally, no matter what Captain Briggs thinks."

Turner smiled into the phone. "Good. Then there's no reason for you not to talk with the desk nurse."

He heard the chief sigh. "I'll take care of it. I'll give the hospital a call as soon as we hang up."

"Thank you," he replied. "I'm in the emergency room waiting area. That's where the paramedics originally brought Ronnie. Talk to the nurse working that desk."

He clicked off and stuffed the phone in his back pocket and wandered back over to the waiting area. The emergency room entrance doors swooshed open, and he smiled as Joyce walked in. He waved at her, and she rushed over to where he was standing.

"Any news yet?" she said, wrapping him up in a big bear hug.

"Nothing yet," he said as they both sat down. "He's been in there an awfully long time. I don't know if that's good or bad."

She nodded. "I know you told me not to come, but I wanted to be here to support you. And besides, I've known Ronnie and his family for a long time and I'm just sick over what that young man has gone through." She paused. "And now this…"

They both looked up as a doctor wearing blue scrubs came through the double doors marked *Surgery, Authorized Personnel Only*. She walked up to the nurse on duty. The same nurse Turner had spoken with earlier. He hoped Tommy had made the call.

He and Joyce jumped from their seats and watched them talk for a moment; then the nurse pointed at Turner.

The doctor strode across the floor to where they were standing. "Mr. Turner," she said. "I'm Doctor Jennifer Pope. I performed the surgery on Ronald Spatch. He's in the recovery room, but he's not out of the woods yet.

"There was a lot of internal damage caused by the knife wound. The next twenty-four hours will be crucial to his healing. He's sleeping now. If he makes it through the night with no complications, I believe he has a good chance of a full recovery."

Turner nodded. He felt Joyce take his hand in hers.

He gently squeezed it, feeling appreciative of her standing there beside him. "Thank you, Doctor," he said. "I understand I can't speak with him, but will we at least be able to see him tonight?"

"Not tonight. He'll be in recovery for a while and then assigned a room. I don't want to take any chance of him being disturbed. He needs the sleep. Now, go home. You should also get some rest. Later this evening, check with the nurse for his room number. You can see him tomorrow morning, say... around eleven, after we've had time to assess his progress."

Joyce squeezed Turner's hand. "She's right. It's been a long day. Let's go home for tonight. Let the medical professionals do their job."

Turner blew out a breath and nodded. "Okay," he said. He glanced over at the doctor. "Thank you again, Doctor Pope."

Joyce reached into her purse and pulled out a pen and one of her realtor business cards. "I'm writing Brandon's number on the back," she said, jotting down the information. She handed the card to the doctor. "And my number is on the front. Please call us if anything changes."

Doctor Pope pocketed the card. She nodded at Joyce and then, her eyes finding Turner, gave him a compassionate look. "I understand you slowed down the blood loss by keeping pressure on the wound before the paramedics arrived. You most likely saved his life, Mr. Turner."

Turner began to choke up and slowly nodded his head. "Thank you," were the only words he managed to get out of his mouth.

CHAPTER FIVE

Turner walked Joyce to her car. They were both parked in the visitor's lot outside the emergency room's main entrance.

"Are you okay, Brandon?" she said when they reached her vehicle.

He took hold of her hand and pulled her close to him. "I am now." He leaned in and gave her a kiss. "I'm glad you came, even though I told you not to."

She gently pulled back and stared into his eyes. "I feel like you're not being completely honest with me."

"Ah," he said with a slight grin. "But I am being honest. It was comforting to see you walk through those hospital doors. You being next to me in there and here with me right now makes me okay."

"Thank you. But that's not what I meant, and you know it."

"I'm fine." His eyes looked past her as he drew in the night air. "Or at least I will be."

"Then why do I sense some tension?"

"I don't know," he said. "I guess I'm tired." He stretched his neck from side to side, trying to release some of those tense feelings Joyce obviously picked up on. "I barely know Ronnie. Outside of the one time I interviewed him during that drug investigation a couple of years ago, I haven't even thought about the guy. That is until he appeared in my backyard the other day. And now, after seeing him on that barn floor..." His words faded, and he slowly shook his head.

"You feel responsible for him," said Joyce.

"No, that's not it," he said, puffing out his lips. "Well, maybe that's a part of it. I feel bad for the boy. He's had a rough time. His mom dying so young, then his dad being murdered, and now he's in the hospital fighting for his life."

"And he can thank you for that last part. He's lucky to be alive. If you hadn't acted so quickly and put pressure on the wound to stop the bleeding... who knows what would've happened?"

"All I did was push some old rags down on the wound until the paramedics got there. It was not a medical miracle."

"Don't be so modest. You heard what Doctor Pope said. You most likely saved his life." She took hold of both his hands. "And I know you felt the weight of her words. I could see it in your eyes and hear it in your voice when you answered her."

Turner grew quiet and nodded.

"Are you coming over?" she asked, changing the subject.

His solemn expression gave way to a smile. "Yes. I'm gonna run by my place and pick up Max. We'll meet you at your house in about thirty minutes."

"Sounds good," she said. "If you're hungry, I've got some leftover pizza from Olivia's I can heat up."

"Now that you mention it, I haven't eaten anything since this morning. And that was a donut. Leftover pizza sounds great." He gave her a kiss on the cheek and watched her get into her car. "I'll see you in about a half hour."

After she'd backed out of the space and was on her way, he headed to the other side of the lot and hopped into his truck.

Max greeted Turner as soon as he walked through the front door. "Hey, buddy," he said as the big Labrador bounced up on his hind legs and licked his face. "I hope you had a better day than I did."

He walked down the hall and into his bedroom. Max entered right behind him and leaped up onto the bed. Turner sat down, pulled off his shoes, and tossed himself backwards onto the mattress. Max curled in next to him and they both closed their eyes.

After a few minutes, Turner cracked one eye open, lifted his phone to his face and checked the time. It had been a long day, and he was exhausted. But it was time to go.

He glanced over at his dog. Max was fast asleep. He envied how easily his best friend could drift off into dreamland.

Turner lightly jostled him, but Max only snorted and curled up tighter. Turner smiled and shook his head. *What a bum*, he thought. He sat up on the bed, nudged his dog a little harder, and said, "Do you wanna go see Joyce and Jason?"

Max's head shot up. He let out a small howl and immediately jumped down and ran from the room. Turner grinned as he followed him down the hallway toward the door. "I knew that would get you moving," he said with a chuckle.

As soon as he opened the front door, Max blew past him and ran over to the pickup. He always chuckled at how patiently the big lug would sit there near the rear of the truck waiting for him to lock up the cabin and join him.

After ensuring his home was secure, he walked to his vehicle and opened the rear driver's side door. Max jumped up onto the seat and made a few tight circles before finally settling himself. Meanwhile, Turner pulled his door open and got in behind the wheel.

With a quick glance to confirm Max was laying down and not standing on the seat, he hit the engine start button on the console and drove up the long driveway.

They had just pulled out onto Burnet Reservoir Road when his phone rang. He glanced down at the screen on the dashboard console but didn't recognize the number. He was going to let it roll over to his voicemail when it occurred to him it might be the hospital calling about Ronnie. With a click, he activated the phone function on his steering wheel. "Hello, Turner speaking."

A man's voice bellowed over the speakers. "Turner. Palmer Kraus here. Chief Jager gave me your number. Hope you don't mind. Any chance of us getting together? I'd like to discuss a few things about the Spatch case. Maybe pick your brain a bit."

"I could do that," replied Turner. "When?"

"How about now? Is that good for you?"

"Unless it's critical that we meet tonight, I'd rather wait until tomorrow. I'm headed over to my girlfriend's house for the evening. And I'm sure you know that the hospital won't let anyone see Ronnie until tomorrow, anyway."

"Yes, I'm aware," Kraus said. "I spoke with the surgeon earlier. I was just hoping that we could talk. Get to know each other a little better since we're going to be working parallel on this investigation."

"I think that's a good idea, Sergeant. How about I meet you at the Really Good tomorrow morning around ten?

We can talk over coffee and then head over to the medical center to check on Ronnie. The doctor said we can see him any time after eleven."

"Sounds good. I've got a few hours free in the morning. Enjoy your evening, Turner."

"You too, Sergeant. See you in the morning." He clicked the off button and smiled. This guy was nothing like Sovern.

He made the left by the Burnet College of Fine Arts and then five minutes later made another left into the Magnolia Estates neighborhood where Joyce lived. He turned right onto Oakdale Lane, drove to the end of the cul-de-sac, and pulled into her driveway behind her silver Toyota Camry.

Max, recognizing where they were, danced around the back seat and pushed on the inside of the door in anticipation of getting out of the truck.

Turner cut the engine and hopped out of the vehicle. He waved at Joyce, who popped out from underneath the garage door as it opened. "Brace yourself," he said as he pulled open the rear door and Max exploded from the cab.

He watched as Joyce stood there, arms extended wide, waiting for the black Lab to dive bomb into her. He always marveled at how Max knew just when to slow down enough so he wouldn't hurt her as he jumped into those outstretched arms. Turner couldn't resist smiling. Max loved both Joyce and Jason and could be very protective if someone tried to harm them. But right now, he was acting like a playful puppy. He really was a gentle soul.

He walked past them and went into the garage while they rolled around on the front lawn. Grabbing a Lone Star out of the mini fridge, he popped the top off on the bottle opener, and went back outside to see if his girlfriend had enough of his dog licking her face yet.

With a laugh, Turner drank some of his beer. Max was lying on his back, and Joyce was rubbing his belly. Each time she withdrew her hand, Max pushed it back down onto his stomach with his paw. It was apparent he didn't want his tummy rub to end anytime soon.

Turner pressed the Lone Star bottle against his lips, tipped his head back, and took a big swig. After wiping the back of his hand across his mouth, he said, "I'll be inside heating up that pizza in case you two wanna join me."

Joyce giggled like a six-year-old little girl. "As you can see, our boy here is clearly not ready to let me get up." She gave him a wink and waved him away. "Go eat your pizza. I'll be in shortly."

On his way through the garage, he grabbed another beer from the fridge, opened the door leading into the house, and stepped into the kitchen.

Joyce had a combination toaster oven and air fryer that sat on the counter near the refrigerator. Turner pulled the pizza from the fridge and then stared at a bunch of buttons and knobs on the large countertop oven that all did various things related to cooking. He found the button marked *pizza* and pushed it. He laid five slices on a sheet of aluminum foil and placed it on the middle rack. Then he set the temperature for 375° and turned the timer on for fifteen minutes.

Once he had his meal heating in the toaster oven, he wandered down to Jason's bedroom to see what the boy was up to. The door was closed. "Hey, Jason," he said, knocking lightly. "It's Brandon. Okay to come in?"

A couple of seconds later, he heard the lock unlatch, and the door swung open. Jason stood on the other side and waved him in. "Hey, Brandon," the sixteen-year-old said. He turned around and walked over to his gaming chair and sat down. "Mom said you were coming by tonight. What's up?"

Turner followed him into the room, and planted himself on the corner of the bed. "Nothing really. Just wanted to say hi. I'm warming up some pizza. Wanna join me?"

Jason glanced over Turner's shoulder at the clock on his nightstand. "Naw," he said. "I already ate. And besides, I've gotta get signed into the big game in a couple of minutes. Appreciate the invite, though."

Turner nodded. It didn't surprise him. He knew the boy was a big gamer and spent a lot of his evenings planning some kind of world domination with his online group of friends. "What planet are you and your buddies destroying tonight?"

Jason laughed. "Nothing like that. We're going old school tonight. We're rolling with GTA."

Turner cast a side glance at the young man. "Grand Theft Auto," he said. "Which version?"

"The new one."

"Isn't there nudity in that one?"

"There's nudity in all of 'em," shrugged Jason.

Turner smiled knowingly. "Well, don't let your mother find out."

"Why do you think the door was locked?" the boy quipped.

"Well," he said, rocking himself off the bed. "Have fun. But keep in mind it's just a game. It's not real. If you kill someone in real life, they don't come back. No reboot. No second chances."

Jason rolled his eyes. "I know."

Turner lowered his gaze. "I know you know," he said. "You've got a good head on your shoulders. My job is to make certain you never forget that." Smiling, he turned and left Jason to his fun evening of animated carjacking and mass murder.

He returned to the kitchen just in time to hear the toaster oven ding. He reached in and grabbed the foil by its corners, pulled it off the rack, and put it on the counter.

The door from the garage opened, and Max tore down the hallway to Jason's room. Joyce came through the door behind the big dog. She was carrying a couple of Lone Star bottles. "Figured you might need a refill," she said, wiggling the bottles at him.

Turner's face brightened. "You figured right," he said. "You're just in time. Pizza's ready."

"Oh, good," she said, setting the beer on the table. "I'll let Jason know in case he wants to join us."

Turner took two plates from the cupboard, placed them on the kitchen table, and sat down. "Don't bother. I just left his room. He said he wasn't hungry and was getting geared up for some online battle game with his buddies. And he doesn't need us. Max will keep him company."

"Of course," she sighed. She pulled the chair out next to Turner and sat down. "I really wish he'd spend less time playing those games and more time reading."

He grinned. "Good luck with that."

"I'm serious. I've tried talking to him about it, but…"

"Not very receptive?"

"Not really. I don't know. He says he's not playing as often as he used to, and I suppose that's true. But it's not enough of a cutback for me."

"Want me to talk to him?" offered Turner.

She smiled. "I appreciate it, but I think I can handle it."

He nodded and placed a slice on each of their plates, grabbed a third from the foil, and took a bite. "I got a call from that new detective, Palmer Kraus, on the way over here."

Joyce took a bite of her slice, followed by a sip of beer. "And?" she said after swallowing.

"He wanted to meet tonight to talk about the investigation. I put him off until tomorrow since there's no new information at the moment. He wants to get to know me better since we're gonna be working on the same case."

"What do you make of that?"

"Not a hundred percent sure yet, but he seems like he's a decent cop."

She shot him a grin. "So, you approve of Detective Sovern's replacement?"

"Yes," he admitted. "I may have judged him too harshly before meeting him."

"I was right, then."

Turner's forehead crinkled. "About what?"

"About Officer Nick Vandegan not recommending someone he didn't believe could do the job."

Turner shook his head while a slight smile crossed his lips. "Yes, you were right. I will never doubt you again," he said, before downing the rest of his beer.

CHAPTER SIX

Morning came early at the Blackstone house. Turner had called the hospital before he and Joyce turned in for the night. He'd been able to get an update on Ronnie's condition and his room number.

Tossing and turning most of the night, he'd finally drifted off in the wee hours of the morning. He floated in and out of a dreamy state between sleeping and waking, his senses tingling all the while.

His mind felt like it'd been coaxed awake by the sweet smell of maple syrup and oatmeal pancakes dancing across his nose. His tastebuds had been on high alert while his tongue darted around his mouth, searching for pay dirt.

The brain fog finally gave way to full consciousness, and it registered he was actually still in bed rather than enjoying a pancake breakfast. His eyes opened as soft sunlight filtered through the bedroom curtains, prompting him to take a deep, cleansing breath.

He sat upright as he recognized the tasty scent of syrup and pancakes still lingering in the air. He smiled. It wasn't a complete dream after all.

Turner pulled a t-shirt and a pair of gym shorts from "his" drawer and put them on. He and Joyce had given each other a drawer a few months back, so there were clothes to wear no matter which house they slept at. Of course, "her" drawer at his place was actually three drawers and extended to half his closet as well. He was perfectly fine with giving her the space. His bedroom closet was less than half full and he wasn't using all the dresser drawers at his cabin anyway.

After a quick trip to the bathroom, he made his way to the kitchen where Joyce was plating up a stack of pancakes hot off the griddle pan on her stovetop.

"That smells delicious." He gave her a peck on the cheek, looked around, then said, "Jason already left?"

"He did. Fed him his breakfast about an hour ago. He promised to help Hank and Ann out on their farm today."

Turner smiled. "Help on the farm, huh? Sounds more like an excuse to see Camila."

"I'm sure you're right," she said with a giggle. "That boy was downright thrilled to get over there. He practically ran out of the house when Hank pulled into the driveway to pick him up. I'm just glad to see he's interested in something other than those damn video games."

"He likes baseball too," Turner said with a sarcastic grin.

"Oh, you know what I mean." She laid a plate full of pancakes, sausage links, and bacon on the table next to a bottle of maple syrup and a butter dish. "This is for us," she said, turning to pull two more plates from the cupboard. She handed one to Turner, then sat down next to him. "Let's dig in."

They both put a couple of pancakes on their plates. Joyce stabbed one sausage link and ignored the bacon. He knew that's all she would eat, so he slid the remaining three links and all four strips of bacon onto his plate, picked up the syrup bottle and covered everything in the sweet, amber colored liquid.

Using his knife, Turner pushed a little bit of everything onto his fork and lifted it to his mouth. When he'd finished chewing, he grinned at Joyce. "Why are you so good to me?"

"Because I love you," she replied softly. "And... I want to ask you a favor."

He put his utensils down on the corner of his plate and found her eyes. "You don't have to bribe me to get a favor." He shrugged his shoulders and smiled at her. "You just have to ask."

"I took the day off because I want to go with you when you speak with Detective Kraus." She paused. "I also want to be at the hospital when you talk to Ronnie."

"I understand why you'd want to go to the hospital, but why see Kraus?"

"You said he wanted to get to know you. Well, getting to know you means getting to know me. He needs to understand he can talk to me... trust me, when you're not around. And that you trust me."

"You don't think I can convey that message without you being there?"

"It's not that," she said with a slight grin. "I'm not sure it'll even come up in the conversation if I'm not there to bring it up."

Turner put another heaping forkful of pancake in his mouth and chewed while he thought about her comment. "Okay," he said after swallowing. "You can come. We're meeting him at the Really Good at ten."

Joyce nodded. "Oh good," she said. "I don't stop by the coffee shop as often since Harry and Ember decided to take a yacht trip around the world. It'll be nice to see Estrelita and Miguel."

"Yeah," said Turner. "I feel a little guilty for not going to the Really Good as much as I used to." He offered a slight shrug. "It just seems different without Harry there to overload me with all his obscure coffee knowledge on why I need to try his latest brew from some exotic part of the world I'll never visit." He paused. "A lot sure has changed over the last six months."

"It has," she agreed.

Joyce gazed down at her breakfast and was quiet while she used her fork to push the food around her plate. He could see she was deep in thought. He leaned over and gave her shoulder a gentle rub. "Hey," he said. "You okay?"

She laid her fork down and shifted her gaze over to him. "I was thinking about what you said about things changing so much over the last few months." She breathed out a sigh. "And then I thought about Ronnie's dad getting killed, and how nothing's changed—Magnolia Bluff is still full of senseless murders."

"You're right. All the more reason we have to track down whoever did this and make them pay." He glanced up and checked the digital clock display on the stove. "We'd better get dressed. It's almost time to go. Don't wanna start off on the wrong foot and keep Kraus waiting."

Joyce leaned over and gave him a kiss on the cheek. "I'm proud of you."

"Why is that?" he said, looking totally confused.

"It obviously matters to you to get along with Detective Kraus." She smiled. "I like that."

"We both know my first encounter with Sovern was a bit... challenging," he said. "I'd prefer to have a better working relationship with Palmer Kraus. Who knows how long he's gonna be here in town? Might come in handy as a PI if Kraus and I got along. And besides, I like him better than Sovern."

When Turner and Joyce walked into the Really Good, Jack Bonhoffer greeted them. "Long time, no see," he said. "Glad to see you guys remembered where we're located."

Turner shook hands with the floor manager. "Hi Jack. Good to see you."

Joyce leaned in and gave Jack a hug. "How are you, Jack?" she said. "I'm not going to insult you by saying I've been too busy. The truth is, it feels weird knowing Harry's not here."

"Don't feel bad. You're not alone on that. The business has never been overwhelmingly busy, but nowadays, I see more strange faces coming through the door than I do the regulars. Even the Niners' Coffee Klatch doesn't show up every day like they used to."

"Wow," said Turner. "Must be quiet around here without Huston's big mouth in here every day."

Jack let out a belly laugh. "Oh, no... he still comes in every morning," he said.

"Lucky you," Turner replied, joining in with his own hearty laugh.

Jack grabbed a couple of menus from behind the counter. "You guys here for breakfast? We've got a scrumptious western egg omelet as this morning's special. Miguel said it was his abuela's special recipe. When he was a boy, she used to let him help her prepare the veggies, ham, and the cheese. He adds it to the menu every once in a while, and today's that day."

"No offense to Miguel's grandmother," said Turner. "But I don't see what's so special about it. Sounds like the same recipe a little greasy spoon served up in Greenwich Village back when I was a cop in New York."

"Ah," said Jack. "But do they top it with a sour cream

mixture that includes ground beef, cumin, pepper, and just a hint of lime?"

"You got me there," grinned Turner. "They do not."

"And as wonderful as that sounds," Joyce said, "we're just having coffee today. We already ate breakfast."

"Now why on earth would you eat before coming in this morning?" The slight grin on Jack's lips betrayed the hurt look on his face. "Just kidding," he laughed. "But I'll be so disappointed if you don't at least pick up a couple of cinnamon rolls on your way out."

"We're meeting Sergeant Kraus here this morning," explained Turner. "And you got a deal on the cinnamon rolls."

Jack signaled Estrelita over to where they were standing. "Please take Joyce and Brandon to a table. They're just ordering coffee but box up a half dozen fresh cinnamon rolls for them to take home. On the house."

"Of course," she said. "Happily." She looked at them and said, "Follow me, guys."

Joyce smiled and nodded at the floor manager while Turner shook his hand. "Thanks, Jack," he said. "We appreciate it." He patted his stomach. "I'll make sure those rolls find a good home."

"And next time we come in, we'll come to eat," added Joyce.

"You better," Jack said, smiling and waggling a finger at them.

They followed Estelita across the room to a booth and slid in next to each other, first Joyce, then Turner. After they placed their coffee orders, Turner said, "When Sergeant Kraus gets here, will you please point him to our booth?"

The waitress nodded and left to fill their order.

"Do you think the sergeant has any further updates about Ronnie?"

"I hope so," replied Turner. "When I called last night, all the nurse could tell us was that he was breathing and sleeping on his own."

"Considering how it looked when we left the medical center yesterday, that's very good news."

"It was great news. But hopefully, Kraus spoke with either the nurse or the doctor this morning and they gave him the green light to question Ronnie about what happened to him."

They both looked up when Estrelita came back with their coffees and the sergeant. "Look who I found," she said, placing the steaming mugs in front of them. "A distinguished member of our law enforcement." She looked at Kraus as he slid into the booth across from Joyce and Turner. "I'll be right back with your coffee, Sergeant." She let out a giggle and walked away.

Kraus watched the waitress make her way behind the counter and get to work on his order. "What's she laughing about?"

Turner looked across the table and grinned. "Don't take this the wrong way," he said, "but the Magnolia Bluff PD isn't exactly known for its ace detective work solving the crimes that have plagued this little town over the last few years. My guess? She's pegged you as just another ineffective part of the problem."

"And she thinks that's funny?"

Joyce piped in. "Hi, Detective Kraus. I'm Joyce Blackstone." She glanced over at Turner. "Brandon's better half. She thinks it's funny because you're here talking to Brandon. Everyone in this town knows Brandon's been Magnolia Bluff's white knight when it comes to solving the murders that your team hasn't been able to solve. She assumes that's why you're here—you want his help."

There was a loud banging sound when a man walked into the building and the door slammed shut behind him. Everyone, including Turner, looked up toward the front of the restaurant just in time to hear a larger-than-life voice boom across the coffee shop. "TURNER, WHAT THE HELL ARE YOU DOING SITTING THERE WITH MY OFFICER?"

"Oh crap," muttered Kraus, as they watched Captain Davis Briggs marching across the room in their direction.

CHAPTER SEVEN

When Briggs reached the table, Joyce looked up at him and smiled. "Care to join us, Captain?"

The scowl on his face immediately dissolved. "Uh, hello, Ms. Blackstone," he said, managing a less intrusive tone. "I didn't realize you were also sitting here."

"That's because you were too preoccupied with drawing conclusions about my presence here with Sergeant Kraus," said Turner. "Last time I checked, it wasn't a crime to be out having a friendly coffee with a colleague."

Briggs snorted. "You're not a colleague. You're a former cop who's now a PI." He looked over at Kraus. "I demand to know why you're having coffee with this man."

Turner stood up abruptly. "That's none of your damn business, Briggs. I think you're stretching your authority pretty thin here."

Joyce touched Turner's arm. "Captain Briggs," she said, before anyone else could say a word. "The three of us are simply trying to get to know each other better. The sergeant is new to our little town, and we thought it would be nice to let him know we're glad he's here. Sergeant Investigator Sovern's shoes are hard to fill." She glanced over at Kraus and smiled and then turned her focus back to the captain. "We wanted him to understand the whole town is behind him and he's doing a good job." She leaned forward around Turner so she could look Briggs in the eyes. "I can assure you Sergeant Kraus is not sharing any case secrets with us."

Captain Briggs stared at his sergeant. "Is this true?"

"Every word, Captain. We have discussed nothing about any ongoing investigations. We're just having coffee."

"Make sure it stays that way," said Briggs. He nodded at Joyce, turned, and marched off, banging through the front door as he left the coffee shop.

Turner shook his head in disbelief. "How do you work with a guy like that?"

"It's not so bad," replied Kraus. "He's a good cop. Just has some hard ass feelings about cops asking civilians for help on any police investigations. Which I'm sure he felt we were guilty of doing." He glanced over at Joyce and grinned. "I'm glad you're on my side. I don't think I'd want to go up against you in a fight."

She returned his smile. "Thank you. But in this case, I was more the calm voice of reason than a fighter," she said, then quickly cut her eyes over at Turner and winked.

"Well, at least I didn't lie to him," observed Kraus. "We hadn't gotten into anything about the Spatch case before he blew in here and interrupted us." He looked at Turner and grinned. "So whatdaya say we change that?"

"I like the way you think, Sergeant," Turner said.

"How about we start with you guys calling me Palmer?"

"You got it. But only if you call me Brandon."

Joyce smiled at Kraus. "And I expect you to call me by my first name, too."

Kraus nodded just as Estrelita showed up at their table with his coffee and a cinnamon roll. She laid both in front of him, smiled, and left.

"She didn't giggle at me this time," Kraus said, as he

watched the waitress head to another table to take an order. "I'll chalk that up as progress." He picked up the cinnamon roll. "I hope you guys don't mind. I didn't eat breakfast before I left my apartment this morning."

"Of course not. Enjoy. Brandon and I love the cinnamon rolls from here. Best in town."

"I agree," replied Kraus. "I had one a few weeks back and now I have one every time I come in here." He took a bite of the pastry, closed his eyes, and dropped back on the bench. "Hmm… perfection."

"So, Palmer," began Turner, "I'm curious. Were you reassigned and told to come to Magnolia Bluff, or did you volunteer to come here? And if it's the latter, why?"

"Good question," replied the sergeant. He laid the confection on his plate, picked up a napkin and wiped the sugary icing off his face. "I got a call from Nick Vandegan. We worked together at the Austin PD. He transferred here a year or so ago and loves the small town life. He told me about Sergeant Sovern leaving on a special assignment and asked if I was interested. Long story short, we talked about it. I put in for the transfer and when Chief Jager asked Nick about me, he recommended me as someone who would fit what they were looking for here. Figured it would be a nice change of pace." He took a sip of coffee. "What about you? I know you were a cop up in New York, but how did you end up here?"

"We had a big drug bust. We seized a lot of heroin, coke, and money. A chunk of the money went missing. I was in charge at the time and coordinated the take down. When the smoke cleared and the money came up short, I was accused of lining my pockets with it."

Kraus shook his head and let out a low whistle.

Turner continued. "Let me just say up front—I am not

and never was a dirty cop. Of course, they put me on paid leave while Internal Affairs investigated. They dug into every nook and cranny of my life." He paused. "I prided myself on being an honest cop. It was humiliating."

"So what happened?" Kraus asked. He'd leaned forward across the booth, intently listening to the story.

"They cleared him," said Joyce. "Cleared him of everything."

Turner nodded. "That's right. Turned out two officers under my watch during that investigation were dirty. Had been for some time. They'd always been careful. Nobody had caught them with their hands in the cookie jar… until then."

Kraus straightened and took a sip of his coffee. "What got 'em caught this time?"

"The money was too rich for them to lay off. We had seized a half million dollars during that bust. They logged it into evidence as half that amount and forged my name on the paperwork." Turner was quiet while he thought about that. "Dumbasses. They were setting me up. After a lengthy IA investigation, in the end, it all came down to a handwriting analysis to clear my name."

"Damn," said Kraus.

"Yeah… damn," replied Turner. "Anyway, my captain never one hundred percent believed I wasn't a part of it."

"He said that? Even after they cleared you?"

Turner nodded. "Even after they cleared me. Well, he never actually said the words, but I felt it. Felt it every time he looked at me. Every time he spoke to me. I probably could've transferred out of narcotics, but I had twenty-plus years in, so I took my retirement and moved to Magnolia Bluff to do some fishing and live out the rest of my life in peace and quiet." He snorted. "Course, with the amount of murders this little town seems to have, it's been anything *but* peace and quiet since I got here."

"What a story," replied Kraus. "Well, it's New York's loss and Magnolia Bluff's gain." He glanced over at Joyce and smiled. "How'd you get mixed up with this character?"

She shrugged her shoulders. "He bought a house from me."

"Really?" He glanced over at Turner. "That must be some house."

"It's the only way I could get her to go out on a date with me," joked Turner.

Joyce gave him a light slap on the wrist. "That's not at all true," she said. "I would've said yes even if you just rented the house."

"You two are funny," said Kraus. "And I'm sure there's more to the story."

"There is," admitted Turner, offering no more details.

"Okay," said Kraus. "I get it. You wanna keep the details secret for now. We'll circle back another time."

Joyce rolled her eyes at Turner's short answer. She looked at Kraus. "No secret. Just a longer story better suited for another time," she said, then added, "What about you, Palmer? Anyone special in your life?"

"There used to be," he said, lowering his eyes. "But it didn't work out. We wanted different things out of life, so we decided to pursue our dreams separately."

Joyce reached across the table and lightly patted the back of his hand. "I'm sorry."

He withdrew his hand and put them both in his lap. "Don't be. It was mutual."

Observing the sudden uneasiness of the sergeant, Turner said, "Sounds like you wanna keep your details secret for now, too."

"Yeah," he admitted. "But like you guys, no real secrets here, either. Just not ready to talk about it. At least for now."

"Fair enough," replied Turner. "How about, as you said, we circle back another time on this entire conversation?"

They all nodded, and Joyce added, "Besides, you boys have to concentrate on catching the person who killed Ronnie Senior and put Ronnie Junior in the hospital." She grinned at Kraus. "We'll have you over for dinner one night after y'all put the murderer behind bars and swap relationship stories."

The detective returned her grin. "Sounds perfect." He glanced over at Turner, the smile gone. "We did a full sweep of the property after you left the farm."

"Didn't you guys do that after you found Ronnie Senior dead?"

"Not a whole sweep. We did a basic search of the house, since Junior said there was nothing missing or out of place. So we originally focused mainly on the area where Senior's body was found."

"I'm guessing something turned up during the new search?"

"Were you aware there's an old bomb shelter underneath the house?"

"Seriously?" replied Turner. "I saw the storm cellar door on the backside, but didn't really think much about it?"

"This room is much more than a storm cellar. We found two twin beds, an AM/FM transistor radio, an eight pack of nine-volt batteries with a five-year shelf life, a ham radio setup with a twelve-volt lithium battery power supply, and a four-tiered shelf with a year's worth of canned goods, along with an old crank-style can opener. There were also paper plates and plastic silverware in a box on one of the shelves."

"I guess Ronnie Senior feared the possibility of a nuclear war."

"Maybe," said Kraus. "Who can say what the man was thinking? But there was more thing down there. We also found a heavy duty safe sitting flat against the back wall with its legs bolted into the cement floor." He paused. "The door was wide open."

"Empty?" assumed Turner.

"As empty as my refrigerator is by the end of each month," said Kraus.

Turner shifted in his seat and nodded at the sergeant. "Whatever was in that safe is probably our motive for murder."

CHAPTER EIGHT

At noon, **Turner** and Joyce walked into the Burnet Medical Center and took the elevator up to the third floor. They'd left the Really Good Wood-Fired Coffee and Ice Cream Emporium sixty minutes after Sergeant Kraus had left the restaurant.

Turner thought it was wise to have Kraus leave first, and he and Joyce would lag behind at the coffee shop for another hour, just in case Captain Briggs was watching.

Turner followed Joyce out of the elevator. They walked past the nurse's station and down the hall toward room 309. Officer Schreiber was standing guard at the door entrance when they arrived at the room.

Joyce smiled at the officer. "Hi, Dick," she said. "Are you all moved into the new place yet?"

"Sure are," he beamed. "We love the house. And you were spot on about redoing the kitchen. The contractor completed the remodel last week. Thanks, by the way, for recommending him. He was great."

"I knew you'd like him. Jim and his team do quality work."

"Ginny liked him enough that we're having him turn the patio into a sunroom next month."

"Good for you guys," said Joyce. "And say hello to your beautiful wife for me."

"I will," said Dick. "Oh, and I gave my brother your card. His son is going to be looking for his first house this fall. Told him how pleased we were with you as our realtor."

She smiled at him. "Thanks, Dick. Referrals are a great source of business for me. And you'll be happy to know, if your brother's son buys his home from me, I'll pay you a referral fee. So make sure I get that call. It'll be worth it. Trust me."

"You got it," he replied. "And thank *you*." The officer looked over at Turner. "The captain called earlier and told me if you showed up, not to let you in to see Mr. Spatch. But no worries. Sergeant Kraus was here a little while ago. Before he left, he told me you'd be coming by soon and it would be okay to let you in. Said he'd handle the captain if it came down to it." He leaned over and continued in a mock whisper. "If Briggs asks, as far as I'm concerned, you were never here."

"Appreciate it, Dick," said Turner. He smiled. "Say hi to the wife from me, too."

He and Joyce stepped past Officer Schreiber and into the room. Ronnie was lying on the bed with his eyes closed. A nurse taking his vitals glanced up when they walked in. "I assume you must be family," she said as she gave them both the once over, "or the officer shouldn't have let you in here."

"That's right," lied Turner. "Family."

"How's he doing?" asked Joyce.

The nurse walked over and pulled a clipboard from the plastic box hanging off the end of the bed. She flipped through a couple of pages, jotted a few quick notes, and returned the chart to the box. "Mr. Spatch is doing much better today. But he still needs his rest, so please don't stay long."

As soon as the nurse left, Joyce walked over and took Ronnie's hand in hers. His eyes flittered open at her touch. A weak smile appeared. "Hey there, Ms. Blackstone," he said, his voice shaky. "Thanks fer comin' by."

"I'm so sorry you're experiencing all this pain in your life," she said. "Remember, Ronnie, seasons come and go. And no matter how bleak this time may be, it's just a season. Eventually, it'll pass and take all the pain away with it."

There was a tear in his eye. He lightly squeezed her hand. "Thank you, Ms. Blackstone."

"Ronnie," she said, returning the squeeze. "Brandon's also here. If you're up to it, he'd like to ask you a few questions."

Turner stepped closer to the bed. "Hey, Ronnie," he said. "How you feelin', bud?"

The young man winced in pain as he inched his way into a seated position. "Like a big 'ol Mack truck run over me," he said.

"I'll bet," replied Turner. "Any idea who did this to you?"

"Like I tole the sergeant when he was here, I didn't see nothin'. I heard a noise out in the barn and went inside to see what it was." He paused to catch his breath.

"Take your time, Ronnie," offered Joyce. "There's no hurry."

He nodded and took in a couple more shallow breaths before continuing. "I knew there was nothin' in there that should've been makin' any noise 'cept maybe a few chickens. And it didn't sound like no chickens. Me and Daddy sold off the milkin' cows and our two horses to hep pay the bills a couple months back."

Turner thought about what he saw inside the barn. "Why didn't you sell that big red tractor in the barn instead of your animals?"

Ronnie spit out a laugh and then immediately

clutched his abdomen. "Ow. I guess laughin's not such a good idea," he said. "That ain't no tractor. It's a combine harvester. Daddy wanted to continue farmin' the land. He thought it was better to keep the equipment and sell the cows and the horses. It's good land for crops."

"Okay. I guess that makes sense," said Turner. Not being a farmer, he really didn't understand the logic but wanted to get back on track. "Tell me what happened when you went inside the barn."

"I looked around a bit and called out to see if anyone would answer. Next thing I knew, I got jumped from behind. Don't remember nothin' else till I woke up here this mornin'."

Turner nodded. "I'm sure you're aware that the police searched your home."

"Yep," replied Ronnie. "Sergeant Kraus tole me so when he was here. I'm figurin' you wanna know the same thing he did—what was in the safe my daddy had in the bunker?"

"That would be extremely helpful," said Turner.

"First off," said Ronnie. "I never been in that safe. Had no need. Daddy tole me it's where he kept all the important papers about the farm and the land. He wanted me to know in case somthin' ever happened to him." He lowered his eyes. "I'm ashamed. I didn't think to look inside it when daddy was kilt. I plum forgot all about that safe till the sergeant asked me 'bout it."

Joyce gave Ronnie a caring smile. "Nothing to be ashamed about."

"She's right," said Turner. "Too much going on. I'm sure in time, you would've remembered."

"I reckon so," said Ronnie. "But all my thoughts have been on how to catch whoever kilt my daddy... not about checkin' some paperwork in his safe after he died."

"So when you said, 'all the paperwork about the farm,' did you mean things like the deed to the house and the land? Insurance policies? Maybe a will? That kind of paperwork?"

Ronnie scrunched his nose. "I reckon," he said. "Didn't never get into the details with him. Always figured me and daddy had plenty of time for that later."

Turner shook his head and glanced over at Joyce. "I wish we knew for certain if that's the type of paperwork that was inside the safe," he said. "Otherwise, it's still just speculation. And if it was the property deed or insurance policies in the safe, I'm sure there are several reasons someone would want to take it."

Joyce agreed. "It could be anything from insurance fraud to using the property as collateral for a fraudulent loan to stealing the house and land right out from under the Spatch family." Addressing Ronnie, she said, "Do you know if anyone approached your daddy recently about wanting to make an offer on your land?"

The boy shook his head. "I don't know," he said. "Daddy said nothin' 'bout speakin' to nobody 'bout sellin' the house or any of the land."

"How big is your property?" asked Turner.

"Just shy of thirty acres," he said, sitting up a little straighter. "But I don't believe Daddy would've sold any of it to nobody. He was proud of what we had. The land's been in our family for three generations, and I know he wanted to pass it on to me when he was gone."

Turner was taken aback. "That's a good chunk of land. Ever had it surveyed, to be sure?"

"We had someone come survey the property last month. Daddy wanted to better understand exactly where the property lines was drawn and to confirm the total acreage."

"Are you positive about him not wanting to sell?" asked Turner. "That's a lot of acres. Worth a pretty penny, I imagine. And you already said he sold off the cows and horses recently to make ends meet. Could be why he wanted the survey done. Maybe he was considering sectioning off a few parcels to make life a bit more financially stable for both of you."

"That don't make no sense," said a visibly upset Ronnie. "Why not tell me 'bout it? Why go and sell off the animals if he was gonna sell off a piece of the property? And iffin' he was gonna sell, why kill him and steal the papers outta the safe?" He paused. "No, it don't make no sense."

"I want you to take a couple deep breaths, Ronnie," Joyce said in a soothing tone. "Why don't you take a minute to rest while I talk to Brandon?"

The young man nodded and let out a deep sigh. "It don't make no sense," he muttered quietly to no one in particular.

Turner followed Joyce outside the room so they could talk and give Ronnie a minute. Officer Schreiber closed the door behind them. "Are you guys through in there?" he asked.

"Not quite yet," said Joyce. "Brandon and I need a minute to go over something and then we'd like to go back in to say goodbye to Ronnie before we leave."

"You got it," said Schreiber.

"Thank you, Dick," said Turner. "We'll only be a minute."

They walked down to a small waiting area near the elevators and sat down.

"I agree with him," Joyce said. "If Ronnie Senior was planning on selling any or all of his property, it stands to reason he would've talked with his son about it."

Turner nodded. "You're right. And he brought up a good point—why kill Senior and steal the paperwork if he was going to sell?"

"If he agreed to sell," Joyce reminded him. "It's all speculation, like you said."

"I know," replied Turner. "It's all so frustrating. I was hoping to get some positive answers from Ronnie, but it feels like we're still stuck on square one."

"It's not a total loss," she said. "We know Ronnie's going to live, and that's something positive."

Turner nodded and gave her a smile. "Thanks for keeping my head on straight."

She leaned over and kissed his cheek. "Anytime," she said. "Let's go back and say goodbye to Ronnie and let him know that you're just getting started on the investigation and what you said in there about his daddy selling his land is only one avenue to pursue. It's not the only thing you're going to look at."

They stood up and strolled hand-in-hand back down to the room. They found Ronnie sound asleep when they walked in. Joyce sighed and looked at Turner. "Tell you what," she said. "I'll come back tomorrow and let him know you're investigating all the reasons someone might've broken into the safe and not just the idea of his daddy selling off any of the land. It's possible it's not even related to Ronnie Senior being murdered. I'll make him feel better about things, okay?"

"Yeah. Probably better you have that conversation without me. He seems a tad upset with me at the moment."

"Don't worry," she said with a grin. "I'll smooth things over. Can't have you getting fired from your first PI gig, now can we?"

CHAPTER NINE

After he and Joyce left the hospital yesterday, they took advantage of her having the rest of the day off. They lazed around eating and sipping wine while chatting about everything they'd learned while visiting Ronnie.

Jason had not arrived back home last night until after dinner, opting to eat with Hank, Ann, and their daughter, Camila. Of course, Turner understood Camila was the driving force behind the young man's decision

His mind wandered back to the first time he'd fallen for a girl. He was right around the same age as Jason was now and could relate to what the kid might be going through with his feelings.

He wondered if he should let him know he was available if he ever needed to talk. Or maybe he should leave that up to Jason's father. Sometimes it felt like he was walking a delicate line. Denny was still a big part of the boy's life. It had always been that way, even after Joyce and Denny divorced.

Turner shook his head slightly and refocused.

He'd had a good night's sleep—much better than the night before. He woke up later than usual and discovered Joyce had already left the house. She had a twelve-thirty appointment to show a townhouse to a pregnant young couple relocating from Grand Prairie.

Turner knew she couldn't skip another day of work. She told him the night before she'd planned on leaving a couple hours earlier, so she'd have enough time to swing by the medical center and speak with Ronnie. It was important to make sure he was no longer upset about his suggestion that Senior might've been thinking about selling their home, or perhaps maybe just some of the land.

After taking a quick shower, he was ready to get down to business. He was curious about the missing contents from inside the safe. Were the documents valuable enough for someone to commit murder to get their hands on them? Answering these questions started with going back out to the Spatch farm.

Turner wanted to see the bomb shelter, but more importantly, he wanted to see the safe inside the bomb shelter. According to Kraus, his team had done a complete search of the house the same day he'd found Ronnie on the floor inside the barn. The only thing they'd uncovered of any interest was the safe, or more to the point, that there were no documents inside the safe.

Even though he told Ronnie he'd back off on the idea of his father wanting to sell some or all the land, the current pieces of the puzzle seemed to fit that scenario best. Didn't mean it was the only viable solution, but it was a place to start.

In the spirit of playing nice, he placed a call to Sergeant Kraus to keep him in the loop. The line rang twice, then clicked over to voice mail. "Hey, Palmer," he said after the beep, "It's Brandon. Had an interesting discussion with Ronnie yesterday. I'm on my way back out to the farm to nose around a bit more. Call me when you get a chance."

He clicked off his phone and wandered down to Jason's room to tell the boy he was leaving. No surprise that Max was lying on the bed when he walked in. He scratched his pooch under the chin, gave him a pat on the head, said goodbye to Jason, and wandered back up the hallway to the kitchen.

He opened the fridge, grabbed a bottle of water and the last slice of the leftover pizza from the other night, and threw it on a paper plate. Then he cut through the garage and went out to the driveway. After tossing the plate with the cold pizza on the passenger seat, he walked around to the driver's side and got inside the truck. He sat in the cab and scarfed down the slice and drank half the bottle of water before pulling out of the driveway.

He drove up State Highway 38, crossed over Blossom Street, and took the right onto Cemetery Drive. After passing the Magnolia Bluff Cemetery, he turned onto Muskrat Road.

Like the last time he was at Ronnie's place, Turner parked behind the small red pickup. But instead of stepping up onto the porch, this time he went directly behind the house to where the storm cellar was located.

Crime scene tape draped across the doors and a shiny new chain and padlock had replaced the rusty lock and hasp.

"Hey, Brandon."

Turner whirled around and saw Sergeant Kraus walking toward him. He stared at the detective.

Kraus smiled. "Got your message," he said, waving a silver key in the air. "Figured I'd join you."

"Glad to see you. I was just about to check the toolbox in the back of my truck for a pair of cutters so I could take this lock off."

"No need to commit a B&E," chuckled Kraus. "I'd hate to arrest you so early in our friendship." He stuck the key in the lock, turned it, and slid it out from between the metal links.

Turner nodded at the big, thick chain wrapped through the door handles. "Your handiwork?"

"You should've seen how quickly the team was able to break the old hasp off the door. They didn't even bother with the lock, just pried the rusty hasp off on one side with a crowbar and bent it back," he said with a shrug. "Didn't want anyone nefarious getting the same idea. The big ass chain is a deterrent."

"Nefarious?"

"Yeah. Nefarious."

Turner's lips twisted into a smirk. "Good word."

Kraus grinned. "Yeah, I thought so."

"Ready to go in?" Turner asked while he unwrapped the chain from the handles.

They both grabbed a door handle and lifted, then peered down the stairs into the cellar. "After you," said Kraus.

Turner trotted down the steps first, followed by the sergeant. When Kraus hit the bottom step, he reached to his right and pulled a string hanging down from the ceiling. Light flooded the room.

Even though it was now bright enough, Turner pulled out a pencil thin flashlight and began searching the room. He focused the pinpoint beam under the beds, behind the shelving against the wall, and all around the canned goods that lined the shelves.

After examining every nook and cranny he could find, he turned his attention to the ham radio. "Does this thing work?"

"Don't know," admitted Kraus. "Didn't turn it on the other day. But the transistor radio works."

"You turned on the transistor radio, but not the ham

radio?"

The detective shrugged. "I wanted to listen to some music while I searched the room. I know my way around an FM dial. The ham radio didn't interest me. Figured it's not that much different from the ten-code radio in my cruiser."

"Yeah, but you can't talk to someone across the country on your police radio."

Kraus let a small grin appear. "I think I'll live," he said, while swinging the safe door open. "You wanna look in here?"

Turner shook his head. "Naw, I know it's empty," he said with a wry grin. "I trust you checked it over for secret compartments."

"Did everything to it except push it away from the wall," the sergeant replied. "The damn thing must weigh upwards of five-hundred pounds. I assume Spatch didn't hide anything behind it."

Turner nodded. He tried to move the safe. It didn't budge. Then he tried to get a look behind it. It sat tight against the wall. He glanced over at Kraus. "Good assumption."

He walked over to one of the beds and sat. "I spoke with Ronnie yesterday. He's got thirty acres here. That's gotta be worth a pretty penny. If the missing paperwork is actually the deed and other land-related documents, I'm leaning toward the idea of Senior being murdered to get a hold of the land."

"Maybe," said Kraus. "But why? Farmland isn't hard to find around here. Farming is a tough way to make a buck. People are getting out. I see 'For Sale' signs all over Burnet County every day. Even the farm down the road from this one has a 'For Sale' sign on it. Why would someone kill

Ronnie Senior for his?"

"Don't know," admitted Turner. "I'm just spitballing here. Ronnie said his father had a survey done a month ago. I think he may have been thinking about selling off some of his land."

"If that's true, why wouldn't someone just buy it? Why kill him?" wondered Kraus.

"What if someone approached him about selling? Maybe he agreed and then changed his mind?" offered Turner.

"Again, why kill him over it?" said Kraus. "The house is a piece of crap."

"The house can be torn down. And besides, Ronnie claims he didn't have any knowledge of his father thinking about selling all or any part of the farm," said Turner. "He said his dad told him he wanted the farm to go to him one day. Senior wanted to keep the home and land in the family."

Kraus sighed. "Which puts a hole in the theory about him wanting to sell at all."

"Agreed. Except Senior was getting old. The land had to be worth enough to give him a comfortable retirement if he sold it and set Junior up for quite a while."

The sergeant disagreed. "Guys like Ronnie Senior don't retire," he said. "They work the land until they die. Then they're buried in a patch of that same dirt they worked and sweated over for years."

"You just said yourself that you see farmland up for sale all the time."

"And I'd bet money on it that the folks selling are the grown kids who inherited the farms and didn't want the same rough life their parents had. Not the situation here. Senior was still working his farm until someone put a knife in his belly."

Turner nodded. Maybe the land wasn't the reason Ronnie Senior was murdered.

He would have to keep digging.

CHAPTER TEN

Turner spent another hour or so at the Spatch farm after Kraus left. Although he got along with the sergeant much better than he had with Sovern, he still didn't want him crawling up his butt all day. So, when Captain Briggs called Kraus to the station, Turner happily remained by himself to explore the property.

Since he'd only taken a cursory look the other day, the first thing he did was check out the scene of the murder. He walked over to where Ronnie Senior's body was found and inspected the tractor and surrounding grass. Someone other than Junior, most likely the killer, had removed the crime scene tape and washed all the bloodstains from the tractor.

After a thorough examination of the area surrounding the tractor, and finding nothing of substance, Turner wandered the property for a little while. He guessed he probably searched about three of the thirty acres before deciding it would be more useful riding an all-terrain vehicle. He made a mental note to look into that before he made another trip back to the farm.

His stomach started complaining, alerting him it was lunchtime. He glanced at the time on his phone and sighed. It was one-thirty, which meant Joyce was most likely still showing that couple the townhouse.

He figured he could wait a little longer to eat, so he decided to check out the barn again before calling Joyce. Finding Ronnie bleeding on the floor certainly had distracted him. Maybe he missed something the last time.

He understood the sergeant had his team search the barn when they conducted the search of the house. But just because he liked and trusted Kraus didn't mean he had any faith in the rest of the MBPD to recognize a clue. He'd seen them in action too many times to have any confidence in any of them identifying a clue, even if it jumped up and bit one of them on the face. Besides, maybe Joyce would be free for lunch by the time he finished searching the building.

Turner pulled his small flashlight from his pocket, opened the barn door, and went inside.

"Combine harvester," he grumbled as he walked around the big farm machine. "Still looks like a big tractor to me."

He got down on his hands and knees, clicked on his penlight, and peered underneath the vehicle. Next, he made his way over to the two horse stalls. As expected, they were empty except for some hay scattered on the floor inside each stall.

Aside from some tools on the bench, the box of rags, a few rakes, and some different size shovels, the rest of the barn was also empty.

He stared at the box of rags. *What am I missing?* he thought. *Thank God those rags were sitting there. Stopping the bleeding might have been impossible otherwise.* He inhaled sharply and started to walk away when something caught his eye.

He leaned down to get a better look. There were a few footprints in the dirt, but that's not what made him stop. The prints probably belonged to whatever officer clomped around the bench area where the tools and rags were located. Hell, one pair he recognized as his own. What caught his eye was the dirt that appeared to be pushed around underneath the prints. It looked like someone used their hand to sweep away what might've been some other footprints.

Now he was curious. Why would somebody take the time to erase their tracks? Unless they didn't want to leave any evidence that they were near the area.

At first glance, Turner saw nothing on or around the bench that piqued his interest. Frustrated, he took a step back and took in the scene in front of him.

Again, what was he missing?

His stomach growled, adding to his frustration.

Perhaps it would be easier to focus after lunch. He pulled his phone from his pocket and checked the time.

Two-fifteen. He smiled. Surely her appointment had ended by now.

He lifted the phone to his face and said, "Call Joyce."

After two rings, he heard a faint voice say, "Hey, hon. I'm starving. I was hoping you would call."

"Hold on a sec. I've gotta turn up the volume so I can hear you." He pulled his phone away from his ear so he could find the correct button on the side. As soon as he pushed it, the phone slipped from his hand and landed in the box of rags.

"*Dammit*," he said, then called out loud enough so Joyce could hear him. "Hang on. I dropped my phone." He stuck his arm down into the box and fished his hand around, trying to locate the device.

It was as if the soft rags swallowed his phone.

He dug deeper.

Finally, his hand grasped a solid object, and he knew immediately it wasn't what he went fishing for. When his hand came out of the box, it was grasping a wooden handled hunting knife sporting a four-and-a-half-inch high carbon steel blade.

He shook his head slightly, laid the knife on the bench, then dove his hand back into the rags and retrieved his phone. Putting it up to his ear, he said, "I'm sorry to do this, but I'm not gonna make lunch."

"What's going on?"

"I've gotta get in touch with Palmer. I'll explain later," he said, then ended the call.

Turner heard the barn door open and watched the silhouette of Sergeant Kraus enter through the bright sunlight.

"What took you so long?"

"I was in the middle of having lunch when you called," replied Kraus.

"I told you I found something."

"Yeah, but you didn't tell me what you found, so I figured it could wait until I finished eating."

Turner mumbled something undecipherable about not getting to eat under his breath.

Kraus gave him a puzzled look. "I didn't understand what you just said."

Turner shook off his frustration about missing lunch. "I said, your team missed a major piece of evidence when they searched the barn." He nodded his head at the knife still sitting over on the bench.

"Where the hell did you find that?" asked the wide-eyed detective.

"Buried in the box of rags."

Kraus pulled a pair of latex gloves from his pocket, along with a large plastic bag. He strapped on the gloves, walked over to the bench, and picked up the knife. He turned it over in his hands while giving it a close inspection. "The blade was wiped clean," he said. "Probably won't find any prints on it either."

"You'll find my fingerprints on the handle."

Kraus nodded. "Well, no usable prints anyway," he said, correcting himself. He carefully placed the knife inside the bag and sealed it. Then he pulled out a marker and jotted the date and time on the bag. He also recorded the location and Turner's name as the person who found the knife and reported it to the police. "I'll have this checked for prints, anyway. You never know, we might get lucky."

"Maybe," agreed Turner. "Even a partial would be better than nothing."

Kraus nodded again, then said, "Tell me everything you did after I left earlier, right up to finding the knife in the box. And by the way, I'm going to record this to save you a trip down to the station. So hold on a second." He took his phone from his pocket and pushed the voice memo app, then gave his name, their location, the date and time, and whose statement he was recording. When he was through, he pointed the phone at Turner and said, "Okay, go."

Turner accounted for all his movements from the time he and Kraus parted ways. He began with his inspection of the tractor and the surrounding area. Next, he gave the details of his walk around the property, which entailed just the first three acres. He expressed that an inspection of the remaining twenty-seven acres using an all-terrain vehicle should take place.

Next, he moved on to his search inside the barn. He gave the details of everything he inspected—under and around the big red harvester, the horse stalls, and the dirt floor near the box of rags that looked to him like someone tried to sweep away their footprints. He ended with how he dropped his phone inside the box and found the knife when he fished through the rags searching for his phone.

He left out the part about being hangry because of missing lunch.

Kraus stopped the recording and slid the phone back into his pocket. He glanced down at the box, then asked, "How do you think the knife ended up inside a box of rags?"

"My best guess," said Turner, "is that when I opened the door to the barn the other day, I alerted whoever was in here with Ronnie that they were not alone. I'm figuring they must've panicked. Then they quickly stabbed Ronnie, saw the box filled with rags, wiped the knife down, and threw it in with the rags. Take a look around. It's dark in here. They probably hid in the shadows and slipped out when I found Ronnie."

"You said, 'they'," replied Kraus. "You think there was more than one person?"

Turner shook his head. "I don't know," he admitted. "Could've been just one person. My gut's telling me different. If it is some kind of attempted land grab, it makes sense that it's not someone acting alone."

"Well," stated the sergeant, "the way Chief Jager talks about the success you've had solving those other murders, I'm willing to trust that gut of yours."

"I appreciate that, Palmer."

Kraus smiled, then nodded at Turner's midsection. "Sounds like your gut's trying to tell you something right now."

Turner winced as his stomach growled. "Yeah," he said, rubbing his belly. "It's telling me to get some food in there before there's an act of mutiny against my body."

CHAPTER ELEVEN

Turner swung into a gas station convenience store and grabbed a large fountain drink and a couple of hotdogs from the heated rollers near the counter. He slapped them on some buns and slathered them with mustard. It wasn't the best choice, but it was fast, and he was beyond starving.

The first dog was on its way to his stomach before he was back inside the truck. He hopped into his pickup, finished off the second wiener, and washed it down with half his soda.

He exited the gas station, returning to Burnet Reservoir Road, and headed to Joyce's house.

By the time he was sitting in her driveway, he'd managed to down the rest of his thirty-two ounce Big Gulp.

As he got out of his vehicle, the garage door opened and Max came bounding from beneath the door into the driveway, followed by Joyce.

"Thank God you're all right. I've been worried all afternoon," she said, wrapping him up in a hug. She planted a kiss on his lips, then added, "What happened?"

"I love you," he said, handing her his big empty drink cup. "And I promise I'll tell you everything. But right now, I've got to hit the head."

Joyce looked at the cup and rolled her eyes in amusement. She giggled and stuffed the cup into the trash can as they all went inside the garage. "Come on, Max," she said, following Turner into the house. "Let's go wait for Daddy in the living room."

"Thank you," he yelled as he rushed down the hallway toward the bathroom.

A few minutes later, a relieved Turner sat down on the sofa between Joyce and Max. The big dog laid his head on Turner's lap and looked up at him. "You look pathetic," he said, laughing. Then he kissed Max on the head and gave him the attention he was craving. "You're such a good boy. I'm sorry I ignored you when I first got here, but when ya gotta go, ya gotta go." Max reached up and licked him right on the mouth. Turner gave his dog one last flurry of petting and scratching and then turned his attention to Joyce. "Hey there," he said, a sexy grin on his face.

"Hey there, back," she replied with a grin of her own.

He leaned over and nuzzled her on the neck. She playfully pushed him back and waggled her finger at him. "Uh-uh," she said. "No fooling around until you tell me everything that happened today."

A dejected Turner leaned back against the sofa and blew out a breath. "Okay," he said. "You're right. You already know I went back out to Ronnie's farm this morning. Palmer showed up, and we did another search of the bunker and the safe. We came up empty-handed. Anyway, Briggs called him, and he had to leave. So I stayed around and searched the property on my own. I started over by where the tractor was becau—"

"That's all well and good," she said, interrupting him, "but can we skip ahead to the part where you hung up on me?"

Turner shrugged. "You said you wanted to hear everything. I was just complying with your wishes."

She shook her head, sighed, and gave him a light slap

on the arm. "Fine," she said. "Ya got me. Now, can you please tell me what happened that made you hang up on me?"

"I found a hunting knife inside that box of rags in the barn. It's probably the weapon used to stab Ronnie and might be the same knife that was used to kill Senior. Palmer's checking it for prints and we'll see where it takes us."

Joyce sat there speechless for a minute before saying anything. "My God," she said softly. "The same box you pulled rags from to save Ronnie?"

"The same."

"And you didn't notice it in the box then?"

He shook his head and lowered his eyes. "I took the first few rags from the top of the pile. I never stuck my hand all the way into the box that day."

She leaned into his shoulder. "I didn't mean anything by what I said."

"It's not that. Whoever hurt Ronnie was still in the barn when I walked in. If I was better tuned into my senses, I might've been able to catch them before they escaped."

"You don't know that. Don't put yourself through that. Your focus was where it needed to be—saving Ronnie's life. If anyone's to blame, it's the police for not doing their jobs."

"That's not fair either," he said. "The police weren't even there. They arrived on the scene after the fact. Their blame lies with conducting a piss-poor search of the barn… twice. They should've found the knife during their initial search, or at least during the second search."

Joyce nodded. "Just as long as that damn Captain Briggs doesn't somehow place the blame on you with some trumped up obstruction charge or whatever."

"Don't you worry about Briggs. I can handle him. And besides, he has no justification for even suggesting blaming me. As soon as I found the knife, I called Palmer. He came and took over the scene from that point forward."

She lifted herself from his shoulder so she could find his eyes. "I know that. But the man I saw marching across the Really Good is hell bent on keeping you from being involved in this investigation."

Turner nodded. He couldn't deny the fact. "You're right. He is. He also can't stop me," he said. "I'm working on this case as a private investigator on behalf of a client who willfully hired me to do so. And just as long as I don't cross a legal line, he can stew about it all he wants for all I care."

"Just be careful and don't cross any of those legal lines. I don't wanna have to bail you out of jail anytime soon." She paused. "On a good note, I saw Ronnie today, and he's doing better. Dr. Pope was walking out of his room right as I showed up and she told me they're going to keep him there until the wound in his abdomen heals enough that he's able to walk on his own."

"I guess it would be challenging to walk after that kind of trauma. I'm glad he's staying put for a while. Makes it harder for whoever attacked him to come back and finish the job."

"From your lips to God's ears," she said, then added, "And Ronnie's not upset with you pushing him about his father maybe wanting to sell. He understands you are trying to catch whoever murdered his daddy, and you have to look at every possibility."

"Good," replied Turner. "Because I have a nagging

feeling that might be the direction we're headed. I just have to figure out who and why?"

Joyce nodded and rubbed his leg. She gave him a suggestive smile. "So what's next, Mr. Big Shot PI?"

"Where's Jason?"

"He's been out at Hank and Ann's farm all afternoon. He and Camila went horseback riding. I heard from him a little while ago. They're all going out for pizza at Olivia's tonight. Hank will drop him off later after they eat."

"Hmm... that means we've got the house to ourselves." The corners of his lips turned upward. "Can you guess what's next for the big shot PI?"

She put her arms around his neck and leaned in so close he could feel her breath against his ear as she spoke. "I think it's time for you to investigate my bedroom," she said, as a seductive smile played across her lips. "And leave nothing untouched."

CHAPTER TWELVE

Turner looked across the kitchen table at Joyce and said, "I've got to go over to my place this morning. If I don't cut my lawn soon, the HOA is probably going to fine me."

Joyce rolled her eyes. "You live in a cabin on a lake. You don't have an HOA."

He cracked a smile her way. "Just making a point. My grass is getting tall."

"Why don't you ask Jason to cut it?"

"That's not a bad idea," he said. "I'll offer to pay him to do it. Maybe get him to trim those bushes around the side of the house, too."

"Exactly," agreed Joyce. "That way, you can stay focused on the investigation."

"I would've stayed focused. I planned on doing some deep thinking while cutting," he said. "What time are you going to work today?"

"In about an hour." An amorous grin appeared on her face. "Why? You wanna quick repeat of last night before I go?"

"As much as I would love nothing more," he said, matching her grin. "As you said, I need to stay focused on the case today. But I'll certainly take a raincheck for tonight."

"I think we can arrange that," she said, giving him a wink. "If you're not planning on taking me this morning, was there another reason you asked when I was leaving?"

"I wanted to pick your realtor brain and ask you a

couple of questions that might help me sort some things out."

"I'll do my best," she said. "What do you want to know?"

"When we were at the hospital, you said something about fraud that involved stealing the house and land without the owner's knowledge. How hard would it be for someone to steal a property like the Spatch farm out from under the owner?"

She let out a sigh. "Unfortunately, not that hard at all. There's even a name for it—home title theft."

"How does it work?"

"Well," she said. "First thing to know is that it's not a common form of theft. But it is identity theft, and most people don't even know about it. Which makes it even more dangerous. Someone gets a property owner's information and opens a line of credit against their home, usually either a home equity loan or a prime equity line that's loaded onto a credit card. The owner finds out when they start getting the bills in the mail or creditors start calling demanding money for payments that haven't been made. Or even worse, they discover that someone has sold their property without their knowledge." She shuddered. "There are other ways besides those, but these are the biggest. It's scary to think about."

"So, if Ronnie Senior kept all his homeowner's documents in his safe and someone stole them, whoever killed him would have total financial control over his home and land."

"Conceivably, yes." Her eyes widened. "Do you really think that's why someone attacked Ronnie and murdered his daddy?"

"Could be," he replied. "I believe it's all somehow connected. I just have to figure out how and why."

Joyce leaned across the table and took his hand in hers. "If anyone can, it's you. I have faith in you."

Turner nodded. "Thanks for the vote of confidence. And thank you for the info. It's reason enough for me to visit the courthouse this morning." He looked up over her shoulder as Jason walked into the kitchen.

The teen let out a yawn. "Mornin', peeps," he said while grabbing the milk from the refrigerator and cereal and a bowl from the cupboard. He rummaged through a drawer next to the sink and pulled out a spoon.

Turner waited until the boy filled his bowl with frosted flakes and milk. After watching him shovel in an overflowing spoonful, he smiled and said, "Breakfast of champions."

Jason shrugged. "Don't blame me," he said. "I don't do the grocery shopping around here."

"Would you rather I bought you a box of plain oats for your breakfasts?" countered Joyce.

"I never said I didn't want frosted flakes," Jason said. "I merely pointed out I'm not the one who chose them." He glanced over at Turner and grinned. "Brandon's the one criticizing your choice, not me."

"You're right," she said, agreeing with her son. She turned her focus to Turner and raised her brows. "What've you got to say for yourself, mister?"

He looked across the table at his two most favorite people in the world. They were both staring at him with a playful smirks on their faces. "I'd say it's time for me to change the subject before this hole gets any deeper." His eyes moved to Jason. "How would you like to make some money this afternoon?"

"I'm in. Whatdaya need done?"

"I'd like you to cut the grass and trim the bushes over at my place," he said. "I'll give you twenty-five bucks."

"I don't know," said Jason. "That's a lot of work. Twenty-five seems a bit light."

Turner leveled his gaze at the boy. "I've got a riding lawn mower."

"But it's gonna be really hot today. I'll still be sweating big time. I'll do it for fifty."

"Wear a hat," Turner replied. "I'll bump it up to forty and all the lemonade you can drink."

Jason let a wide grin spread across his face. "half up front," he countered.

He had to admit, he liked the boy's negotiating style. "Ten up front. The rest when you're done, and I'm satisfied with the job."

"You gotta deal," smiled Jason. He thrust his hand out.

Turner grabbed it in his and gave it a hearty shake. He looked at the boy with respect and smiled. "Not bad, Jason. Not bad at all. Where did you learn to negotiate like that?"

"My dad," he said. "He bought a new car last year, and I went with him. I paid close attention to what he did and said, trying to get the best deal he could. I know this wasn't the same thing as buying a car, but I figured I'd try out what I learned watching my dad."

"Well, you impressed me. Maybe you should go into sales."

"Not a chance," replied Jason. "You know I want to be a doctor."

"Yes," said Joyce, looking at Turner. "So let's not distract him from that goal."

"Wouldn't dream of it. Just saying the boy's got skills,

that's all."

"Good," she said with a nod.

Turner pulled a ten-dollar bill from his wallet and handed it to Jason. "Not sure if I'll still be at home when you get there. All the lawn equipment is in the shed, which has a combination lock on the door." He pulled out his phone and started typing. "I'm texting you the combo now."

Jason took his phone from his front pocket. "Got it. I think I'm going to get it cut earlier before it gets too hot." He glanced over at his mother. "Can I borrow the car?"

"Not today," she said. "I've got to work. But you can catch a ride with me when I leave, then call me when you're done, and I'll come pick you up."

"When's that gonna be?" said Jason, the disappointment clear on his face.

"How about as soon as you finish your cereal?"

He spooned the rest of the flakes into his mouth, then lifted the bowl to his lips and gulped down the milk and cereal together. After letting out a belch that would wake the dead, he said, "I'm done."

Turner and Joyce looked at each other, then at Jason. "That was quite the burp," said Turner. He smiled. "Hall of fame caliber."

Jason smirked. "Thanks. I've been practicing."

Joyce looked at them both. "I guess it's true what they say."

"What's that?" asked Turner.

"Men never really grow up," she said, shaking her head.

Once Joyce and Jason were on their way, Turner went down to Jason's bedroom and rousted Max off the bed.

He let him outside using the garage door and prepared a couple bowls of food and water for him while he was out doing his business.

Turner felt bad about leaving Max at Joyce's alone all day, but he knew that having his dog with him at the courthouse would probably not be acceptable. He gave his buddy some attention, then locked up the house and headed to the center of town.

The courthouse sat on the Green kitty-corner from the *Chronicle*, Magnolia Bluff's newspaper. Turner pulled his truck into the parking lot on the north side of the courthouse building, got out of his vehicle, and went inside.

After he cleared the metal detector, he checked the directory, then rode the elevator up to the second floor where the Burnet County Register of Deeds office was located.

When he walked into the office, there was a woman in her mid-thirties standing behind the counter sliding a stack of papers, one by one, into an automatic stamping machine. She stopped what she was doing and looked up as he approached. "Hello," she said. "Is there something I can help you with?"

Turner glanced at the nametag pinned to her blouse. "Yes. Hello, Celia. I would like to look at any information you have on a property. The address is twenty-three Muskrat Road, here in Magnolia Bluff."

"Are you the property owner?"

"No, I'm not," he said. He pulled out his ID and held it up for her to see. "My name is Brandon Turner. I'm a private investigator working alongside of the police. The case I'm working on involves the home at this address."

"Do you have a warrant or something?"

"No. I'm not a cop. I'm private. But isn't what I'm asking for public information? As in, no warrant needed?"

Celia forced out a breath. "Yes, I suppose it is," she said. "However, it will take some time to gather up what you want." She glanced up at the clock hanging on the wall by the door. "Give me a couple hours and I should have everything pulled for you to look at. Come back after lunch."

Turner gave her a tight smile and said, "I don't understand why my request is going to take so long to fill. But fine, I'll see you this afternoon."

"Small town. Small office. And I'm by myself most of the time." She gave him a meaningless shrug and went back to work, feeding papers into the stamping machine.

He exhaled through pursed lips, nodded, and walked out of the office.

CHAPTER THIRTEEN

Turner left the courthouse and drove around the corner to the police station. Chief Tommy Jager pulled into the lot right behind him and pulled his police SUV into the space next to his. Both men got out of their vehicles at the same time.

"Hey, Brandon," the chief said as he walked around to where Turner was waiting. "To what do I owe the pleasure?"

"Just thought I'd stop by and catch you up on what I've been up to on the Spatch investigation."

"Unless you're about to give me the name of the killer, it's not really necessary. Sergeant Kraus has been keeping me in the loop."

Turner nodded. "I figured he was. Where is the sergeant this morning? I was hoping to give both of you guys an update together, since I'm here, if that's okay?"

Tommy smiled. "Course it is," he said. "But it'll be just me. Sergeant Kraus is out interviewing a witness for another case he's working on." He glanced up at the sky. "Let's get outta this bright sunshine and talk in my office."

Turner followed Tommy into the building. After chatting with Gloria at the front desk for a couple of minutes, the two men went down the hallway to the chief's office.

"Have a seat," Tommy said while walking around the desk. He plopped himself in his chair. "What can I do ya for?"

Turner quickly got down to business. "As you're

probably aware, Sergeant Kraus and his team discovered an old bomb shelter out at the Spatch farm that contained an old floor safe. You also know the safe was empty when they opened it."

"Yep. Sure wish we knew what was inside that big 'ole safe. Might lead us to who killed Ronnie Senior."

"I agree," said Turner. "I believe the missing contents of the safe are the key to this murder. I'm sure Kraus told you our theory about Senior maybe reneging on selling either his house or some of his land."

Tommy nodded and leaned forward across his desk. "I thought after you both spoke with Ronnie Junior, that theory didn't have any legs? What're you thinking?"

"My gut's telling me those legs are still walking. It makes little sense to me that the land's been in the Spatch family for almost a hundred years, yet Senior decided to get it surveyed last month. Why? He told his son he wanted to make sure where the property lines were. All of a sudden? And for no other reason than doing an inventory of the land? I don't buy it. I think he planned on selling, then for some reason, changed his mind."

"Maybe so," said Tommy. "Maybe he started feeling guilty about selling his family's heritage right out from under his son."

"That's just it," replied Turner. "Thirty acres is a lot of land. Selling it would've set them both up for life. Most people couldn't walk away from that much money. Especially if you've struggled your whole life, like Ronnie and his son have."

The chief shrugged his shoulders. "Some things are more important than money. Or maybe Ronnie Senior didn't need the money. I've seen it before—run down lookin' house, beat up old truck, and a pile of money hiding under the mattress. Maybe Senior was sittin' on a pile of cash that nobody, including his son, knew about."

Turner shook his head. "I don't think so. Ronnie told me his father sold off the cows and their two horses a few months ago so they could make ends meet. Does that sound like something a man would do if he was harboring a fortune somewhere?"

Tommy let out a sigh. "No, I guess not," he said. "But that still doesn't mean he was ever thinking about selling the farm."

"You're right. But what if someone approached him to sell? Maybe the idea of giving himself and Junior a better life was enticing enough for him to say yes?"

"If that was the case, then why change his mind?"

"And therein lies the rub," said Turner.

"If he agreed to sell after being approached, and then changed his mind, something must have triggered it," said Tommy. "But why was he approached in the first place?"

"I think he discovered something on that survey that changed his mind. Something that perhaps someone else already knew about when they approached him."

"I guess it could've played out that way," said Tommy. "But what could be so important about the Spatch farm that would cause somebody to kill Ronnie Senior if he wouldn't sell?"

"Hopefully, I'll have the answer to that question later this afternoon," replied Turner. "I was at the County Register of Deeds before coming over here. Apparently, the woman working there was too overwhelmed to find the deed information for Ronnie's place while I waited. She told me to come back later."

Tommy let out a laugh. "Celia's new," he said. "Cut her

a break. She's only been there about six months or so. And she's by herself most of the time."

"Don't know if I'd call six months 'new'," argued Turner. "But I guess I've got no choice."

Tommy shot him a grin. "You've been living here a couple of years. You must know by now that life moves at a slower pace in a small town. Magnolia Bluff's no exception."

Turner gave him a sour look. "Whatever." He stood up and turned to leave. "I'll let you and Kraus know if anything pops when I get a look at the survey paperwork."

The chief nodded. "Okay," he said, then added, "I hear you and Sergeant Kraus had a run in with Captain Briggs over at the Really Good the other day."

"Let me guess," said Turner. "The jerk couldn't wait to rat out that his sergeant investigator was having coffee with a civilian, and possibly spilling department secrets?"

"Surprisingly, no. Jack Bonhoffer told me when I was there this morning. He said Joyce put the captain in his place." Tommy slapped his knee and guffawed. "Man, I would've liked to have seen that."

Turner smiled. "That's my girl," he said. "The man was way outta line. She shut him down fast."

"All kidding aside," said Tommy. "I'll have a little chat with him. If he had a problem with Kraus having coffee with you and Joyce, he should've addressed it with Kraus later, back here at the station. Not out in public for all to see."

"Yeah, well, his problem was with me being there, not Joyce. Either way, the man has a quick fuse. Maybe you should suggest he go to an anger management class."

"I'll take it under advisement," the chief replied.

Turner nodded and walked out of the office. Gloria

was on the phone, so he waved to her as he went out the door of the station house.

He got into his truck and looked at his phone. Too early to go back to the deeds office. *Maybe I'll drive over to the cabin and check in on Jason.*

He pulled out onto School Street, made the left onto Burnet Reservoir Road, and headed for his place.

When he arrived, Jason was just coming around the side of the cabin, hedge trimmer in hand. Turner waved and got out of his truck. He watched as the boy quickly shaped up the two bushes on either side of the front door.

After he'd finished with the shrubbery, he turned off the trimmer, laid it on the ground, and pulled off his work gloves. "Good timing. I just finished. Let's go walk the yard, see what you think."

Turner smiled. "All right," he said. "Let's go."

They walked around the side of the cabin and the boy pointed out how the bushes were now trimmed evenly across the top. Next, they walked through the grass down to the lake, turned and walked back up to the patio.

"Looks great," proclaimed Turner. "You did a really nice job. I appreciate all your hard work. Thank you." He reached into his back pocket and pulled out his wallet. He extracted two crisp twenty-dollar bills and held them out to Jason.

The boy waved him off. "That's too much. You already gave me ten, remember? You only owe me thirty."

"I know. But after walking the property and seeing the effort you put into making it all look good, you earned the extra ten bucks."

Jason took the money and smiled. "Thanks. I appreciate it."

"You know what else you earned? A free lunch. Go

get cleaned up and I'll take you over to Olivia's for pizza. Unless you want something else since you had pizza last night."

Jason stuffed the money into his pocket. "Nope. Pizza's awesome," he said with a fist pump into the air. He opened the sliding glass door off the patio and went inside to wash up.

Turner sat down in one of the Adirondack chairs and called Joyce. When she picked up, he said, "Hey there, good looking. You got time for lunch? I'm at my place with Jason and we're going over to Olivia's in a few if you'd like to join?"

"Sounds perfect. How about I meet you guys there in about twenty minutes? I'm just finishing up printing out some new listings for a client I'm meeting first thing in the morning."

"Jason's in the bathroom getting some of the dirt and sweat off before we go. So twenty minutes works. See you soon. Love you."

"Love you too," she said.

He clicked off his phone and went inside to grab a bottle of water from the fridge. Twisting the top off the bottle, he plopped down at the kitchen table and took a sip. He sat back and thought about where he was in the investigation. What if he continued to pursue his current line of thinking and it ended up going nowhere? He would've wasted a lot of time for nothing.

He rubbed his temples, trying to clear his mind. No. He'd always trusted his gut in the past. He should trust it this time, too.

Turner hoped Ronnie wouldn't get upset at him again and fire him over this. Logically, the boy would be shaken if he discovered his father planned to sell the farm without including him in the decision. Even if Senior did change his mind before going through with it. Assuming that's what happened. It's all speculation right now. But what other explanation could there be?

He forced some frustrated air past his lips. He had to get a look at a copy of the survey. That'll either confirm his gut or not. And if not, then what?

"You ready to go?"

Turner shook his head and looked up. "Huh? What?"

"Earth to Brandon," chuckled Jason. "I asked if you were ready to go."

"Oh, sorry," Turner replied. He rubbed the inside corners of his eyes. "Yes, I'm ready. By the way, your mother is joining us."

"Mom's coming? Cool."

They climbed into the truck and fastened their seatbelts. Before Turner pressed the ignition button, his phone rang. He smiled at the name on the screen and pushed the talk button. "Hi Joyce. We're leaving for Olivia's now."

"I just got a call from the nurse at the hospital," she said, her voice shaky. "Ronnie's blood pressure dropped, and they think he's bleeding internally. He's in surgery. I'm on my way to the hospital."

"I'll drop Jason off at home and then meet you there," he said.

"This is serious, Brandon. I'm not sure if he's going to make it…" Her voice dropped, and he heard her begin to cry.

"Ronnie's in excellent hands," he said, trying to console her. "Dr. Pope is good at her job. His best chance of survival is her being in that operating room. We have to believe he'll be okay."

"I hope you're right," she said. "I'll see you there."

Turner heard the phone click off. He pounded the steering wheel with his fist. "Dammit," he said through clenched teeth. "This can't be happening." He looked over at Jason, who was sitting quietly in the passenger seat. "I'm sorry about that outburst."

Jason nodded. "I understand."

Turner managed a thin smile. "Raincheck on the pizza?"

"You got it," the boy replied. "Just take care of mom."

"You know I will."

Jason nodded again. "Oh, and I hope Ronnie's gonna be all right."

"Me too," replied Turner. "Me too."

CHAPTER FOURTEEN

After a quick pit stop at Joyce's house to drop off Jason, Turner drove to the hospital. He parked in the visitor's lot and rushed into the main lobby and over to the elevators. As soon as he heard the ding and the door opened, he entered and began banging on the buttons until the door slid closed.

The ride up to the third floor took forever. When he finally exited, he immediately saw Joyce sitting in the same small waiting area they used the other day.

She looked up as he approached, and he saw her eyes were wet from crying. Turner took the seat next to her. She leaned over and wrapped herself around him. "Ronnie doesn't deserve this," she said. "He's had so much pain in his life already."

"I know," said Turner. He gently massaged little circles on her shoulder. "He's gonna be all right."

She pulled back from him. "You don't know that."

"You have to have faith, Joyce."

"I know," she said softly. "You're right." She leaned back into him and sighed, then closed her eyes and whispered, "I have faith that Ronnie will be all right."

They sat in silence for a while. Turner said an internal prayer that Ronnie would pull through the surgery. Joyce was right. Ronnie's had a hard life. The boy deserved a break. And Joyce would be devastated if he didn't make it after all he'd been through.

He glanced at the clock on the wall above a snack machine in the corner of the waiting area. How much longer before they heard something? Ronnie had been under the knife for over an hour.

"Mr. Turner? Ms. Blackstone?"

They both looked up. It was Dr. Pope.

Joyce took a step toward the doctor. "Ronnie...is he...?"

The surgeon gave them a smile. "He's going to be fine," she said. "A stitch loosened on one of the blood vessels I repaired during his initial surgery. Blood seeped through the opening and into the stomach cavity. I was able to stop the bleeding and restitch the vessel. He'll need to rest, but he'll be okay."

"Thank you, Doctor," he said.

Joyce puckered her brow. "How does something like that happen?"

"The vessel was weaker than it looked during the first surgery. The blood flowing through pushing against the inner wall eventually caused enough pressure and popped the loose spot in the suture."

"Can it happen again?" asked Turner.

"No," Dr. Pope assured them. "I used a stronger thread to repair the bad suture and then went through and reinforced all the others to be sure there won't be a repeat performance."

Turner nodded. "How long will he be in recovery?"

"He'll be in there for a while before he's transported back to his room. And even then, I'm going to prescribe something to keep him sedated for the rest of the day." She offered a smile. "You can see him tomorrow during visiting hours. He'll be out of commission for the rest of today."

Joyce breathed out a sigh of relief. "Thank you so much, Doctor."

Dr. Pope smiled and gave them a slight nod of her head. Then she turned and walked down the hall toward the nurse's station.

Turner looked at Joyce and gently placed his hand on her cheek. "Faith," he said, softy. "He made it through because we both had faith."

She put her hand on his, drew it over to her lips, and kissed it. "I love you so much," she said. "Thank you for reminding me about the power and strength in having faith."

He gave her a tender kiss on the top of her head. "Why don't you go home for the rest of the day? Jason's there, so you won't be alone."

"You're not coming?"

"I made a trip over to the Register of Deeds office inside the courthouse this morning," he said. "The woman I dealt with didn't have time to gather up the deed and survey information for Ronnie's place until this afternoon. She told me to come back after lunch. It's important I get a look at the paperwork so I can see if there's a reason to stay the course or if my gut's wrong."

Joyce nodded. "I understand. You'll be over later?"

He pulled her in close and hugged her. "Wild horses couldn't keep me away."

Turner walked her out to her car and kissed her goodbye. His truck was across the other side of the visitor's lot from hers. He jogged over to his row, weaving between the other parked vehicles on the way. He got in and fired up the pickup, then headed across town to the courthouse. It was four-thirty, and the deeds office closed at five. He punched the gas pedal and prayed the green lights were on his side.

It took him seventeen minutes to reach the

courthouse. He breathed a sigh of relief as he pulled into the parking lot off Main Street.

By the time he was out of the truck, and on the elevator to the second floor, he had ten minutes to spare.

Celia was not happy to see him when he walked into the office. "I see you're back," she said. "I'm just getting ready to close up for the day."

Turner leveled his eyes at her. "You've still got ten minutes," he said. "Give me the copies of the deed information I asked for, and I'll be on my way."

She let out a disgruntled sigh. "I'll be right back." Then she disappeared behind a wall.

Turner tapped his fingers on the counter while he waited. As much as he hoped this wasn't an identity theft situation for Ronnie, if he turned out to be correct, then at least he and Kraus could effectively plan out their next steps toward finding Ronnie Senior's killer.

Celia came around the wall and plopped an envelope on the counter. "Here you go," she said. "Now, if there's nothing else... I'm closed."

Turner ignored her attitude and opened the envelope before leaving. He wanted to avoid having to return if anything was missing. He pulled the documents from the envelope and quickly sorted through them. After flipping through them a second time, he looked across the counter at Celia and said, "Where's the survey? You didn't make me a copy of the land survey."

She pointed at the documents in his hand. "I made you a copy of everything in the file. If you don't have a copy of a survey, then there wasn't one in there."

He lowered her brows at her. "I know for a fact the property owner had a survey done a month ago. Why would it not be in the file?"

She shrugged. "I don't know what to tell you." She pointed at the door. "Now, if you don't mind…"

Turner stuffed the documents back inside the envelope and left without saying another word.

CHAPTER FIFTEEN

Turner tossed the envelope on the passenger seat and hopped up into his truck. He slammed the door closed and expressed his frustration by spewing out a few choice words before pulling out of the courthouse parking lot.

He tapped the phone button on his steering wheel and then tapped Kraus's name on the console screen. The phone rang twice and then he heard, "What's up, Brandon?"

"Hey Palmer. You got a minute?"

"I do," replied Kraus. "What's going on?"

"I just came from the Burnet County Register of Deeds office. I requested copies of the deed and all the property paperwork for the Spatch farm."

"Hey, that's a good idea," said Kraus.

"I thought so, too. Until I opened the envelope and there was no survey."

"What do you mean, 'no survey'?"

"There wasn't a copy of the survey Ronnie Senior had done last month. When I asked the clerk about it, she said there wasn't one in the file."

"That's odd," said Kraus. "Unless Junior was mistaken and Senior never had one done."

"Do you believe that? Because I sure as hell don't."

Turner heard a sigh come through the phone. "No, I don't," admitted Kraus. "Maybe someone mistakenly put the survey in the wrong file jacket. Since it was only completed a month ago, it's also possible that the land surveyor hasn't registered it with the county yet. That kind of thing's not unheard of."

"I suppose," said Turner. Maybe he jumped at Celia without knowing all the facts. "I doubt someone filed it incorrectly. That doesn't sound right. It's more likely that the survey company hasn't registered it yet. Hopefully, Ronnie knows the name of the company his dad hired."

"Tell you what," said Kraus. "You follow up with Ronnie on the land survey company, and I'll look up the County Register of Deeds website and search for it there. That way, we cover all the bases."

"We can do that?"

"It's the twenty-first century. Of course we can do that."

"So, I could've avoided the trip to the courthouse?" said Turner. "I wish I knew that ahead of time."

He heard Kraus chuckle. "That's why we make such a good team, Brandon."

Turner laughed. "I guess you're right."

They hung up. Turner couldn't help but smile. Palmer Kraus was a good guy. So much better than trying to work with Sovern. Maybe he could talk Tommy into sending Sovern to Austin and keeping Palmer in Magnolia Bluff.

When he pulled into the driveway at Joyce's house, she and Jason were outside playing with Max on the front lawn. He smiled at them rolling around in the grass. He was still a little surprised at how right it all felt. The idea that he would meet a woman and fall in love with not just her, but her son, was something that would've been unbelievable to him a few short years ago. He thought he'd be a confirmed bachelor for the rest of his life. And certainly never a father figure. He chuckled to himself. How things had changed since moving to Magnolia Bluff.

How domesticated he'd become.

Joyce broke away from the acrobatics happening on the lawn and walked over to meet him. She gave him a peck on the cheek. "You seem to be in a good mood," she said. "I'm guessing things went well at the courthouse?"

"Quite the opposite," he said.

"Then why the big grin on your face?"

"When I pulled in and saw you guys out here playing and having fun, I couldn't help but think about how much I love my life with you and Jason in it."

She looked over at her son, still rolling around on the ground with Max. "Looks like Max loves his life, too."

"You're right. He thinks the world of you and Jason."

"Good," she said as she threw her arms around him. "I can't imagine our lives without you and Max. I love you two big lugs." She smiled. "And I know Jason does too."

Turner leaned down and planted a deep, passionate kiss on her lips.

"Hey, you two," Jason called out from the front yard. "That's a little too much PDA for my taste." A big smile appeared on his face. "Don't make me have to poke my eyes out."

Turner and Joyce broke from their kiss. "See that?" Joyce said with a grin. "Nothing but love from the boy."

They both laughed and went up to join Jason and Max in the front yard.

Turner gave his dog a few good scratches behind the ears, then said, "Since we missed lunch today, how about I order up some pizzas for dinner?"

"*You* guys missed lunch," Jason said. "I made myself a PB&J with a side of chips."

"So, then you're good?" said Turner, already knowing what the kid's answer would be.

"That's not what I meant," Jason replied. "I was just pointing out that I didn't miss lunch since you dropped me off before going to the hospital. I'm down for pizza."

"Sorry, Jason," said Turner. "I thought it was best to bring you home first."

"I know. It's cool," the boy said. "How is Ronnie? Is he okay?"

"Yes," said Joyce. "It's going to be a long road to recovery, but he's going to make it."

Jason nodded. "I'm glad."

Joyce glanced over at Turner, then back to Jason. "Thank you. We are too."

Turner looked at them both and said, "Okay, here's the plan. Joyce, you give Olivia a call and let her know I'm on my way to pick up our usual. I'll head over to the restaurant and grab the pies. Jason, do you have one of your on-line games lined up for tonight?"

"No. why?"

"Can you set one up?"

"Wait. You're *asking* me to play a video game? That's new."

"I need some time to talk with your mom tonight. It's case related, and I'd prefer you weren't a part of the conversation."

Jason rolled his eyes. "If you guys are gonna talk more about what happened to Ronnie, you know I can handle it, right? I'm practically an adult."

"We know you can," Joyce said, before Turner could answer. "You've been exposed to a lot over the last couple of years. Between the drug overdose murders at your school, and then you finding the body of that little girl on the school bus last year…" She paused and took in a breath. "I just don't want you to be involved with this.

Play your video game. You're sixteen years old. Enjoy being a kid. You'll be an adult before you... or I know it. So don't rush it. Okay?"

"Okay. I can probably rustle up a game with some of the guys tonight. But I still think it's weird that you actually want me to play a video game."

Joyce lowered her eyes at her son. "Don't get used to it, bub," she said, then flashed a quick smile at him.

Turner grinned at the two of them. "Now that we've got that settled." He pointed a finger at Joyce. "You make the call to Olivia. Jason, go into your room and try to set up your game for after dinner. I'm going to go pick up the grub."

CHAPTER SIXTEEN

As expected, Olivia had a large pepperoni and a small spinach pizza waiting when Turner arrived. He was there and back in twenty minutes.

After dinner, Jason disappeared into his room, with Max following behind him. Joyce and Turner retired to the sofa in the living room.

"What happened at the deeds office this afternoon?" asked Joyce. "You glossed right over it earlier."

"I know," he said. "It's just when I saw you all on the lawn, I didn't want to think about it any longer. I wanted to be in the moment with you and Jason."

"And Max," she smiled. "Don't forget Max."

Turner grinned. "No chance of that. Max won't let me forget Max."

"That is so true," she said, her own smile stretching further across her face. She placed a hand on his knee and leaned toward him. "So, tell me what happened."

"The land survey Ronnie told us his dad had done wasn't in the envelope with the other paperwork the clerk gave me. When I questioned her about it, she said she made copies of everything in the file and if it wasn't in the envelope, then it wasn't in the file. I was angry when I left that office, so I called Palmer on the way over here. He helped me think through the most likely reasons for it not being included in the paperwork."

"Let me guess," she said. "The surveyor company hadn't registered it yet."

Turner nodded. "That's the most plausible

explanation. Palmer's going to check on-line at the County Register of Deeds website and look up the Spatch file there to see if the survey is in the file or not."

"You think the clerk may have lied?"

He shook his head. "No. She was unpleasant, but I don't see why she would lie to me about the survey not being in the file. Palmer thought that if the surveyor company had already registered it with the county, they may have misfiled it. I doubt that's the case, though. Which is why I'm going to talk with Ronnie again to see if he knows what land surveyor company his father hired."

"That's a good idea. Even if they haven't filed it with the county yet, they should be able to provide you with a copy."

"That's what I'm betting on," he said. "Figured when we went to visit Ronnie tomorrow, I could ask him."

Joyce crossed the index and middle fingers on both of her hands. "Here's hoping he's feeling well enough and is up to answering some questions."

Turner nodded. "Yeah, there's that. You know, I've never been a big believer in superstitious things like crossing your fingers for luck, but I guess in this case, Ronnie needs all the luck he can get," he said, joining her with crossed fingers of his own.

She put her head on his shoulder. "Not to mention you could use a little luck yourself."

"You're right about that."

"Maybe I should get you a rabbit's foot to carry in your pocket while you're out there investigating."

He gave her a wry smile. "Let's not get carried away."

She snuggled in closer and giggled. "Just trying to help."

"Hmm...thanks," he said.

"Was there anything else from today you wanted to tell me about?"

"Nope. You're all caught up."

She nodded and climbed off the sofa.

He reached out and took hold of her arm. "Whoa," he said. "Where do you think you're going?"

"I was going to let Jason know we were through talking about the case so he could come out of his room."

"What's the rush? He's probably off fighting some aliens that are looking to destroy all of humanity right about now. Why not take advantage of that?" He grinned at her while patting the seat cushion next to him. "Come on, sit back down."

She curled back up on the sofa and leaned against him. "What do you have in mind?"

"I thought maybe we could Netflix and chill."

She sat up, looked at him, and giggled. "Netflix and chill?"

He smiled and wiggled his eyebrows at her. "Yeah. Isn't that what all the big kids are saying nowadays when they put a movie on and don't end up watching it?" He pointed the remote at the TV and clicked on the Netflix app.

Joyce nuzzled into him and took his hand in hers. "You are so bad."

Everyone was up early the next morning and ready to get their day started. Turner and Joyce were finishing their coffee when Jason walked into the kitchen. "Ann asked Camila to text me about going to their farm today. Hank is out repairing a few sections of fence on their property, and Ann thinks he might need my help. She's gonna come pick me up… if that's okay with you?"

"I'm good with that," said Joyce.

"Sounds like an excuse to see Camila again," joked Turner.

Jason forced a smile. "You guys have a great day," he said. "I'll be in my room until Ann gets here."

As soon as Jason walked out of the kitchen, Joyce said, "Why would you say that to him?"

"What?" Turner said. "I was kidding around. He seemed okay with it. And besides, he knows we know he likes her."

Joyce slowly shook her head. "Tread lightly, okay? If he believes we think his crush is something to joke about, he won't share his feelings with us. I don't want him to feel like he can't talk to us about her."

"Never thought of it like that. Sorry. You think I should apologize to him?"

"No, I think he'll be okay, like you said. Just think before you make any comments to him about Camila. That's all I'm asking."

"Understood. You about ready to go to the hospital?"

"Yes. Let me just say goodbye to him. I'll meet you at the truck."

Turner nodded and watched as she headed down the hallway to her son's bedroom. When he saw her disappear into the room, he went out the front door.

He got in his truck, started it up, and then took in a deep breath. What Joyce said in the kitchen now had him wondering if Jason took his comment the wrong way. He agreed he needed to learn to think before he said anything to Jason involving Camila. Even after two years, he was still getting used to what his boundaries should be regarding the boy. Maybe he should sit down with Jason and clear the air… see if there was any air to be cleared.

Hell, he didn't know. He and Joyce had never really discussed what his role was with the kid. It's just kind of gradually developed over the past couple of years.

It's been a great relationship, and he's blessed to have Jason in his life. But when it comes to girls and first crushes, he's going to have to learn how to navigate that better.

The passenger side door opening snapped him from his thoughts. Joyce climbed into the seat and gave him a double take. "You okay?" she asked.

"Yes… yes. I'm fine." He gave her a quick smile. "You ready to go?"

She stared at him for a few seconds, then said, "Are you still thinking about what I said? You know I wasn't scolding you, right? I was trying to give you some advice, that's all. I don't want things to get tense between you two. You've got such a good relationship."

"We do." He considered his next words carefully. He turned toward Joyce. "How do you see my role with your son?"

She gave him a funny look. "What do you mean?"

"Jason and I are close, but I'm not his father. So, what am I? Just a guy who's nice to him, who's dating his mother?"

"Where is this coming from? You know you're much more than that. Much more. You got all this from me saying something about one little comment?"

He sat back and gazed out the windshield. "No. Well, maybe." He let out a sigh. "Actually, yes. It got me thinking about how much I don't know about raising a kid. I spend a lot of time with Jason. I don't want to become someone he can't look up to… or even worse, someone he doesn't want to look up to. And I don't really know how I fit in when it comes to any of that. I mean, what can I or should I talk to him about? Am I overstepping if I guide him or try to give him advice on stuff he should be talking to his dad about?"

She leaned over and gave him a kiss. "Just the fact that you care enough to think about this makes me love you even more. Let me make this easy for you. Yes, Denny is Jason's father and is in his life. There are conversations they will have, and questions Jason will want to ask his dad as he grows into adulthood. But Denny and I are not together, and we won't ever be again. You are the man in my life, which makes you the man he will most likely spend more time with. He will come to you for advice, and he will ask you questions too. He might even ask you and Denny the same questions because he respects you as a man. But more importantly, he respects your relationship with him. And so do I." she paused. "We should've had this conversation when we started getting serious. That's on me. But we're having it now and I hope it helps clarify things for you."

He turned toward her again and took her hand in his. "Thank you for saying that. And yes, it does. Ever since I realized he was starting to have feelings for Camila, I've wanted to make sure he knew I was there for him if he had questions. But I didn't want him to think I was trying to replace his father with that kind of thing."

"You don't need to worry about that," she assured him. "I know my son. He's a typical teenager. He won't want to talk with anybody about that. Not until he's ready. And when he is, don't be surprised when he comes at you with both barrels full of questions."

Turner nodded and squeezed her hand. "I love you."

"I love you, too." She buckled her seat belt. "Now let's

go see how Ronnie's doing."

Turner backed out of the driveway at the same time Ann pulled up to the house. He rolled down the window and he and Joyce waved to her as she got out of her vehicle. "Jason's in his bedroom," he said. "The front door's unlocked. Go on in. His room's down the hall, the last door on the right. It'll probably be closed. Just knock and he'll come right out."

Ann gave him the okay sign, waved at them both, and went inside. Turner rolled up his window and headed for the hospital.

CHAPTER SEVENTEEN

Turner followed Joyce into the elevator inside the main floor of the Burnet Medical Center and pushed the button for the third floor. Right before the door slid closed, a hand appeared between the sliding door and the frame, popping it back open. Sergeant Kraus stepped through the doorway and smiled.

"I saw you two get on as I walked around the corner. Figured I'd hustle and join you."

Turner looked surprised. "I didn't expect to see you here this morning. I thought you were following up with the deeds office online."

Kraus leveled his eyes at Turner. "You know that only takes a few minutes, right?"

"How would I know that?" he replied. "I didn't even know you could look that information up online until you told me. I certainly had no idea how long it would take you to cut through whatever red tape you would need to get through."

Kraus grinned at him. "Do you even own a computer?"

"That's not the point," shot back Turner.

Joyce touched his shoulder. "Okay, boys," she said. "Let's not take our eyes off the bigger picture." She looked at the sergeant. "What did you find out? Was the survey in the Spatch farm online records?"

"No, it wasn't," replied Kraus. "The surveyor company probably didn't file it with the county yet."

Turner nodded. "So, it comes down to hoping Ronnie

knows who his father hired to do the survey of the farm."

"Seems so," said Kraus. "It's one of the reasons I'm here."

"You didn't need to come all the way down to the hospital," said Turner. "I would've called you once I had that information."

"I know. But I had a few questions for Ronnie, anyway. I was going to make the trip later this afternoon, but had some time, so here I am."

The elevator dinged, and the door opened. Joyce stepped off first, then Kraus, followed by Turner. They walked down the hall toward Ronnie's room.

Officer Schreiber was sitting in a folding chair guarding the door. He stood up when he saw them approaching. "Hey, Sergeant," he said, then nodded at Joyce and Turner.

"Good morning, Officer Schreiber," replied Kraus. "How's our patient doing today?"

"Near as I can tell, he's been sleeping most of the morning. The doctor was here earlier, and the nurse has been in and out a few times. Other than that, been pretty quiet."

Kraus nodded. "Thanks," he said, then pushed open the door and went inside. Turner held the door for Joyce, then entered the room behind her.

Ronnie was lying in bed with his head elevated. His eyes were closed when they walked in but fluttered open by the time they all reached his bedside. A weak smile crossed his lips. "Hey there," he said, his voice sounding rough.

Joyce leaned over and placed her hand on top of his. "How are you feeling, Ronnie?"

"Like someone backed a dump truck up over my

belly," he said as he wrapped his hand around hers.

"I can imagine," said Turner. "You up to answering a couple of questions this morning? The sergeant and I need to see if you can clear a few things up for us." He glanced over at Kraus and gave him a quick nod to jump in.

"Hey, Ronnie," said Kraus. "I know you've been through a lot, so I promise we won't take up much of your time." His eyes softened, and he edged out a smile. "I want you to be able to get as much rest as you can, so I'll make this as painless as possible."

Ronnie snorted out a laugh, then grabbed his stomach and winced.

Joyce tightened her grip around his hand. "Are you okay?"

"I'm fine, Ms. Blackstone," he said. "I just thought it was funny what the sergeant said." He pushed out a couple of breaths before continuing. "Him sayin' he'd make his questions painless caught my funny bone. If'n he can do that, it might be the least amount of pain I've suffered so far." He looked over at Kraus and gave him a another weak smile. "Whatcha wanna know, Sergeant?"

Kraus hesitated before answering. He glanced over at Turner. "We're having a hard time finding a copy of the land survey for your property. Any idea what company completed the survey?"

Ronnie shook his head. "Like I said before, my daddy took care of all that. I don't rightly know if he ever mentioned who done the survey."

"Take your time," said Turner. "It's important. So far, we can't find any evidence of a survey being completed. We really need you to think about it. Did he ever mention anyone by name? If he did, we can probably track down the survey company with a person's name. We just need something to go on."

"I wish I could hep, Mr. Turner," replied Ronnie. "But I don't remember my daddy ever tellin' me who was gonna do the survey."

"Are you sure the survey was ever done?" asked Kraus.

Ronnie nodded. "I'm sure. I was there the day the men came to do it. There was two of 'em. They had a bunch of fancy surveyin' equipment in the back of their pickup truck. I remember they drove all over the property with their electronic gadgetry and everything. Took 'em most of the day."

Kraus nodded. "I want you to close your eyes and think back to that day," he said. "Try to remember what was written on the side of the truck." He waited until Ronnie had closed his eyes. "Can you see it? Can you see the name on the truck?"

Ronnie pushed his eyes together. His face scrunched up as he appeared to be concentrating on what Kraus had asked him. Except for the rhythmic beeping of Ronnie's heartbeat on the machine next to his bed, the room was quiet. Finally, he opened his eyes and said, "I can't see a name, but I can tell you the truck was white. There was a picture of a brown dog's head on the front doors on both sides of the truck. There's some printin' underneath the dog, but I can't make it out." He looked up and Kraus. "Sorry."

"Don't be sorry," Kraus said, smiling. "What you told us helps. We should be able to find the company based on what you said the truck looked like. Thank you." He took a small spiral notepad and pen from his pocket and wrote down a description of the pickup and handed it to Turner.

Turner put the paper in his pocket. He looked at

Ronnie. "I know this has been hard on you," he said. "We haven't had much luck finding any real clues that would point us in the direction of your father's killer. But the information you just remembered about the truck will help me locate the surveyor company. And I think that's a step in the right direction."

Ronnie tried to push himself up a bit. "I don't understand how knowin' who my daddy hired to do the land survey is gonna hep find out who kilt him."

"I'm not sure it will," Turner admitted. "But my gut tells me it's all somehow connected. I'm hoping by tracking down the company and getting a look at the survey they performed at your place, maybe we can get an answer to that question."

"I hope yer right, Mr. Turner," Ronnie said just before closing his eyes.

"So do I," he replied.

Joyce gently moved her hand from Ronnie's. She looked up at Kraus and Turner. "He's asleep. If either of you have any more questions for him, they're gonna have to be asked another time."

The sergeant nodded and glanced over at Turner. "I'm headed back to the precinct for now. Briggs wants me to give him a full update on the Spatch case."

Turner snorted. "Keep my name out of it."

Kraus cracked a smile. "You don't have to tell me."

CHAPTER EIGHTEEN

Turner and Joyce left the hospital and walked across the visitor's parking lot toward his truck.

Once they were back on Burnet Reservoir Road, Joyce said, "What do you say we head over to the Really Good, grab a coffee, and discuss everything from the hospital there?"

"Sounds good to me," he said, then cut over to Main Street toward the coffee shop.

They drove around the square twice without finding an empty spot to park the pickup. Joyce glanced over at Turner, who had his neck stretched out his window, trying to manifest a parking space to open up. "Hey, I've got an idea," she said. "Let's park over at the Flower and have our coffee there. We haven't seen Lily in a while. It would be nice to pay her a visit."

Turner smiled. "That's a great idea. It has been a while." He completed his circle past the shops on Main Street, took the left onto Magnolia Street and pulled up to the Flower Bed and Breakfast.

He put the truck in park and, instead of getting out of the vehicle, sat back in his seat. Joyce looked at him and said, "Something wrong?"

"No, not really. I just wish we had Max with us. He loves seeing Lily. And she's gonna be sad that we didn't bring him along. The Flower is like a second home to him." He thought about for a second. "Well, actually, I guess it's more like a third home to him."

She gave him a curious look.

Turner laughed and then clarified. "The cabin's his first home. Your house is his second home, making the B&B his third home."

"Nope," she said with a corrective smile. "You're still wrong. I think there's a case to be made for the Flower being his first home since you both stayed here for almost a year when you moved to Magnolia Bluff."

"I guess you're right about that," he said. "Never thought of it that way."

She laid her hand on his leg. "Tell ya what. We'll schedule a play date to bring Max over to the Flower and we'll all have a proper visit with her once you've put Ronnie Senior's killer behind bars."

Turner nodded his head and grinned. "Perfect. I know that'll make her happy. Let's go in and get that coffee."

They got out of the pickup and walked up the steps to the front porch. Lily came bursting through the front door and embraced both him and Joyce in a group bear hug. "Well, ain't you two a sight for sore eyes," she said, wrapping them up tight. "Two of my favorite people on the planet." She let go and turned her head from side to side and then looked past them. "Where's Maxie? I know you didn't come over to see me without bringing the best dog this side of the Mississippi with you." She took a second look around her. "Where is that big teddy bear?"

Turner offered her a sheepish grin. "He's over at Joyce's place," he said. "Sorry, but he's not here with us this time."

Joyce stepped in to explain. "We just left the Burnet Medical Center. We came straight here from there."

"Let's go inside and I'll tell you all about why we were at the hospital," he said, trying to put a Band-Aid on her disappointment. "And we'll also set a date to come back *with* Max. I promise."

Lily gave him the side-eye and then added a toothy grin. "As long as yer promisin' to bring that big boy with you the next time, I guess I can forgive ya." She turned, opened the front door, and waved them inside. "Well, whatcha waitin' for? Let's get in here and talk."

Turner and Joyce followed the innkeeper inside. She led them over to an empty table in the restaurant area where they all took a seat.

Joyce lifted her head up and filled her lungs. "What smells so incredibly delicious?"

Lily's eyes twinkled. "I just took a brisket out of the smoker out back. Renata is in the kitchen carving it up right now. We're offerin' a smoked brisket sammy on the lunch menu this afternoon."

"Wait," said Turner. "When did you get your own smoker? I thought you got all your smoked meats from Jumbo Jim's Barbeque."

"Used to. But ever since old Jumbo was murdered a few years back, the place just ain't what it used to be. You know Jim was Buck's daddy, right?"

Turner and Joyce both nodded.

"Well," continued Lily, "with all the crime and murderin' that goes on around here, Buck hasn't been able to spend the time there he wants to. Keep tellin' him he should retire from the sheriff's dept and devote his time to makin' barbeque. He's real good at it. A chip off his old man's block. Anyway, Buck shared his daddy's recipe with me and gets me the meat at cost. I went out and got me a smoker, set it up out back near the garden, and smoke everything that needs smokin' in house. Cheaper that way... and fresh, tender, and tasty."

Turner sat back in his chair. "I'm sold. Any way we can

get some of that brisket for ourselves?"

Lily glanced down at her watch. "I reckon so," she said. "It's just about lunchtime, anyway. Lemme grab you two a cup of coffee and I'll let Renata know to put two brisket sammy plates together, and I'll be right back." She looked directly at Turner. "Then I expect you to spill yer story."

"For one of those sandwiches, I'll tell you anything you wanna know."

Lilly leveled her gaze across the table at him. "I guess you forgot where you're livin', Brandon. It's called a sammy here in Texas. Don't make me have to knock the New York outta you." She gave him a wink and a wide grin and sauntered off to the kitchen.

"I guess she told you," laughed Joyce.

"She certainly did," he said, sharing her laugh. He paused, then snapped his fingers. "I just had a thought. Lily knows everybody in Magnolia Bluff. I'll bet she knows the name of the survey company that uses a white truck with a dog logo on the door panels."

"Sure do," Lily said as she took two mugs of coffee off the tray she was carrying and laid them on the table in front of Turner and Joyce. She put a third mug down near where she'd been sitting and set the tray on the empty table behind her. Then she took her seat next to Turner, who was staring at her. "Don't look so surprised. I heard whatcha said as I was walking over here. That truck belongs to Pyramid Land Surveying. John Seeley's the owner. Well, I guess his son Jake runs the company now. Has ever since his daddy passed last year."

Turner nodded. "And where can I find Jake?"

"They're located over on Sunrise Chapel Road. It's off State Highway 28 about a mile past Doyle's Garage. Just ask for Red."

Turner cocked his head. "Red?"

"Jake goes by Red. Always has since he was a young boy."

"I'm guessing he's a redhead?" asked Joyce.

Lily shook her head. "You'd think. But no. The boy was constantly in and out of trouble. His daddy tanned his hide so often, his skin had a red hue to it."

Joyce made a face. "That can't be true."

"It's partly true," admitted Lily. "Jake really was a pain in the butt kid. He was always in some kind of hot water. Don't know if his daddy ever spanked him or not. His skin was red because he had a severe case of psoriasis. Not sure if he still does. Haven't seen him since he moved back to Magnolia Bluff to take over his daddy's business."

"If his skin was red because he had psoriasis," asked Turner. "Why on earth would he ever want to be called Red?"

"He didn't. He hated it. The other kids called him that," Lilly said, then shrugged. "After a while, it just sorta stuck. Not sure if he still goes by that or not."

"Then why did you tell me to ask for Red?"

"Never liked him when he was a kid," she said. "And last I knew, he hadn't changed much as an adult. 'Course that was before he moved out west to Arizona. Not sure how he is since he's been back. No need to call him Red. Probably wouldn't answer ya anyway."

"Wow, Lily," said a surprised Joyce. "I never knew you not to like anyone."

"Well, the boy got on the wrong side of my smile when he was sixteen."

"He must have done something fiercely wrong if he pissed *you* off," said Turner. "You're the nicest person I know."

"I agree," said Joyce. "What did he do?"

"That boy was foolish enough to walk into the Flower one afternoon and break into my office. He took a week's worth of cash deposits right off my desk." She shook her head. "I was putting together my deposit for the bank and only stepped away from my office for a few minutes to use the bathroom. And before you ask, Brandon... yes, I locked the door. He must've been waitin' for me to leave the office. He jammed a crowbar in and cracked the doorframe to get in."

"How did you know it was him?" asked Turner. "Did you have surveillance video?"

"Hell no," she said. "That was almost twenty-years ago. I didn't have any security cameras back then. Didn't need 'em up to that point. But I sure got me one after he tried to rob me."

"Then how did you catch him?" asked Joyce.

"He walked right by me as I came out of the bathroom. Crowbar under one arm and my bank deposit bag under the other. I told that boy to drop my money, or I was gonna take that crowbar from him and make sure he walked funny for the next month or two. Oooh whee, he dropped that bag and ran outta here faster than a polecat chasin' a squirrel up a tree."

Lily was a small, feisty woman. Barely five feet tall, if that. And Turner thought she must've been in her early forties twenty-years ago when that happened.

Turner smiled to himself. He wouldn't want to get, as she put it, on the wrong side of her smile now. He could only imagine what she would've done if that boy hadn't dropped that bag full of cash when she was in her prime. Jake Seeley would probably still be walking funny today.

"Enough listenin' to my stories," Lily said, pulling Turner from his thoughts. "Tell me about your trip to the hospital. I'm guessin' it has somethin' to do with Ronnie Junior recoverin' from being almost stabbed to death."

Turner was not surprised that she heard about Ronnie Spatch. Word gets around pretty quick in a small town. Especially Magnolia Bluff. The folks in this town are notorious for the speed at which news and gossip reached everybody's ears.

"As you know," began Joyce, "Ronnie lost his mom when he was a young boy."

Lily slowly shook her head back and forth. "I remember. Such a tragedy," she murmured.

Joyce continued. "Then his daddy being murdered right there on the farm. And now Ronnie Junior is in the hospital after being attacked in his barn." She paused. "Brandon found him and was able to keep him alive until the paramedics got to him and rushed him to the hospital."

Lily got up from her chair, walked to where Turner was sitting, leaned over and hugged him. "You saved my life when that maniac tried to blow me up last year, and now you've done the same for that poor, sweet boy." She leaned back with a wet tear in her eye. "You really are this town's knight in shining armor."

Lily's reaction surprised Turner, and he didn't know how to respond. Finally, he smiled sheepishly and said, "Just doing what I was trained to do as a police detective."

Joyce had taken a napkin and was dabbing the wetness from her eyes. "He's being modest," she said. "He helps people because he cares." She looked at Turner. "You do your best to save people in terrible situations not just because you're trained to do so, but because it's in your

DNA. It's why you're going to be such a good private investigator."

Lily put her hands on her hips. "Now hold on, you two," she said, then glanced at Turner. "You're a PI now? This is great news. Magnolia Bluff needs someone like you. Once the word gets out, you're gonna be a busy man. When were you plannin' on telling me?"

Turner shrugged. "It's brand new," he said. "Decided to hang out my shingle when Ronnie asked for my help in solving his father's murder. He had concerns that with all the recent changes in the police department personnel, they might not be giving his father's death top priority. I agreed with him. He offered to pay me, but I told him no. I would look into it at no charge. He's my first case as a bona fide gumshoe."

"You really are a good man," said Lily. "You're doin' the right thing. He definitely needs someone like you in his corner. That boy ain't got a pot to piss in." She gave him a sly look. "I'll bet you were glad to see Sergeant Sovern leave town for a while."

"Let's just say his leaving without a goodbye call didn't hurt me. Although, it's a shame he had to take Georgia Jean along with him. She's a talented investigator."

"It's not just them two," replied Lily. "Seems like the whole town decided to up and leave all at once." She lowered her voice so the folks that recently took a table close to them couldn't hear. "I really do miss Harry and Ember, but I was glad to hear that awful Mary Lou Fight also went on an extended trip. Hope she stays put wherever she is and never comes back."

Turner and Joyce laughed. "No argument here," they both said in unison.

CHAPTER NINETEEN

He now had a name. After he dropped Joyce back home, Turner set out for Sunrise Chapel Road. With any luck, Jake Seeley would have the Spatch farm survey available, and he could get a look at it this afternoon.

It was about twenty minutes before he pulled into the parking lot of Pyramid Land Surveying. The building was small. One story, all brick with two large, reflective glass windows that spanned out from both sides of the entrance door. There was no sign attached to the building confirming where he was. The only evidence he was in the right place being the white etched letters on the entrance door glass that read PYRAMIND LAND SURVERYING, PA. Under the company name were the hours of operation and a phone number.

Turner pulled the handle on the door. Nothing happened. The door didn't budge. He cupped his hand over his eyes and peered through the glass. It looked quiet. No sign of anyone inside. He stepped back and looked around the parking lot. He hadn't paid attention when he parked and marched up to the front door. His was the only vehicle in the lot.

He fished his phone out of his pocket and called the number etched on the door. A recorded message told him they were closed and then stated the same business hours that were printed on the glass in front of him.

He took a closer look at the glass. Pyramid closed at noon on Fridays and was closed on the weekends.

It never occurred to him they wouldn't be open. He

looked at his phone. It was after one o'clock. And it was Friday. He hadn't kept track of the days lately. Since he'd begun working on this investigation, the days had all blended together. Or at least that's how it felt. He would have to wait until nine o'clock Monday morning to get a look at the survey.

Reluctantly, he returned to his truck and considered his options. He'd felt excited about finally being able to get his hands on a copy of the Spatch survey. The company being closed had forced the wind out of his sails. He sat back in his seat and closed his eyes while he contemplated his next move.

Stealing homes and property out from under the owners seemed to be a growing trend in the world of identity theft. He wondered if what he suspected was happening to Ronnie's farm had happened to any other farms in Magnolia Bluff. He would need some outside help to get that information, and he knew the prefect person to ask.

With a renewed sense of purpose, he started the truck, threw it in gear, and drove back toward town.

Twenty minutes later, he parked out front of the *Chronicle*, hopped down from his pickup, and went inside.

Monica Crow, Graham Huston's all knowing, all seeing, all hearing, right-hand gal was sitting at her desk attacking the keyboard on her laptop when Turner walked in.

She tore her gaze away from her computer screen and looked up at him over the top of her glasses. "Hi, Brandon. What brings you over to our fine news establishment? Looking to purchase some advertising for your PI business?"

Turner grinned. "I would question how you could

possibly know I just started a private investigation business, but I can only assume the 'Monica Hears' columnist knows everything happening in this town."

She cast a smile at him. "You'd better believe it. As a matter of fact, you caught me in the middle of putting the finishing touches on my column for the Saturday edition. So, are you really here to drop some advertising dollars, or are you looking for some information for your case?"

"Considering I'm working this first investigation *pro bono*, there aren't any advertising dollars to drop."

She nodded. "Information it is then," she said. She turned her chair toward him and crossed her legs. "How can I help?"

Turner took a beat before he answered. "Have you heard anything about any farm owners losing their property in any kind of fraudulent manner? Specifically deed fraud?"

Monica put a finger to her lip and looked up. "Hmm, I don't remember anything ever being reported in the *Chronicle*," she said. "Hang on... something's nagging in the back of my head about this." She turned back toward her desk and started typing on her computer. After a few minutes, she looked up and said, "Here it is. A year ago, a farm owner in Lampasas County reported they were victims of identity fraud. Apparently, they applied for an equity loan against their farm and were told the deed to the property was not in their name."

"Lampasas County. Never heard of it. How far away is it?"

"It's practically right up the road," she said. "Almost all farm country. Maybe twenty-five, thirty miles north of here."

Turner nodded. "Any way you could send a copy of

what you're looking at to my phone?"

"No problem. It's an article from the Lampasas Dispatch Record. That's the local paper up there. Give me your email address and I'll forward it to you. I know you've been working on the Ronnie Spatch Sr. murder investigation. Do you think this is why someone murdered him? Identity fraud?"

"I have a theory I'm working on," he said. "Please keep this to yourself for now. I don't need this showing up in the *Chronicle*. At least not until I've confirmed what I'm thinking."

She gave him a nod. "You have my word… as long as I get the scoop on the story when you're ready to spill."

"I promise," he said with a grin. "Besides, I'd rather give it to you than your boss." He gave her his email, and a few seconds later, he heard his phone ding. "Thanks, I appreciate it, Monica."

She grinned back. "If you really appreciated it, you'd buy some advertising for your PI business."

"I'll think about it," he said. "Gotta start getting paid for this gig first."

"Tell you what," she said, laughing. "Since you can't drop the bucks on an ad just yet, I'll drop a line or two in my 'Monica Hears' column about you opening a new private investigation business. A little free advertising for you until the money starts rolling in."

"You're the best," he said. "Thank you. Not sure how long it'll be before the money starts rolling, but thanks."

"You got it. Now go catch the bad guy."

He nodded, then left Monica so she could get back to whaling away on her laptop.

CHAPTER TWENTY

Turner sat in his truck out front of the newspaper's office and read the article Monica sent to his phone.

After thirty-six years of operating a dairy farm in Lampasas County, Texas, Angus Sorrel Price and his wife Rita Lynn Price discovered that a Richard J. Smith had transferred the deed to their property from their name to his. The new deed's date was six months before they applied for an equity loan on what they thought was their property.

Turner sat back in his seat. Richard J. Smith. Obviously a fake name. And one very hard to trace.

The problem he had was there wasn't anything that connected to Ronnie Senior's death. The Lampasas Dispatch Record article mentioned nothing indicating physical harm to anyone. It was a terrible tragedy for Angus and Rita Price, but there was no bloodshed.

Still, it might be worth a thirty-minute drive to hear their story just to make sure. Besides, he was at a dead end until Monday, when Pyramid Land Surveying would be open, and he could speak with Jake Seeley. Of course, if Ronnie Junior was mistaken and Pyramid never did a survey of their farm, he was back at square one.

He started up his pickup, then pressed the phone button on his steering wheel and called Sergeant Kraus. When he answered, Turner said, "Hey Palmer, you got time to make a quick road trip with me?"

"Depends. Where we going?"

"Lampasas County. I've got a lot to fill you in on. I'll

catch you up on the way if you're coming."

"Okay. You've got me curious. When?"

"If you're not busy, how about now?"

"Where are you? I'll come to you."

"If you're at the station house, I'm not that far away. I'm sitting in my truck outside of the *Chronicle*."

"Gimme ten minutes and I'll meet you there," said Kraus, then clicked off.

As it's been known to do in the middle of July in Texas, the afternoon temperature was quickly rising. Turner glanced at his fuel gauge, and not wanting to waste gas while waiting for Kraus, rolled down his windows and shut off the ignition on his truck.

He sat back in his seat, closed his eyes, and tried to envision a snowy day back in New York. After the third drip of sweat rolled off the tip of his nose and hit the leather seat between his legs, he fired up the pickup and rolled up the windows. He set the air conditioner on high and said out loud to no one, "Screw it, I'll fill the tank on the way to Lampasas."

The ten-minute wait was more like a twenty-minute wait before he saw the sergeant's cruiser pull in next to him.

Kraus got out of his vehicle and hopped up into the truck. "Sorry about that," he said. "Briggs called me into his office right after I hung up with you. Apparently, he overheard my conversation with you and gave me the third degree on where I was going and with who."

Turner shook his head. "He thought you were talking to me? You never mentioned my name."

"I know. But ever since he saw us at the coffee shop, he's been hell bent on catching me working this case with you. Took me a minute to convince him it wasn't you on the phone."

"I think your captain might be a psycho," grinned Turner. "Even if he found out we were collaborating on the investigation, you'd think he'd appreciate the extra manpower. It's not like I'm some rando calling in a fake tip for attention."

Kraus nodded. "You'd think. But Briggs is old school, and he doesn't believe in outside involvement from anyone, especially a PI, who isn't currently wearing the blue. Doesn't matter to him you used to be on the job. You're not now, so he doesn't want your help." He gave Turner a smirk. "Luckily for you, I don't have those old-world views."

Turner chuckled. "Thanks. I'd bow down to your greatness, but I don't wanna risk puking all over your shoes."

Kraus smiled and shook his head. "So, what's in Lampasas County?"

Turner filled him in on finding out who the surveying company was and that they were closed until Monday. Then he told him about his conversation with Monica, which led him to wanting to take the drive up to see if they could speak with Angus and Rita Price.

When he'd finished speaking, Kraus said, "It might be a wild goose chase."

"You're right," agreed Turner. "But you never know. I'd rather go up there for nothing than not and then find out later we might've missed a shortcut to catch whoever killed Ronnie Senior."

"Know how to find them?"

Turner shot Kraus a grin. "That's why I asked you along," he said. "Thought we'd stop by the local police station and ask them."

"And you figured they'd be more willing to talk to me than you."

"Precisely," admitted Turner. "Didn't wanna run into a carbon copy of Briggs. Seems there's a lot of his type that don't appreciate what a PI can bring to an investigation."

"Well, to be fair, there are a lot of gumshoes out there that don't exactly run an ethical PI business."

"I won't argue with you. But I guess I never saw a little outside help as an issue. As a narcotics officer, my network of CIs directly helped me achieve some of my biggest busts. Admittedly, I never worked with any private investigators, but I did rely on outsiders to help me bring down some pretty awful drug dealers. And some of those confidential informants were pretty unethical people."

"I think most of the captains that feel that way have forgotten what it was like to be out in the streets," said Kraus. "Still doesn't mean there aren't any scummy PIs out there." He glanced over at Turner. "I know this PI thing is new to you. Just don't become one of 'em."

Turner nodded as he put the truck in drive and pulled away from the *Chronicle* building.

The Lampasas County Police Department was larger than Turner expected. He pictured another Podunk department filled with a bunch of country bumpkins masquerading as cops. What he found was a well-run, mid-sized organization.

He parked his truck in the lot and he and Kraus went inside.

There was a main desk staffed with several people dressed ranging from business casual to suit and tie, to uniformed officers. As they approached, Turner leaned over to Kraus and said, "Remember, you're taking the lead on this."

Turner followed Kraus as he walked over to where a uniform was sitting behind a computer. He looked at the nametag on the man's chest, then pulled out his shield and ID and said, "Sergeant Garcia. I'm Sergeant Investigator Palmer Kraus from the Austin Police Department. We're on loan to the Magnolia Bluff Police Department working on a murder investigation." He glanced over at Turner. "This is my partner, Detective Brandon Turner. We'd like to speak with whoever was in charge of the property fraud case involving Mr. and Mrs. Angus Price."

Garcia gave both men the once over. "Hold on a second," he said. He slid the mouse around on his desktop, then began tapping his fingers on the keyboard. After staring at the screen for a minute, he picked up the phone and pushed a couple of buttons. He told whoever was on the other end of the line to send Detective Clark down to the front desk. Then he pointed at a group of chairs over by the wall. "The detective will be down in a few minutes. You can wait over there."

Turner and Kraus both nodded at Garcia, then walked over and took a chair.

"Nice touch telling the desk sergeant you're with the Austin police and we're just on loan to the MBPD."

Kraus smiled. "Yeah, I thought it might give us more clout than telling them we were with the Magnolia Bluff police. Saying we were on loan made it seem like we were the big guns called in from the big city to help the small town force solve a complicated murder case. Figured it would be easier to get the information we needed. And now that we're through the gate, I'm tossing the ball back over to you to question Detective Clark."

Turner nodded his approval. "Fair enough."

They both looked up as an attractive woman dressed in a light gray pantsuit walked up to them. Turner guessed she was in her mid-thirties.

She offered her hand, and said, "I'm Detective Donna Clark. I understand you're both detectives in from Austin? How can I help you?"

"I'm Detective Turner, and this is Sergeant Investigator Kraus," he said as they both took turns shaking hands with her. "We're in from Austin helping the Magnolia Bluff police on a murder investigation that may involve property title fraud. I understand you worked the property fraud investigation for Mr. and Mrs. Price last year, and I wanted to ask you a few questions about that case."

Clark didn't say a word. She just stood there, sizing them up.

Turner cocked his head slightly. "Is there a problem, Detective?"

"I called Chief Jager and had a brief but very interesting conversation with him before coming down to meet you gentlemen," she said. "The chief and I go back a few years, and I wanted to ask him why he would send a couple of his detectives up here about a year old case without calling ahead. You wanna know what he told me?"

This time it was Turner who didn't say a word. He stood there waiting for the other shoe to drop.

A slight grin crossed her face as she stared at him. "Chief Jager said he didn't send any of his detectives up here for any reason, and that you do not work for him. He said you were a retired New York City police detective.

He also said you were now a private investigator and no longer a cop." She turned her attention to Kraus. "You're half of the story actually checks out. He confirmed you were indeed on loan to him from the Austin Police Department and are currently working on a murder case in Magnolia Bluff." She looked over at Turner again. "Care to explain?"

"Okay, you got me," he said. "Yes, I'm a PI, but I really am working on this murder investigation. And no, I'm not actually working the case for the police. The victim's son hired me. That being said, Sergeant Kraus and I have decided to share information since we both have the same goal, which is to catch the person who brutally murdered an old man. My investigation led me here. In the interest of sharing, I asked Sergeant Kraus to tag along since—"

"Since you thought he would get further walking into another police station to ask for information than you would've alone," Clark said, cutting him off.

Turner lowered his head. "Yes. I'm sorry we tried to deceive you, but can't you put that aside for now? Look, you can hate me and still help me. We're trying to put a killer behind bars."

The slight grin on Clark's face had expanded from ear to ear. "You're lucky Tommy and I are good friends," she said. "He also told me how you've helped him and his department on a couple of nasty murder investigations in the past. Said you were smart and still had good cop instincts. He actually had a lot of nice things to say about you. Although I suspect you may hear from him about this little incident you tried to pull." She shook her head at both of them. "Follow me up to my office and I'll show you the file on the Price case." She turned and strutted off toward the elevator.

Turner and Kraus tagged along with their tails tucked between their legs.

CHAPTER TWENTY-ONE

Turner and Kraus were on their way to see Angus and Rita Price. Detective Clark had made copies of the file for them. She also called ahead and spoke with Mr. Price. She wanted to ask him if they'd be willing to speak with the detectives before the two men appeared on their doorstep. What they had gone through was hard on them, and they still felt somewhat embarrassed a year later.

Clark wanted to ensure they both understood the Price's mental anguish about what happened to them before questioning them. She glared at them both while reminding them that Mr. and Mrs. Price were the victims and not to treat them like a perp.

Turner assured her they would not upset the couple. They had no desire to dive into their personal anguish about what took place. They were only interested in seeing if there were any similarities to the Spatch case.

Detective Clark had sighed and handed Turner the file, which contained the address to the Price farm. He could tell she was hesitant as he took the file from her hand and knew it was because she caught him in a lie.

He glanced over at Kraus, who seemed to be interested in watching the country landscape outside his window as they drove past several farms. "Think Tommy will tell Briggs about his phone call from Clark?"

Kraus pulled his stare away from the window and looked at Turner. "I was just thinking about that very thing," he said. "Although, I guess if he does, it really won't affect you."

"Oh, come on," said Turner. "It's not like I planned that to happen. What were the chances a detective in Lampasas County was friends with Tommy and would call him about us?"

"I know, and I don't blame you. Doesn't change that it happened, though. It also doesn't change if the chief does tell Briggs about our little adventure, that it won't affect you the same way it'll affect me."

"You're right," conceded Turner. "Of course, there's always the chance Tommy won't tell Briggs about it. He knows how Briggs feels, so he may stay away from it all together. But just to be sure, I'll talk to Tommy when we get back. I'll make sure he understands this trip was all my idea, and I convinced you to come along."

"I appreciate it. I do. But if he does mention it to the captain, it'll probably happen before we get back to Magnolia Bluff. So you telling Jager anything about this will be too little, too late."

Turner nodded and pushed the phone button on his steering wheel. He scrolled across the screen on his dash until he found Tommy's name and then tapped the screen.

"What're you doing?" asked Kraus.

I'm gonna talk to him right now. Like you said, if I wait until we get back, it might be too late."

"Think now's a good idea? He's probably still mad at us."

Turner heard the click as the chief answered. He looked over at Kraus and silently mouthed, "Too late now." Into the phone, he said, "Hey Tommy, you got a minute?"

"What the hell, Brandon?" the chief blurted out. "It's

bad enough you went to a different county and tried to pass yourself off as an Austin police detective, but you dragged Sergeant Kraus into this."

Turner glanced over at Kraus as he spoke. "I know, I know. You're right. And I apologize for bringing Palmer into this mess."

"What are you doing in Lampasas County, anyway?"

"It's a long story. I'm following my gut. And we're on our way to find out if my hunch pans out."

They could hear Tommy grumbling through the line. Finally, the chief said, "Obviously there's a lot you haven't told me. I want you in my office first thing in the morning. I'm assuming Sergeant Kraus is sitting next to you listening to this conversation?"

Kraus spoke up. "Yes, Chief. I'm here."

"I want you to join us," he said. "You'll need to tell me everything about why both of you went to Lampasas County. And why you felt the need to lie about who you were to Detective Clark."

Kraus glanced over at Turner. "Yes, sir. We'll be there."

"Tommy, I need to ask you something," said Turner. "Have you said anything to Briggs?"

The line was silent for about fifteen seconds before the chief answered. "No, I have not spoken with Captain Briggs about this… yet. I will reserve my position on that until I hear what you have to say in the morning."

"Thanks, Tommy. I appreciate that."

"I'm not doing it for you, Brandon," replied the chief. "I'm doing it for Sergeant Kraus. No need to have the captain ripping into him until I see if there's any disciplinary action needed."

"Fair enough," said Turner. "Still, thank you for smoothing things over with Detective Clark so she would share the information with us."

"You put me in a tough position, and I didn't appreciate that," replied the chief. "Nine o'clock tomorrow morning. Don't be late." The line went dead as Tommy clicked off without another word.

"He's not too happy," said Kraus.

"He'll get over it."

Kraus nodded. "Thanks for having my back on this."

Turner grinned. "It's the least I could do. You're a big part of why we got the information from Detective Clark."

"Speaking of her," said Kraus. "Think she'd go out with me?"

Turner's grin widened. "Are you serious?"

"Well, yeah. I mean, I know we got off to a rocky start back there, but I thought she was kind of cute. I wouldn't mind taking her out on a date."

Turner pulled into the driveway in front of a large farmhouse style home and put the truck in park. "I say, go for it. What've you got to lose?"

"I think I will," smiled Kraus. "Once we've solved Ronnie Senior's murder, I'm gonna take a trip back up here and invite her to lunch. I'll say I want to make it up to her. You know? How we came off today. Hopefully, she'll agree and then I can charm her into an actual date during lunch."

"That's your plan?"

Kraus shrugged. "Well, yeah."

Turner nodded, a grin on his face. "Want me to tag along? Since it's an apology lunch and all."

Kraus lowered his eyes at him. "Not funny."

"Seriously," said Turner. "I hope you do pursue it. And you're right. She is cute. Now, are you ready to get out of my truck and talk to the Prices, or do you wanna swoon a little longer over your new love interest?"

Kraus sighed and shook his head. "I'm beginning to see why Sovern hates you," he said with a grin. "Let's go." He opened his door and got out of the vehicle.

Turner glimpsed a pair of eyes staring at them from a front window just as the curtain dropped back into place. The door opened, and a man stood in the doorway waiting for them to step onto the porch.

Kraus reached into his jacket pocket and retrieved his ID. He held it up for the man to see as they approached. "Mr. Price?" he said. "I'm Sergeant Investigator Palmer Kraus." He glanced over at Turner. "This is Brandon Turner, a private investigator from Magnolia Bluff."

The man nodded. "Yes sir," he said. "I'm Angus Price. Detective Clark called. We've been expecting you." He stepped out of the doorway and gestured for them to come inside. "Do you gentlemen want coffee?" he asked over his shoulder as they followed him into the house.

Turner and Kraus glanced at each other and shook their heads. "No thank you," Turner said. "We don't plan on keeping you long. We just have a few questions to ask, and we'll be out of your hair."

Angus Price took a seat in one of two well-worn recliners that sat side-by-side. He cranked it back and said, "Please, make yourselves at home."

Turner and Kraus both nodded and took a seat on the sofa across from him. There was a glass top coffee table positioned between them and where Angus Price sat.

A woman appeared carrying a tray with a small ceramic pot and four cups stacked on top of four saucers. There was also a small bowl containing perfectly square sugar cubes, and a small ceramic carafe filled with creamer.

She slid the tray onto the table and took a seat in the other recliner. Angus Price smiled at the woman and said, "This is my wife, Rita."

"Nice to meet you, ma'am," said Kraus. He gave her the same introduction he had given to her husband in the doorway.

At the mention of his name, Turner nodded at the woman and said, "You have a lovely home, Mrs. Price. Thank you for allowing us in so we could have this conversation with you."

A smile appeared on Rita Price's lips. She leaned over the table and began putting the cups on the saucers. She looked at Turner. "How do you take your coffee, Mr. Turner?" She shifted her eyes over to Kraus. "And you, Detective?"

Turner waved her off. "You don't need to go to the trouble, ma'am. We just have a few questions about your fraud case from last year, and we'll be on our way."

"Nonsense," she replied. "No trouble at all. You two are guests in our home. If you'd prefer tea, it'll only take a few minutes to put together."

"Don't fight it, boys," grinned Angus Price. "She won't take no for an answer."

Turner conceded. "Coffee's fine. I take it black. Thank you."

"Two cubes of sugar and a pinch of cream," Kraus said. "Thank you, ma'am."

Rita Price poured the men coffee all around and placed the cups and saucers in front of Turner and Kraus. She also handed a cup, without the saucer, to her husband. Finally, she fixed herself a cup and set in on a saucer on the table in front of her.

Once they were all settled, Turner began. "First, I

want to say we appreciate you taking the time to see us this afternoon. I know what you went through wasn't easy." He paused and took his phone out and set it on the table. "Do you mind if I record our conversation?"

The couple looked at each other. Mrs. Price reached her hand out to her husband. He sat up straight and placed his hand in hers. They looked at Turner and shook their heads. "No," said Mr. Price. "We don't mind if you record."

Turner nodded, then dialed up the voice memo app on his device and tapped the red record button. He glanced up at the couple. "Please tell us how you discovered you lost ownership of your home and property?"

"We're mostly a dairy farm," Mr. Price said. "Unfortunately, there's not much money to be made as a dairy farmer. Times were hard and getting harder."

"Our son, Jason," his wife said, "was a lawyer. He worked in Dallas. About two years ago, he put his practice aside and came back home to help us. We turned all our finances over to him so he could figure out where we could trim and where it made the most sense to spend our money to get a bigger profit in return." She glanced over at her husband.

"Things were beginning to turn around for us," said Mr. Price. "Our son was a genius when it came to finances."

Turner could hear the pride in his voice. He could also see the emotion on the man's face as well as the tears that began to trickle down his wife's cheek. "Was?" he said.

Mr. Price nodded slowly, then steeled himself. "He was killed six months after coming back home."

Turner and Kraus looked at each other. Both stayed

silent.

Angus Price continued. "He was in the wrong place at the wrong time. I sent him to the feed store to pick up our order. A man and a woman came in right after he did and held up the clerk behind the counter." He paused and stared at his shoes. "Never heard of anybody robbin' a feed store…" his voice faded as he seemed to become lost in thoughts.

Kraus leaned over and gently coaxed him into continuing. "What happened?"

Mr. Price shook his head and glared at Kraus. His jaw line tightened as he forced out the words. "My boy was stabbed. He tried to wrestle the gun from the man who was robbin' the clerk when the woman who came in with him pulled a knife from her pocket. She walked up and pushed it into Jason's gut."

"I am so sorry," said Kraus. He leaned back and glanced over at Turner.

Turner looked at the couple with sadness in his eyes. "I'm sorry for your loss. He focused on Mr. Price. "Did they arrest the man and woman?"

Mr. Price stretched his neck from side-to-side. "Nope. They got away. Cops showed up too late. They were long gone. The feed store's security video caught the whole thing. And even with that recordin' showin' what she did to my boy, the woman who took our son from us is still out there."

Turner quietly nodded. There was nothing he could say that would help take away their pain.

Kraus spoke up. "Did your son's murder have anything to do with someone stealing your property title?"

"Not as near as we can tell," replied Mr. Price. "Jason died months before that happened."

"What did the police say about the your son's murder?" asked Kraus.

"They said they had the video and would let us know when they had a lead," Angus Price said, his words dripping with anger. "They never found any leads that panned out."

"They said it was an ongoing investigation," added Rita Price.

Kraus nodded. "There's no statute of limitations on murder. I'm sure they've got someone working the case," he said, trying to be upbeat.

"Was there any particular reason why fraudsters targeted your home and property?" asked Turner.

Mr. and Mrs. Price shook their heads in unison. "After our son died," said Mrs. Price, "everything fell apart on us. We only found out about the title theft when we applied for a loan against the property so we could pay our bills."

"Yeah," agreed Mr. Price. "That Richard J. Smith feller wasn't gonna get much by stealing the title to our land. We was about to go into foreclosure if we didn't get the loan. The only reason we haven't lost it all yet was because the bank was gracious enough to hold off while we worked at sortin' everything out. Still are."

"Mr. Price," Turner said. "Did you ever have a survey done on your property?"

"We did. But with all that happened to us, I forgot all about it. Hell, I don't think I even got a copy of it."

"Do you remember the name of the company who did the land survey for you?"

Angus Price shook his head. "No sir, I don't. But if you leave your number with me, I can see if I can find who it was and call you with the information. Give me a day or two."

Turner's insides were on fire. Screw a couple of days. He wanted to shout at the old man to go look it up now. Instead, he understood that was their cue to leave. He looked over at Kraus, who was already standing, and stood up from his seat.

They both thanked the Prices for their time and found their own way out.

CHAPTER TWENTY-TWO

As soon as they were inside the truck, Turner said, "Whatdaya think?"

"I think you may be on to something," replied Kraus. "Although their son's murder seems like a robbery gone wrong, the old man was right. Who robs a feed store? Especially one out in the middle of nowhere?"

"I'm with you. There's definitely more to this story."

Kraus glanced over at Turner. "What's your gut telling you about this?"

"I think the feed store robbery was a setup. I'll bet the so-called 'robbers'," he said, air-quoting, "were following Jason Price on his way to pick up that order." They went into that store to commit murder. The holdup was a ruse. That's what my gut is telling me."

Kraus nodded.

"We need to head back over to see Detective Clark again," said Turner. "See if we can get a look at that video footage."

"I agree. But we also don't need to ruffle any more feathers. Let's go back to Magnolia Bluff and speak with the chief first. Once he's up to speed, we'll ask him if he can call Clark, give her our thoughts on Jason Price's murder and set that up for us."

Turner rolled his head, cracking the tension from his neck. He fired up the pickup, threw it in gear and backed out of the Price's driveway. "You're right. Hopefully, he's not still pissed at us, and he'll call her." A teasing grin crept across his face. He cut his eyes over at Kraus. "Of course, if he doesn't agree to call her, it could be a great opportunity for you to call and ask her. Maybe butter her up over a romantic cup of coffee?"

Kraus grunted out a grin of his own and shook his head. "You're an ass."

"Does that mean if Tommy won't call her, neither will you?"

"Oh, no," replied a grinning Kraus. "I didn't say I wouldn't do it. I said you're an ass. Two completely different things."

"I can live with that," said Turner, and then laughed.

They both rode along in silence. Kraus watched the miles of farmland pass by his window while Turner put his thoughts in order. He wanted to be certain he had them straight when they spoke with Tommy.

He knew he crossed a line by letting the Lampasas County cops think he was a detective with the Austin police. He mentally kicked himself for underestimating them. Even after being in Texas for more than two years, he just assumed small town cops meant they weren't all that bright. Then again, all he had to base his assumption on was the police he'd interacted with in Magnolia Bluff. And they'd proven that assumption true time and time again.

He glanced over at Kraus, who was still counting corn fields, and smiled. Of course, there were exceptions.

Turner tapped the phone button on the steering wheel, then tapped Joyce's name on the console screen. The phone rang twice and then, "Hey handsome. You on your way over? I can't wait to wrap you up in my arms and kiss you all over."

His eyes darted over to Kraus, then back to the road in front of him. "That sounds amazing," he said, smiling.

"But I'm not alone, so don't say anything too sexy."

"Let me guess," she said. "Palmer is with you?"

He glanced at Kraus and grinned. "Good guess."

"Hi Palmer," she sang into the phone, sounding somewhat embarrassed. "Sorry. Just ignore my previous comment."

"Hi Joyce," a grinning Kraus replied. "Don't worry... I didn't hear a thing." He looked over at Turner and silently mouthed the words 'I'm jealous', then went back to staring out his window.

Turner shook his head, then turned his attention back to his phone call. "So, not on the way over to your place just yet. My presence has been requested by Tommy. He wanted to see us in the morning, but we're headed over to the station now to give him a briefing on our trip to Lampasas County. I'll explain everything when I see you."

"Hmm... sounds like you had quite the afternoon," she said. "Should I plan dinner? It'll just be us. Jason is eating over at Hank and Ann's place tonight and then they're having a game night. It took them much longer to knock out those fence repairs than they thought. Jason said they felt like they at least owed him dinner and some fun for all the hard work he did today."

He smiled but said nothing about the fact that the boy probably jumped at the invitation so he could spend more time with Camila. "Dinner sounds great," he said. "I can pick something up on the way over."

"No need. I've got two beautiful ribeyes you can put on the grill when you get here. I'll rustle up a couple of loaded baked potatoes to go with them."

"The heck with seeing Tommy," he said. "I'll be there in ten minutes."

He heard her giggle. "Never mind that," she said. "You and Palmer go see Tommy. Shoot me a text when you're leaving the station, and I'll get the grill warmed up."

Turner glanced over at Kraus, who he knew was pretending he wasn't listening, then said to Joyce, "That's not the only thing you're warming up."

"Hey," she reminded him. "Don't say anything too sexy." He heard her giggle again into the phone.

He laughed. "Love you and I'll see you soon."

"Love you, too... bye," she said, then hung up.

Kraus finally pulled his eyes from the passenger window and looked over at Turner. "You two have a great relationship. She's definitely your better half. I really am jealous."

Turner grinned. "Yeah, we do," he said. "All the more reason for you to ask Detective Clark out. Who knows? Maybe she'll turn out to be your better half."

Turner guided his truck into the parking lot behind the Magnolia Bluff City Hall building and pulled into a space in front of the police station.

"Considering I lied to her the first time I ever met her," said Kraus, "there's no guarantee she'll go out with me, let alone be my better half."

"I wouldn't worry about that. She seems like a good cop. I think she understands the 'why' behind our lies. And besides, she lightened up and helped us out in the end." He shot Kraus a grin. "If it would make you feel better, I can talk to Joyce about a double date scenario."

"Thanks, but I think I'll start by asking her for a coffee date. Depending on how that goes, maybe I'll take you up on the double date thing. That is, if she even says yes to the idea of seeing me outside of a work situation."

Turner nodded. "Just remember, I've got your back."

"I appreciate that," Kraus said with a smile. He took a beat, then added, "You ready to go inside and face the chief?"

"Yup. Let's go."

They both got out of the pickup and walked toward the station. Turner opened the door and let Kraus walk in first. Gloria was busy speaking with someone on the phone, so they gave her a quick wave and headed down the hall to see the chief.

Turner watched Tommy sitting behind his desk through the office window while Kraus lightly tapped on the door.

The chief looked up and signaled for them to enter. Once they were settled, Tommy looked directly at Turner and said, "I thought I told you to be here in the morning?"

Turner shrugged. "Why wait? Figured we get this cleared up now."

Tommy gave him a nod. "Fine. When you first told me you were going to work on this investigation as a PI, you promised to provide me with progress updates. Based on today's incident, I'd have to say you've not done that with the regularity I'd hoped for."

Kraus sat forward in his chair and said, "But he has been keeping me up to date, Chief."

Tommy turned his attention to the sergeant. "If that's the case, then why haven't I heard anything about what he's been up to from you? Maybe you've been updating Captain Briggs instead?"

Kraus slid back into his seat and stayed quiet.

Tommy nodded. "That's what I thought." He focused back on Turner with a stern look. "Start at the beginning. And don't leave anything out."

Turner took a deep breath and began.

Once Tommy had dismissed them, Kraus walked Turner out to the parking lot and watched him climb up into his truck.

Turner started the pickup, rolled down the window, and said, "Well, that wasn't so bad."

"Speak for yourself. Jager put me on a leash."

"It could've been worse," said Turner. "At least he wants your full daily updates given directly to him. Better than having to deal with Briggs."

Kraus nodded. "That's only because he knows it would be impossible for me to get through any update with the captain involving you."

Turner offered a slight smile. Even though Tommy had read them both the riot act, he appreciated that the chief also recognized the progress he and Kraus were making by working together. The fact that he was willing to keep Briggs out of the loop gave him the ability to continue his partnership with the sergeant without interference from the captain.

He motioned with his head for Kraus to get in. "Come on," he said. "I'll give you a ride over to the *Chronicle* so you can pick up your cruiser."

"Thanks, but I'll pass. I think I'm gonna walk. It'll give me a chance to sort things out in my head."

"You mean like how the chief said it's on you to ask Detective Clark to show us the footage from the feed store, and now you have to figure out how to manipulate that into a date?"

Kraus let a smirk cross his lips. "Yeah," he said. "Something like that."

Turner nodded. "Alright then. I'll catch up with you tomorrow." He put the truck in gear and gave Kraus a wave. "Enjoy your walk."

As he rolled up the window, he heard Kraus shout, "Say hello to Joyce for me!"

He gave the sergeant the thumbs up sign and drove out of the parking lot.

CHAPTER TWENTY-THREE

All was quiet when he pulled into the driveway behind Joyce's Toyota Camry. He'd shot her a quick text telling her he was on his way when he'd left the police station. She didn't respond, but he knew she'd seen it because he could smell the unmistakable aroma of the grill warming up behind the house.

The garage door was up, so he grabbed two bottles of Lone Star from the mini fridge and walked around to the backyard.

He found Joyce chopping up some fresh veggies on a table near the grill. He took the stairs up two at a time, laid the beers on the table, whirled her around, and planted a kiss directly on her lips. "Yum," he said. "You taste like you've been sampling the cucumbers."

"Not the just the cukes. The carrots, broccoli, and the bell peppers needed a taste test," she said, without without kissing him back. "How did things go with Tommy?"

"Better than I'd anticipated," he said while mentally flipping through reasons why she didn't kiss him back. "He was pissed, but I think it stemmed more from his embarrassment at receiving an unexpected call from his detective friend and having to admit he didn't know we were in Lampasas County following a lead." He paused. "Of course, it didn't help matters that Palmer and I lied while trying to pursue that lead."

Joyce turned from him and continued chopping the cucumber she'd been working on. "Yeah. About your little side trip," she said over her shoulder. "I thought you were going to try tracking down Jake Seeley at the land surveyor company. How did that turn into a road trip with you and Palmer?"

No one ever accused him of being a genius when it came to recognizing a woman's subtle body language cues, but it dawned on him that Joyce might not be happy with him at the moment. "I did try to track him down," he said. "Pyramid Land Surveying was closed for the weekend."

She turned around to face him. "So, you figured you'd give your new bestie a call and drive out to the country rather than come back here and spend time with me?"

He shook his head. "No, that's not what happened. I wanted to see if there was anyone in Magnolia Bluff who might've been through any kind of home or property fraud in the recent past. Maybe find some sort of connection to my investigation." He took a breath and continued. "I went over to the *Chronicle* and spoke with Monica Crow. I thought if anyone knew the answer, it would be her."

Joyce stared at him and waited.

He continued. "None that she knew of in Magnolia Bluff. However, there was one incident of fraud involving an older couple in Lampasas County last year. It's not that far of a drive, so yes, I asked Palmer to ride up with me to see if the police would give us any info on what happened and steer us in the direction of the couple so we could talk to them."

She nodded. "And it never occurred to you to give me a call and let me know?"

Turner offered a small shrug. "I guess I just got caught up in the moment after Monica told me about the couple.

All I could think about was seeing if there was anything about their story that could help solve Ronnie Senior's murder."

"And...?"

"As it turns out, there just might be," he said. "They were approached about selling their property and said no to whoever it was that made the offer. Shortly after, their son was murdered during a robbery at a feed store while he was there picking up an order. After speaking with the couple, Palmer and I believe the son's murder is connected to the parents turning down the offer to sell their farm." He paused. "And get this—the killer used a knife to stab the son to death. Sound familiar?"

Joyce put her hand up to her mouth and gasped. "Oh my God," she said. "Eerily familiar."

Turner nodded. "We thought so too. The store's security cameras recorded the robbery and murder. The Lampasas County police have a copy. Palmer is calling the detective we spoke with to see if she'll let us see the footage. We should know tomorrow."

He took her in his arms and hugged her. "I'm sorry I didn't call you and tell you I didn't catch up with Jake Seeley and was going to pursue something else."

Joyce let out a sigh. "Thank you. But I don't want you to feel like you have to call me every time you have a change of plan. I'm not trying to impede your investigation. I would never do that. It's just that I feel more connected to this case because I know the hard life Ronnie and his dad lived and really want justice for them. I let my emotions get in the way and I didn't mean to make it all about me."

"I appreciate that, but I still should've called you. I know you're invested in this case as much as I am. I'll try to do better." A smile appeared. "Now, how about I grill up those steaks?"

Turner's eyes popped open when he heard the garage door closing and the door into the kitchen open and close. He looked at his phone. It was after nine o'clock.

He was in the process of untangling himself from Joyce when Jason walked into the living room a minute later with a bag of chips in one hand and a soft drink in the other.

"How was dinner? Did you have a fun evening?"

The boy looked at him, still entwined with his mother, and smiled. "Not as much fun as you," he said with a sarcastic tone, then immediately added, "I'm sorry. That was rude. I'm glad you and my mom are together." He blew out a sigh. "I guess I'm just frustrated." He sat down in the chair opposite the sofa where Turner and Joyce sat. "Can I talk to you about something?"

Turner looked over at Joyce, who was still sound asleep, and said, "Of course you can. Should I wake your mother first?"

"No. I want to just talk to you… if that's okay?"

Turner gently pulled his limbs away from Joyce and sat up. "Always okay," he said. "What's on your mind?"

"Camila. I can't seem to get her off my mind. I really like her, but I'm not so sure if she feels the same way about me."

Turner smiled internally. He wasn't certain how much he'd be able to help the boy, but he felt a warm feeling inside that Jason trusted him enough to ask.

"Well," he said, "have you told her how you feel?"

"God no," Jason replied. "I'm afraid to tell her. What if she hates me?"

Boy, did this sound familiar to Turner. A memory quickly flashed through his mind, taking him back to when he was sixteen and had feelings for Jennifer Sills. He was so scared that she would destroy him emotionally if he told her he liked her.

When he finally got the nerve to say something to her, she turned out to be very nice to him. She'd turned him down when he asked her if he would go out with him. But she was kind in the way she'd said no. They'd remained friends throughout high school. She even helped him eventually meet the girl who'd said yes to him.

"I know it can be scary," he said. "But I'm sure she doesn't hate you. I'm not gonna lie to you. She may not feel the same way. And that's okay. But you'll never know the answer if you never ask the question."

"I don't know if I can."

"What do you like about her?" asked Turner.

Jason laid the chip bag and his drink on the side table by his chair. He sat back, his face beaming. "I like her eyes. The way they sparkle whenever she smiles. I can't explain it, but I get a warm feeling inside every time I look into those eyes. And her hair. It always looks so soft, and it smells good. Like she just washed it in fresh rainwater every time I see her. I also like that she's into the same type of music I am. Plus, we both like the same movies, and we agree that Taylor Swift is overrated."

Turner nodded. "I'm with ya on the Taylor Swift thing."

"We both like Ed Sheeran better."

This time Turner shook his head. "I don't know his music."

"Better songwriter and musician," replied Jason.

"I'll take your word for it. The reason I asked you what

you liked about Camila is that I wanted you to hear it out loud. I wanted you to feel the emotion in your heart as you spoke about what you see in her."

Jason slowly nodded his head.

"Now I want you to harness that feeling and understand the confidence you felt when you expressed those words." Turner closed his fist and tapped his chest. "Keep it here so it's not too far away when you're ready to say those words to her."

"How will I know when I'm ready?"

"Trust me, you'll know."

"But what if it doesn't go well?"

"Whether she has feelings for you as more than a friend or not, you will never regret telling her. I'm not saying it'll be easy to say to her but never telling her how you feel will be harder on you in the long run. If you don't, you'll always wonder 'what if?'"

"Thanks. I don't know if this made me feel any better, but I appreciate it. And I'll think about what you said." He picked up his chips and drink and stood. "Goodnight," he said, and then went down to his room.

Joyce opened her eyes and smiled. "Nice job," she said. "You told him the truth. You sugarcoated nothing, and you did it with compassion for his feelings. See that? You're better at this parenting thing than you think."

He looked at her and smiled. "I didn't know you were awake."

"Did you really think you could untangle yourself from my embrace and I wouldn't notice?" She sat up and kissed his cheek. "I didn't want to disrupt your conversation, so I laid here pretending to be asleep."

He grinned at her. "You ready for bed?"

"I'm not tired anymore."

"Good," he replied. "Neither am I."

CHAPTER TWENTY-FOUR

Turner felt the weight of Max hit the bed as soon as he landed on the lower end of the mattress. The big dog wiggling against the side of his body as he made his way further up the comforter and pushed inbetween him and Joyce.

He lifted his head off the pillow and looked over his shoulder. Max met Turner's face with his tongue and gave him a big lick across his nose and mouth. He pushed the dog's face away from his own. "What the hell, Max?" he said while sputtering and wiping the wet saliva off his mouth. "I thought you were sleeping in Jason's room."

He glanced over at Joyce. She was breathing deeply. A soft snore escaped her lips. Turner sat up and pushed the covers off his body. He looked over at Max. "Come on, boy. Now that you've got me wide awake, let's get you outside. And once you've finished, I'll get you some breakfast."

He stood, pulled a t-shirt over his head, and threw on a pair of sweatpants. He looked back at Max, who hadn't moved from the center of the bed, and said, "Let's go, boy."

The black Lab didn't flinch. Instead, he doubled down and snuggled his body against Joyce.

Turner put his hands on his hips and stared at his dog. "Okay," he said. "Suit yourself. If you don't want to eat breakfast, don't cry to me later when you're hungry."

Max's ears perked up at the word 'eat.' He crawled across the mattress, wagged his tail at Turner, and hopped down from the bed.

Turner smiled. "That's what I thought," he said as the

big dog sauntered past him. He followed Max out of the bedroom and quietly closed the door behind him.

While Max was outside taking care of his business, Turner filled his bowls with food and fresh water and laid them on the doggie mat that sat on the kitchen floor in the corner near the doorway.

Next, he went into the garage, walked through to the driveway, and whistled. Max came bolting from around the side of the house, into the garage, and up the two steps through the door into the kitchen. By the time Turner had closed the garage door and walked in behind him, Max had finished his food and was working on lapping down the water from his bowl.

When he'd finished drinking, Max turned, let out a belch, and proceeded to drip water off his chin across the floor as he wandered into the living room.

"Damn it, Max," said Turner as he pulled several paper towels off the roll and cleaned up the mess left behind by the drooling Labrador. "You really need to take a little more time to savor and enjoy your meal. Feeding time doesn't have to be a race to the finish line every time you eat."

He heard Max let out another belch in response to his rant. All he could do was shake his head and laugh while he finished drying the water droplets that trailed across the floor from the bowl to the living room.

He tossed the used paper towels in the trash just as his phone buzzed. He pulled the device from the front pocket of his sweatpants and glanced at the screen. he didn't recognize the number. He slide the green bar across the screen. "Hello," he said.

"Is this Brandon Turner?"

"Yes, and who is this?"

"Angus Price," said the voice on the phone. "I wasn't able to find the name of the survey company. I'm sorry."

"That's okay, Mr. Price," said a clearly disappointed Turner. "I appreciate you getting back to me."

"You're welcome." There was a pause, then, "Good luck with your investigation. I wish I could've been more help."

"Thank you," replied Turner. "You take care of yourself."

As soon as he hung up with Angus Price, his phone rang again. "Hey, Palmer. Little early for a Saturday, don't you think?"

"Never too early to catch a killer," replied Kraus.

"Speaking of that," said Turner. "Angus Price just called me. No dice on the survey company. He couldn't find the information."

"Well, its was a long shot anyway. I wanted to let you know I'm headed back up to Lampasas County this morning. Thought I'd see Detective Clark in person."

"Did you want some company?"

"Nope. I can handle it. I'm bringing along a flash drive so I can ask her about downloading a copy of the feed store footage."

"And…?" prodded Turner.

"And… what?"

"I'm guessing you wanna go alone so you can ask her to get a coffee or something?"

"Yes," replied Kraus. "I don't want you tagging along and screwing things up for me."

Turner laughed. "I get that," he said. "I'm not looking to be your third wheel coffee partner, anyway. Good luck."

"Thanks. I'll call you later to let you know if she gave me the footage. What're you up to today?"

"Maybe I'll go over to the hospital and check in on Ronnie this morning. See how he's doing and if he's remembered anything else that could help us."

"Sounds like a plan," said Kraus. "We'll catch up later."

Turner clicked off his phone and tossed it on the kitchen table. Then he opened the refrigerator and began rummaging around. He pulled out eggs, bacon, a tub of butter, and a carton of milk. He opened the freezer and found a bag of shredded potatoes and tossed it on the counter.

Next, he took out two frying pans and a small mixing bowl from a cupboard near the stove. He melted butter in both pans. Then he whisked eggs, a little milk, and salt together in the bowl and poured the mixture into one of the frying pans.

In the other pan, he laid out strips of bacon on one side and spooned out half the bag of potatoes on the other. He covered the pan to keep the splattering to a minimum. He went back to the first pan and began folding the egg mixture with a wooden spatula until it formed into fluffy scrambled eggs.

The smells emanating from the stove had their desired effect. Both Jason and Joyce popped their heads into the kitchen.

"That smells delicious," she said. She walked over and kissed Turner on the cheek, then smiled at him. "You are the best."

"Yeah, Brandon," added Jason. "This is awesome."

Turner grinned at the boy and said, "You know what really would be awesome? You grabbing us some plates and silverware. This is just about ready to eat."

While Jason set the table, Joyce took three glasses from the cupboard and took a carton of orange juice from the fridge and filled them each about halfway up. She looked over at Turner, who was sliding hot, freshly scrambled eggs from the pan to each of their plates. "You want me to make some coffee?"

He replaced the empty pan back on the stove and grabbed the other one. "No. I was thinking we could go to the hospital after breakfast and check on Ronnie. Thought we could stop by the Really Good for coffee while we're out."

He took the wooden spoon and scooped out some hash browns on the plates, along with a couple of strips of bacon each.

"That sounds like a great idea," replied Joyce.

Jason's eyes darted around the table like he'd lost something. "What? No toast?" he said.

Turner let out a small sigh as he realized his blunder. He shrugged. "I guess I forgot. Sorry. I never said I was perfect." A grin appeared on his lips. "I guess I'll just have to settle for 'awesome' and 'the best.'"

Joyce gave Jason the side-eye. "I think the words you're looking for are, 'thank you for making this wonderful breakfast, Brandon.'"

Jason rolled his eyes at his mother. "That's what I meant when I said, 'this is awesome.'" He looked over at Turner. "Thank you. I really do appreciate you making breakfast this morning."

Turner smiled at him. "I know you do, Sport. If you want some toast, I'll be happy to make it for you."

Jason shook his head. "Naw, this is perfect," he said, smiling. "I'm good without it." He looked over at his mother. "Mom, if you guys are going to the hospital, would it be okay if I used your car to go out to Hank and Ann's? Camila invited me to go horseback riding... if that's okay?"

Joyce glanced over at Turner. He gave her an almost imperceptible nod of the head. She smiled and looked back over at her son. "I think that would be okay. Have a good time. Just don't stay too late. I want the car back before dark. Deal?"

Jason nodded. "Deal."

The conversation quieted as everyone focused on the feast laid out in front of them. Turner looked around the table, relishing the smiles he saw as they all ate.

He was smiling too and realized at that moment how lucky he was.

CHAPTER TWENTY-FIVE

Joyce and Jason pitched in and helped Turner with the after breakfast clean up duty. It took no time at all to get everything washed, dried, wiped down, and put away.

"Now that's what I call teamwork," said Turner, a smile splitting across his face.

"Well, you know what they say," grinned Jason. "Teamwork makes the dreamwork."

Joyce stared at her son and smirked. "Now, if only I could get you to remember that the next time I ask you to pick your clothes up off the floor in your room."

Jason grinned back at his mother. "Oh, come on, mom. Rome wasn't built in a day," he countered. "I'll get there… eventually."

"Boy, you're just filled with all kinds of cutesy idioms this morning, aren't you?" she said.

Jason's face went blank. "What's an idiom?" He waited just long enough for her stare to settle on him, then busted into a laugh. "Ha… gotcha!"

She raised an eyebrow and snorted. "Good. For a minute there, I thought I was going to have to send you back to grammar school."

Turner leaned back against the counter and watched the interaction going on in front of him. A strange, yet warm feeling shot through his body. A feeling he hadn't experienced before. Not one like this, anyway, and he wasn't sure what it meant.

In a sudden move, he popped away from the counter and said, "I'm going to take a shower."

Joyce gave him a puzzled look. "Everything okay?"

"Yeah, yeah... I'm fine," he said. He rubbed his stomach. "Just a little queasiness going on."

Her puzzled look turned into concern. "Maybe you should lie down for a while. We can go to the hospital later."

"Not necessary. I'm fine." He mustered up a weak smile. "Nothing a hot shower won't cure."

"Okay, if you're sure?"

He nodded. "I'm sure."

Jason grinned at him. "Maybe your cooking doesn't agree with you," he quipped.

"You're a funny guy, Jason," he said, managing a quick laugh. He looked over at Joyce. "I won't take too long in the shower, so you'll have plenty of hot water for yours."

He could still feel the concern in Joyce's eyes cutting through him as he walked out of the kitchen.

As soon as he was back in the bedroom, he stopped and took a deep breath. What the hell happened back there? He'd never felt so weird before. All he could think was that he'd never had such a feeling of peace. And that scared him. He loved Joyce. And he loved Jason like he was his own. But this was something different. Why did this, this *thing*, shoot through him at that particular moment?

It was a simple back and forth lighthearted conversation between mother and son. One he'd seen and experienced many times over the last couple of years. What was different about this time? This conversation? He shook his head. It made no sense.

He stripped off his clothes, grabbed the robe he kept at Joyce's house, and went into the bathroom. As soon as the steam began rising from the shower, he stepped in and let the warm water cascade down his face and all around his body.

By the time he'd finished his shower, clarity had hit him square in the face. These two people in the other room were his family. His center of the universe. Something he'd never really had in his adult life. Until now. And he needed to make sure that would never change.

It had been staring him in the face for months now. He'd just been too damn stubborn to admit it.

Now, what to do about it?

Nothing. At least until whoever killed Ronnie's father was behind bars. Then he would concentrate on what was next for himself and what that meant for his future.

Ronnie was awake and sitting up in bed when Turner and Joyce walked into his room.

Joyce leaned over and gave him a hug around the shoulders. "Well, you look like you're feeling better," she said.

"Much better, ma'am. Thank you."

Turner reached over to shake his hand. "You look good."

Ronnie took Turner's right hand in his left and squeezed it. "Can't shake hands proper yet," he said. "They got a needle stuck in the backside of my right hand." He offered his other hand to show him. There was a small tube snaking out of the back of his hand up to a half empty plastic bag hanging from a hook next to his bed. "The nurse said they're addin' some salt back into me since I'm a bit lower than I should be."

Turner nodded.

A big smile appeared as Ronnie continued. "They say I might be able to go home sometime next week, if'n my numbers continue to stay good."

"That's terrific news," said Turner. "Have they had you up and walking around?"

"Every day this week. I can finally stand without crouchin' over. My belly don't hurt as much no more."

Joyce took his hand in hers and gently squeezed. "That's so wonderful to hear."

Ronnie squeezed back. "Yes, ma'am. It is. I'm almost ready to have me a big, fat, juicy cheeseburger. I don't know how much more of this hospital food I can eat. There's only so much Jello and cottage cheese one man can take."

She gave him a nod and said, "Now don't you rush into anything. You may need to work your way up to that cheeseburger."

"I know," Ronnie said with a sigh. "I ain't gonna do nothin' stupid. I'll wait until the doc tells me I can have one 'fore I actually do."

Joyce patted his hand. "Good for you," she said.

"So, Ronnie," began Turner, "have you remembered anything about what happened? Anything that might help us?"

Ronnie lowered his brows. "Well," he said. "Not about when I got stabbed. But I kind of remembered that my daddy did tell me somethin' about when he had that survey done."

Turner took a step closer to Ronnie's bed. "What did you remember? Did it have to do with the results of the survey?"

Ronnie scrunched his face. "That's just it," he said. "I can't remember what he told me. I know he told me somethin' important. I remember that much. And I've been thinkin' real hard about what that was, but it still feels too far away for me to catch just yet."

It was hard for Turner to hide the disappointment on his face.

Ronnie lowered his head. "I'm sorry, Mr. Turner. Really, I am. And I'll keep trying to remember. I will. I promise."

Turner smiled at the young man. "No worries," he said. "I'll come back to see how you're doing in a few days. Hopefully, you'll remember what it was by then."

"I'll keep trying to remember. You have my word," a dejected Ronnie said. "I didn't mean to disappoint you. I know it's important that I remember."

He definitely felt disappointed. But he certainly didn't want to leave Ronnie believing he'd let him down. He needed the boy to concentrate his efforts on continuing to get better so he could leave the hospital. "I don't want you to worry about me," he said. "I want you to focus on getting out of here. Your health is your number one priority. It's mine too. You didn't let me down." He smiled. "You understand?"

The young man nodded. "I understand. Thank you, but I'm still gonna work on rememberin' whatever it was my daddy told me. That's my priority too. 'Specially if'n it heps you catch my daddy's killer."

Turner smiled at the boy and nodded his head. "You're a good man. Your father would be proud of you. And I won't let you... or him down, either. I'll see you again in a few days."

"Okay," replied Ronnie. He looked directly at Joyce, who was still holding his hand. "I want you to come back, too."

Joyce squeezed his hand again and smiled. "Of course I'll come back. I'm there for you," she said. She glanced over at Turner and then back at the young man. "We both are. We'll see you in a couple of days. Stay strong."

She squeezed his hand one more time, then joined Turner over by the door. They both waved goodbye and then left the room.

They went down the elevator and out the main door in the hospital lobby. Once they were back in the truck and headed over to the Really Good, Joyce said, "Ronnie seemed so much better today. The idea that he may be able to go home next week was really good news, don't you think?"

"Yes, it was nice to see him doing so well," he agreed. "Not sure if his going home next week is good news, though."

Joyce twisted in her seat to face Turner. "How so?"

"Well, for one thing, he'll be alone in that house. Until we catch the person who attacked him and killed his father, I'm not sure his being home alone is a good idea."

"Can't you ask Tommy if he'll post an officer at his house?"

"I can, but they might not have enough manpower to keep someone there twenty-four, seven, until we can wrap this investigation."

Joyce twisted back around and slumped down in her seat. She sat quietly. Turner glanced over and saw she appeared to be hard at work thinking.

"What's going through that pretty little head of yours?"

"What if Ronnie stayed at my house for a while? You could still ask Tommy about having an officer posted. It would just be at my house instead of his. It would certainly solve the being alone problem."

"No," Turner replied quickly. "What if the killer finds

out he's there and comes to finish the job? I will not put you and Jason in danger." He paused, then added before she could argue, "But I do think you're on to something. Maybe he could stay at my place? There are no neighbors around. It's quiet, and the cabin has an alarm system."

"Do you even know the code for your alarm? I've never known you to set it once in the whole time you've lived there."

"Of course I know the code. And I use it all the time when Max and I are staying over at your house. But when we're at my place, Max is my alarm system. I trust him more than any store-bought security device to alert me of any kind of threat."

Turner drove up Main Street and circled the Green that split East Main from West Main, looking for a parking space.

On the second time around, Joyce spotted a car backing out of a space in front of the Bluff Bakery. "There," she said, pointing at the space just vacated by a little Mazda Miata.

Turner pulled in and put the truck in park. "Perfect. The Really Good is right next door," he said as he killed the engine, and they unbuckled their seat belts. He grinned at Joyce. "Good eye. I would've never seen that tiny matchbox car leaving."

"Oh stop. It's a cute little car," she said. She gave him a smirk. "You should think about getting one. You'd look good in it."

"Humph," grunted Turner. "If I were ever to buy anything that small, it certainly wouldn't be that."

"Oh, really?" she said, the smirk still evident. "What would you buy?"

Turner sat back in his seat and rubbed his chin while

he thought about the question. "It would have to be the BMW Z4 Roadster."

A smile dance across her face. "Great choice. The convertible?"

He gave her a mock smug look and shrugged nonchalantly. "Of course."

"Well, what're we waiting for?" she said, the smile growing in size. "Let's head to the dealership."

"You're kidding, right?"

"Maybe," she said, then winked at him.

They both laughed and then walked over to the Really Good.

CHAPTER TWENTY-SIX

Turner was surprised to see the Really Good Wood-Fired Coffee and Ice Cream Emporium hopping for a late Saturday morning.

Jack Bonhoffer waved as he strolled over to greet them. "Howdy, Joyce... Brandon," he said, reaching out to shake their hands. "You guys here for breakfast?"

Turner glanced over at Joyce, then back at Jack. "Sorry. Just coffee," he said. Seeing the disappointed look on the floor manager's face, he added, "You're looking pretty busy this morning. Business been picking up on the weekends? I thought you were busier during the weekdays."

"Used to be that way," he said. "Especially when Harry was here. But since he and Em have been gone, it all seems to have changed. And now that the weather is really heating up and schools are out for the summer, we get a lot of families that like to show up on the weekends. The kids come for the ice cream while the parents sip their iced coffees." He waved around the restaurant. "And as you can see, it's mostly out of towners. What I like to call the bounce-back families. The parents work during the week and then they escape with the kids on the weekends to our beautiful lake community. Most rent a spot for the entire summer over at Hayden's Resort and Campgrounds."

Turner frowned at the mention of Hayden's.

Joyce put her hand on his shoulder. "What's wrong?"

He took in a breath. "Nothing, really," he said. "I just

haven't thought about the campgrounds since last year."

Jack lowered his head. "Yeah. Sorry. Didn't mean to dredge up that memory."

Turner offered Jack a smile. "It's okay. Hey, we took care of business, didn't we?"

Joyce leaned up and kissed him on the cheek. "Yes, you did," she said. "Yes, you did."

He was referring to the psycho kidnapper who pushed the Magnolia Bluff police and Turner's investigative skills to the limit last year. He was lucky to come out of that whole mess alive.

Jack looked over Turner's shoulder and smiled. "A booth just opened up. Follow me." He led them across the floor to a spot over by the window. Once they sat down, he offered them menus.

Turner waved him off. "Not necessary. We're not having breakfast, remember?"

"Just in case you decide to have an early lunch," replied the floor manager. "Estrelita will be over in a minute."

"Thanks, Jack," smiled Joyce. She took the menu from him and opened it.

"You can't be ready for lunch already?" asked Turner.

"No, but I just can't resist the cinnamon rolls," she said, smacking her lips. "I'm looking at the menu to see what other baked goodies Jack's serving today."

Turner laughed at that. "Why bother? You know you're going to order the cinnamon rolls, anyway."

They both looked up as Estrelita said, "Hey guys, good to see you again. What can I get you?"

"Jack mentioned you were serving a lot of iced coffees lately," said Joyce. "I think I want in on that. What do you recommend?"

"How about a French Vanilla Caramel Protein? It's got plenty of flavor and the ten grams of protein will keep you going until lunchtime."

"Ooh... yes, please. That sounds scrumptious."

"You got it," replied the waitress. She looked at Turner. "What about you?"

Turner scrunched up his nose. "That sounds way too sweet for me. But I do like the idea of the ten grams of protein. Any other options?"

"You can get a regular arabica iced blend with the protein. It's bold with just a subtle sweetness to it and it's got a deep finish."

"Perfect. Put me down for that," he said. "And can we also get a couple of those delicious cinnamon rolls?"

Estrelita shot him a sarcastic smile. "The coffee's too sweet, but the cinnamon rolls aren't?" she asked.

Turner laughed. "It's all about balance."

With the smile still lingering, she lifted one of her brows. "Hmm... whatever you say, Brandon. Anything else you guys need?"

He glanced across the booth at Joyce, who shook her head. He looked back at Estrelita. "Nope, we're good. Thank you."

She closed her order book and smiled at them. "Be back in a jiff." She turned and hurried off to fill their orders.

"So, what do you think Ronnie's daddy told him?" asked Joyce.

Turner shrugged. "Who knows? My best guess? Maybe something stuck out on that survey. Something unexpected. I mean, what other reason could there be for somebody to break in and steal the survey from the safe?"

Their attention was pulled away from their

conversation when Estrelita appeared with their order. They both sat back while she placed a tall glass in front of Joyce. It was filled with a mix of light brown and cream-colored swirls circling around ice and oozing over the top of the glass. It had a whipped cream finish and a cherry on top.

Turner smiled as he watched Joyce's eyes widen at the sight of the drink laid out in front of her. "Oh my," she said. "This looks incredible." She took a sip and sat back in her seat. "This is heavenly. Thank you for recommending it, Estrelita."

The waitress smiled. "My pleasure," she said, while placing a much more subdued iced coffee in front of Turner.

He looked at his drink, then over at Joyce's drink. "I feel like maybe I made the wrong choice."

"Try it. You will love it or it's on the house," assured Estrelita. She waited for Turner to take a sip. "Well?"

He nodded his approval. "It doesn't have all the bells and whistles of Joyce's coffee, but it's a solid brew." He smiled at her. "It's just as you described it would be. And it's just what I wanted. Thank you, Estrelita."

"You're welcome," she said with a smile. "I'll be right back with your cinnamon rolls. I saw a batch of them coming hot out of the oven. Miguel was getting ready to slather the cream cheese frosting on them while I was mixing your coffees. They should be ready by now." She rushed off to get the rest of their order.

Turner glanced up at the ceiling. "Now, what was I saying? Oh yeah, there must have been something unexpected on that land survey Ronnie Senior had done."

"Something unexpected enough to kill him over? And if that's the case, are we talking about whoever the person was that approached him about selling the property?"

"It makes sense to me," said Turner. He took another sip of his iced coffee.

Estrelita was back and laid a plate stacked with half a dozen cinnamon rolls on the table between them.

Turner looked at the plate. "You must've misunderstood," he said. "We only wanted two of the rolls."

She handed Turner a small, white pastry box she'd been holding. "I know," she said. "No mistake. Jack said to give you guys extras to take home with you... on the house."

"That is so nice of him," said Joyce. "Please tell him thank you for us."

The waitress smiled at her. "I will," she said. "Enjoy." She turned and wandered off to another table.

Joyce reached over and grabbed one of the gooey confections and took a small bite from the corner of the pastry. She chewed much longer than Turner thought necessary considering the size of the bite, then said, "But, if the person who tried to buy the property is the same person who killed Ronnie's daddy, he had to know about what they'd find on the survey."

"Exactly. Which is why I'm hoping Ronnie can remember what his father told him."

"But what if he remembers, and it's not what you're hoping for? Remember, you told me the thief took all the paperwork from the safe, not just the survey."

Turner took one of the rolls from the plate and broke it in half. "I don't know," he admitted. Then took a large bite from the half he was holding.

Joyce giggled at him as he quickly grabbed a napkin to catch the trail of icing running down his chin. Her phone buzzed. She stuck her hand beneath the table and retrieved it from her hip pocket. "Hello," she said, trying to stifle her giggle. There was a pause as she listened to the caller. She glanced up at Turner. "Yes... I can do that." Another pause, then, "Give me about forty-five minutes and I'll meet you at the office. Then we can ride over together... alright, I'll see you then... bye." She put the phone on the table.

"Who was that?" asked Turner.

"A new client. Don Richardson. I showed him and his wife Susie a condo last week. They're both recently retired and moving here from Dallas. Anyway, they want to see the property again before they make their final decision."

Turner nodded. "Jason's got your car, so I'm guessing you want me to drop you off at the real estate office?"

She gave him a little pouty face. "If you don't mind."

He grinned at her. "I don't mind," he said. "After I drop you, maybe I'll go see Tommy and let him know our idea about letting Ronnie stay at my place when he gets out of the hospital. See if he'll assign someone to be there for security."

"Good idea," she said. "And don't worry about having to pick me back up later. I'm not sure how long I'll be. I'll give Jason a call and tell him he's gonna need to be available to pick me up from the office."

Turner nodded while he packed up the extra cinnamon rolls. He waved Estrelita over and paid the bill.

They walked over to where Jack was perched on a stool behind the front counter.

Turner held the box of pastries up and gave it a little shake. "Very generous of you," he said. "But you don't have to bribe us everytime with cinnamon rolls just to come back, ya know?"

Jack shot him a smile. "I know. But I'm counting on all this generosity convincing you two to come by here for an actual meal one of these days. It feels like the regulars just don't show up the way they used to when Harry was here every day."

"I can't speak for anyone else, but you're right. It felt a little weird coming in here that first time after Harry left on his trip, knowing he wouldn't be here to talk to. Nothing against you, Jack, but I feel like Harry gets me. He seemed to dial right in on me from the first day I met him. He was a big reason I would come here. Probably true for a lot of the regulars."

Jack nodded. "I know I'm not Harry," he said. "But I'd like to see you come around a bit more often." He glanced at Joyce. "Both of you. I know you guys have been through some things with Harry. Things that helped you all bond. But the coffee shop's still the same. Nothing's changed… other than Harry's not being here. But he'll be back, and it would be nice for him to know his friends didn't abandon the place just because he'd been gone."

"You're right," said Joyce. She looked up at Turner and then back at Jack. "We'll start showing up more than we have."

Turner nodded. "I agree. We'll get in here more often in the future. Sometimes to eat. Sometimes to get coffee. But I promise we won't abandon you or the shop."

"That's all I'm asking," Jack said with a grin.

CHAPTER TWENTY-SEVEN

Joyce called Jason on the way over to her office. When she hung up, Turner said, "How'd it go? He didn't give you any pushback on picking you up later, did he?"

She smiled. "No," she said. "Quite the opposite, actually. He wanted to know if it was okay for Camila to come along with him and stay for dinner."

Turner nodded. "Hmm," was all he said in reply.

She twisted in her seat so she could face him. "You think he did what you suggested?"

"I'm not sure. But if he did tell Camila how he felt about her, it must've gone well if he's asking to bring her to dinner." He glanced over at Joyce. "Are you crying?"

She used her open hand to fan herself. "Happy tears," she said. "My little boy is growing up." She reached over and patted his knee. "I am so proud of you. Jason came to you wanting to talk. He trusted you and you didn't let him down."

Turner couldn't help but smile. The boy must've taken his advice. Maybe he could handle this parenting thing after all.

They turned his pickup into the parking lot of the Magnolia Bluff Real Estate Agency and pulled up to the entrance.

Joyce unbuckled her seat belt and opened her door. Before stepping out of the truck, she said, "You'll be there for dinner?"

He smiled at her. "Wouldn't miss it for the world. What are you planning on cooking?"

"I don't know," she said with a frown. "I was so excited about Jason inviting a girl over for dinner that it didn't dawn on me until now that I don't really have much in the fridge. With everything going on, I haven't had the chance to go shopping yet."

"Don't you worry about it," he said. "I've got this."

"You've got what? Dinner?"

"Yep. Kids love pizza. I'll swing by Olivia's on the way over and grab a couple of pies, a dozen chicken wings, and a couple of two-liter bottles of soda to go with it." He offered a toothy grin. "We'll have a pizza party."

She leaned over and gave him a kiss. "That sounds perfect. Thank you."

"You got it," he said. "Now go sell a house."

She gave him another kiss, placed her hand on her heart, and smiled. "You are the best. I'll see you later." She got out of the vehicle, waved, and then went inside the building.

The smile didn't leave Turner's face until he pulled into the parking lot behind the Magnolia Bluff City Hall building. He hopped out of his truck and went into the police station.

Tommy was standing by the front desk when he walked in. He looked up as Turner approached. "Brandon," the chief said. "Perfect timing. Your ears must've been burning. I just got off the phone with Sergeant Kraus. If you're here to give me an update on the case, Palmer will be here in about ten minutes. Let's wait for him."

Turner nodded. "I'm not really here to give you an update about the actual case as much as it's an update about Ronnie's condition. And I have a question. Palmer should also hear this, so we can wait."

"Good," Tommy replied. "Let's head down to my office. I instructed him to come right in when he gets here."

Turner followed the chief down the hallway and sat in one of the two chairs in front of the desk. Tommy closed the door, then took his seat behind the desk.

"So, how do you like being a private eye?"

Turner shrugged. "Still getting used to the idea," he said. "I haven't even set up any kind of an office yet."

"You planning on renting space somewhere or using a room at your cabin?"

"Haven't given it much thought. But now that I think about it, probably rent a space somewhere," he said. "I like the privacy I have at the cabin. Not many neighbors around, which is how I like it. Why screw that up by opening up my business at home?"

Tommy knocked his fist on the desk and then pointed at Turner. "Good choice. Keep business and home life separate."

Turner nodded. "Makes things easier that way. Especially in our business."

"Agreed."

The office door cracked open, and Kraus popped his head in. "Okay to enter?"

"Come in, Sergeant," said the chief. "Have a seat."

Kraus smiled as he sat down. He glanced over at Turner. "Didn't expect to find you sitting here."

"I came by to update the chief on how Ronnie is doing," he said. "I was going to fill you in when you called me, but since you were on your way here, Tommy asked me to join so we could all get caught up together."

Kraus nodded. "Works for me."

Chief Jager eyed Turner. "How about you go first?"

Turner nodded, then filled them in on how Ronnie

remembered his father told him something important that may have had to do with the survey but couldn't remember what it was. Then he informed them of the boy's condition and his probable hospital release sometime next week. He capped it off by letting them know he was going to let Ronnie rehab at his place and was hoping Tommy could assist by assigning an officer to be there when he wasn't home.

Tommy sat back in his chair, taking it all in. Finally, he said, "Damn shame the boy can't remember what his daddy told him."

"It is," agreed Turner. "He said he's gonna try hard to come up with whatever it was, though. He knows it could be important to the case."

"Hopefully he remembers soon," added Kraus. He addressed the chief. "I think you should consider placing an officer at Brandon's cabin when Ronnie's released. Better safe than sorry." He looked over at Turner. "Good call on not letting Ronnie go back home. If the perp is looking to finish the job, that's the first place he'd search once his release from the hospital becomes known."

Tommy nodded, then looked at Turner. "I agree. Let me know once he's at your place and settled and I'll get that set up."

"Will do," said Turner. He glanced over at Kraus and smiled. "How about you? Did Detective Clark give up the goods?"

Turner's eyes twinkled as he watched Kraus' mouth drop open while he fidgeted slightly in his seat. The detective stared at him and faintly shook his head back and forth.

"Is everything all right?" Tommy said, eyeballing his detective.

Kraus broke his stare and looked at the chief. "Everything's fine. Just gathering my thoughts." He glanced back over at Turner and leveled his eyes. "I'm sure by 'giving up the goods' you meant, did she agree to give me a copy of the recording from the feed store robbery?" He paused, and a grin formed on his lips. "Yes, she did. Sort of."

Turner looked at the detective, not really sure if Kraus was also answering the question he was really asking. He cocked his head and returned the grin. "Good," he said. "So, she was cooperative? I knew you were worried about how she would react to you asking her."

"Yes. I don't know why I ever fretted over it," replied Kraus, his grin stretching wider. "We got along better than I expected, and she promised to give me everything I needed."

Turner nodded. "I told you not to stress about it."

"And you were right," said Kraus. "Thanks."

Tommy's head was swiveling back and forth between his detective and Turner. Finally, he said, "Am I missing something here? I feel like you two are having a whole other conversation that has nothing to do with the recording."

Turner straightened out in his seat. "Nope," he said. "Still on topic."

Tommy sat back in his chair. "Good." He looked at Kraus. "So, you have a copy of the robbery?" He held out his hand. "Lemme see it. I can plug the flash drive in on my computer and we can all watch it now."

Kraus glanced over at Turner, then focused on Tommy. "Well, that's where the 'sort of' comes in," he said. "During our conversation, a call came in about a bone a farmer pulled out of the mud around a fishing pond on his property. The guy thought it might be human. She had to go but promised to make the recording and upload the link to an email she'll send me by sometime tomorrow afternoon. I'll let you know as soon as I have it."

"Damn," said Turner. "I was hoping you came back with it."

Tommy sat forward and said, "Okay. Nothing we can do about it now." He addressed Kraus. "I don't care if you're sittin' around in your jammies spoonin' cold cereal into your face in front of the TV, watching cartoons. When that email arrives, you call me and Brandon. We'll all meet up here and take a look at it together. Understood?"

Kraus nodded. "Understood."

Turner was visibly disappointed at not being able to view the robbery just yet. He scowled and stood up. "If we're done, I've got some things to do."

"About the case?" asked Tommy.

"No." His face softened. "Jason asked Joyce if he could invite Camila over for dinner tonight."

Tommy nodded his approval and smiled. "This is a big step for the boy," he said. "How're you guys handling it?"

"I think we're both excited. Jason finally admitted to us he has feelings for her. Difficult for a sixteen-year-old to say out loud to his parents. Or in this case, his mom and me."

"What're you serving for dinner?" asked Kraus.

"He caught us off guard. He only asked Joyce a little while ago. We hadn't even thought about dinner for us yet, let alone a guest. So I told Joyce not to worry, I'd be in charge of the food. Thought maybe a pizza party would be in order."

Kraus nodded. "Kids like pizza."

"That's what I said," replied Turner. "It's easy and it'll keep the atmosphere light and fun. Hopefully, help keep Jason's nerves in check."

"Good luck with that part," said Kraus. "I can tell you from personal experience the nerves are never in check in those first stages of trying to get to know someone special."

Turner smiled knowingly. "You're not wrong about that," he said. "We'll talk later?"

"We will," replied Kraus.

Tommy looked at both men. "I feel like y'all are having a whole other conversation again."

"Nope," said Turner, as he stepped out of the office. He glanced back at Kraus and grinned. "Strangely enough, still on topic."

CHAPTER TWENTY-EIGHT

Turner dialed Olivia's pizza to place his order from the Piggly-Wiggly parking lot, before going inside to pick up the drinks to go along with dinner.

The phone rang twice, then he heard a woman's voice answer, "Olivia's Pizza. How are you, Brandon?"

"Uh... hi Olivia," he said, always amazed by her ability to know when he was calling and what his order would be. "How did you know it was me? Those psychic powers on full blast today?"

He heard her chuckle. "Nothing as mystifying as that," she said. "Your name popped up on my phone screen. I'm afraid it was more like the power of caller ID."

"Shoot," he said, clearly disappointed. "I was hoping to experience the magic that is 'Olivia.'"

"Well, then," she said, still with a chuckle. "Your order for one large pepperoni, one medium sausage with extra cheese, a spinach with white sauce, also medium, and two dozen wings, one mild, one hot, will be ready in fifteen minutes. I assume you'll be finished up at the Piggly-Wiggly in time?"

He smiled. "Now that's what I've come to expect, Olivia. You're simply amazing."

"Glad I didn't disappoint," she said, the chuckle still evident. "See you in fifteen?"

"See you then," he said, with a chuckle of his own. "And thank you for making ordering pizza an other worldly experience every time I talk to you."

"Always a pleasure, Brandon. See you soon."

After clicking the off button on his phone, he sat back in his seat and smiled. Olivia was truly a wonder.

He hopped out of the pickup and went inside the grocery store. His soda picks included a two-liter bottle of Coke, a Pepsi, a root beer, an orange soda, and a two-liter of 7-Up. He wanted to cover all the bases since he was out of tune with what kind of soft drinks teenage kids liked to drink.

Next, he rolled his buggy—still something he wasn't used to calling a shopping cart since moving down south—down the beer aisle and grabbed a twelve pack of Lone Star.

After paying the check-out clerk, he loaded everything into the back of his truck, then climbed into the driver's seat and headed over to Olivia's to pick up his food order.

Once he had the pizza and wings secured on the passenger seat, he scrolled his phone and tapped on Kraus's name. Then he put the truck in gear and pointed it toward Joyce's house.

He almost hung up after the fourth ring when the detective answered. "Sorry, Brandon," Kraus said instead of the standard greeting of hello. "I was leaving a message for Donna on the other line."

"So, it's Donna now?" replied Turner. "On a first name basis with the pretty detective, I see. I'm guessing your coffee date was successful?"

"Yes, we are. And yes, it was. She's easy to talk to when I'm not spewing lies at her."

Turner laughed. "Good to know. Maybe I'll try that the next time I see her."

"I explained a bit more about the case we're working on and why you felt the need to be untruthful when you asked for her help. She said she was already over it and for you not to worry about it. She saw the passion you had for wanting to solve the murder."

"So you dropped that whole lying thing in my lap, huh? You didn't happen to mention that part of the plan was your idea?"

"It didn't come up during the conversation."

"Happy to take the bullet for you," Turner laughed. "As long as she doesn't hate me, I'm good."

"Well," said Kraus. "It would be kind of awkward if she did, since we'd like you and Joyce to join us for dinner once we wrap up this investigation. Her idea, by the way."

"Sounds good. Joyce will love it. She's also invested in you meeting someone nice. Are you planning on seeing her again before then?"

"Yes. We're going to try sneaking in a couple dates before the dinner with you guys. I really like her and want to spend some time getting to know her before we do a foursome."

"I think that's a good idea."

"I'm hoping to get up there to see her in a couple of days. Planning on shoring up the details when I speak to her tomorrow. She said she'd call me right after she sends me the recording, so I'll know when it's in my email."

"Don't forget to call me once you've got it," said Turner.

He heard Kraus snort into the phone. "Like that's gonna happen. I won't forget. I'm not sure about the time, though. It depends on when she gets this bone thing wrapped up. She told me before she left she thinks it's probably an animal bone. The guy thinks it's human because of the size. More likely from a horse or maybe a steer. She said they see it all the time but still need to investigate if someone calls and reports finding one, just in case."

"The perils of being a cop from an agricultural heavy county," said Turner.

"You said it," replied Kraus, "not me. But I agree with you."

"All I know is when I was a narcotics cop back in New York, if we got a call about someone finding a bone that might be human, it usually was. Of course, it was also always a possibility it was a finger with a pinky ring attached."

"The perils of being a cop from a drug heavy city," replied Kraus.

"You're not wrong," said Turner as he pulled into Joyce's driveway. "Listen, I've gotta go. Got hot pizza and wings that need to be consumed."

"Have fun at your pizza party," said Kraus. "I hope everything goes well tonight with Jason and his girlfriend. Where will you be tomorrow when I call you about getting the email?"

"I'm gonna see if I can catch up with Jake Seeley over at Pyramid Land Surveying. I'm hoping I can get a look at the Spatch survey from him."

"Okay, sounds good. I'll talk to you tomorrow," said Kraus.

"You got it," replied Turner. "And by the way, I'm glad you took the plunge and asked Detective Clark out. Nothing but good things to come, buddy."

"Thanks, Brandon. Enjoy your evening."

Turner clicked off his phone and smiled. He really was happy for Palmer.

Joyce's car wasn't in the driveway when he'd pulled in. He looked at the time displayed on his phone. It was just after six o'clock. He tapped her name on his phone and waited for her to answer.

She picked up on the second ring. "Are you at the house?" she said, skipping the hellos.

"Just got here. Where are you guys? I've got piping hot pizza and wings waiting to be devoured."

"We should be there in about ten minutes."

"Perfect," he said. "How about I get everything set up on the back deck?"

"Sounds good," replied Joyce. "We'll see you in a few."

Turner walked around to the passenger's side and carefully stacked the food in his arms. He opened the garage door and went inside. Max met him at the door as he walked into the kitchen and laid the boxes on the table.

Max followed him outside as he went to retrieve the beer and soda from the truck bed. Max stayed outside to nose around and take care of his business while Turner brought the drinks inside.

Once he had everything on the table, he went back out to the garage and grabbed the cooler and took it around to the deck. He knew Joyce already had some ice bagged up in the freezer, so he went into the kitchen, grabbed the bags from the freezer and dumped them inside the cooler.

He brought the bottles of soda and the beer out and pushed them into the ice, then closed the cooler top.

Next, he brought the pizza and wings out to the deck and placed them on the table along with napkins, plates, and plastic cups for the drinks.

He'd finished setting up as Joyce and Camila, followed by Jason, came marching through the back door onto the deck.

Joyce sidled up to Turner and gave him a quick peck on the cheek. "Thank you for doing this," she said. "This all looks great."

"I told you I got this," he said with a smile. He looked over at Jason and Camila. "Come on, guys. Grab yourself a drink from the cooler, take a seat, and dig in. We've got enough pizza and wings to feed an army. So don't be shy."

The kids did as they were told. Both poured some Coke into a cup and took a seat next to each other at the table.

"This is awesome," said Jason, a wide grin plastered on his face.

Camila nodded her head. "Yes, Mr. Turner," she said in agreement. "This is amazing." She looked over at Joyce and then back at him. "Thank you so much for having me over."

Joyce smiled at her. "It's our pleasure, Camila. You're welcome here anytime," she said, glancing over at Turner.

"Absolutely," added Turner. "And you can call me Brandon."

Camila nodded her head. She offered him a shy smile. "Thank you… Brandon."

Turner looked around the table as he took in the sounds of people eating, laughing, and just enjoying themselves in general. His people. He smiled and realized he had that same feeling he'd had after breakfast. A feeling of how right this was. An inner peace that said to him this was what it was all about. Family. He sat back, took a swig of his beer, and ate some pizza while he got lost in the moment playing out in front of him.

Joyce leaned over and said, "Everything okay?"

Turner snapped back from his thoughts. "Everything's perfect," he said, smiling. "I was just thinking about how nice this was—Jason asking Camila over, me being able to help with the dinner, you just being… you, which is amazing all by itself, by the way."

He shrugged. "It all makes me feel good."

She smiled at him. "You're right. It does feel good. It's nice to be able to wind down like this at the end of a long day. I imagine even more so for you. The stress of trying to solve your first case as a private detective with all the pressures that must bring…" She shook her head as her words faded.

"Yes," he agreed. "But it's more than that. When I was a cop back in New York and I was having a rough day—and believe me, there were plenty—I would go out with the guys afterwards, have a few beers, maybe spend some time with a lady friend… you know, blow off a little steam…"

"I get it," she said, interrupting him. "You weren't exactly a saint back then. I know there were other women before me. I'd be a fool to think any differently. I don't care about that, Brandon."

"No, no," he said, shaking his head. "I'm not trying to confess anything here. I was a normal, single guy living in the big city. I know you know that. We're both adults. And we both have a past. I don't care about that either. What I meant was the way I used to decompress after a hard day on the job back then left me no satisfaction. It was nothing more than a Band Aid. The feeling was temporary, at best. It didn't come close to how I feel now. Right at this moment. With you. With Jason. With us. I've never had this before. This… this feeling of completeness."

Joyce put a hand gently on his chest, kissed his cheek, and then laid her head against his shoulder. "I feel it too."

"Get a room," Jason howled from across the table.

Camila smiled and gave him a playful slap. "Stop," she said. "I think it's sweet."

Joyce smiled at the girl. "I'm with you, Camila." She glanced up at Turner. "I think it's sweet, too," she said, cutting her eyes at Jason. "Unlike that son of mine."

"Oh, I don't know," Camila said. She took Jason's hand in hers. "I think he's sweet." She smiled and glanced over at him. "Kinda cute too."

Turner opened his mouth to say something but thought better of it when he saw Joyce's eyes boring into him.

Jason mumbled something.

Camila nudged him in the side with her body. "What was that? I didn't quite hear what you said."

Jason took in a breath and looked at her. "I think you're cute, too," he said in a barely perceptible voice. Then he turned to the food on his plate and concentrated on eating his chicken wings.

Camila smiled and took a bite of her pizza.

The rest of dinner was fun with Camila getting to know Turner and Joyce a little better and them getting to know more about her. Turner noticed even Jason joined into the conversation after getting past the slight embarrassment he'd felt after Camila got him to admit his feelings out loud in front of them. He knew exactly how the boy felt in that moment and was glad he didn't appear scarred for life after his admission. Maybe he'd have a follow up talk with him later to reinforce that there was nothing for him to be ashamed about.

By the time the evening ended, it was after nine o'clock, so Turner drove Camila back to Hank and Ann's place. Jason rode along with her in the back seat so he could say goodbye to her when they dropped her off.

Jason walked her up to the door and waited until she was safely inside before getting back inside the pickup.

Once they were on their way, Turner said, "I was proud of how you handled yourself during dinner."

Jason looked at him and said, "What do you mean?"

"I'm sure it was hard to say what you said about Camila while your mom and me were sitting right there."

"Oh, that," Jason said, playing it off. "It wasn't as hard as I thought it would be."

"Well, I just wanted you to know that your mom and I were proud of you. And if you ever feel like you want to talk about anything again, I'm here for you."

"Okay, thanks, but it was no biggie."

Turner nodded as he caught the smile forming on the boy's face as he turned away to look out the window.

CHAPTER TWENTY-NINE

Turner guided his truck into the parking lot of Pyramid Land Surveying, PA exactly at nine the next morning. He'd thought about last night's conversation during dinner with Joyce on the drive over. He pretty much already knew she felt the same way about how things were going with them as he did, but it was nice to hear her confirm that.

But for now, he needed to pack all that away until they caught Ronnie Senior's killer and put him in a jail cell.

He got out of the pickup and walked into the surveying office.

The look and feel of the place was almost museum like. Black and white, glossy photo images of old farmhouses, framed by their surrounding land and crops, papered the walls. There were men dressed in 1900 turn-of-the-century outfits standing in the fields surveying the properties. There were several low-profile glass cases set against the walls showcasing some tools of the trade from that same time period.

Turner took a moment to take in the photographs and the items enshrined in the display cases before making his way over to the receptionist. He guessed the young woman sitting behind the desk was in her mid-twenties.

She glanced over the top of the paperback book she was reading and said, "Can I help you?"

He squinted at the name plaque on the desk, then flashed his best smile at her. "I hope so, Mia," he said. "I'd like to speak with Jake Seeley. Is he in this morning?"

"Do you have an appointment with Mr. Seeley?"

"I do not," he admitted. "Perhaps he can fit me in? I won't take up much of his time."

She let out an audible sigh and stuck a bookmark between the pages she'd been reading and set the book down in front of her. "I'll have to see if he is free. Name?"

"Brandon Turner," he said, flashing his smile again.

She pointed at an area to the left of her desk where two high back leather upholstered chairs were situated around a small cocktail table stacked with several magazines. "Have a seat over there. I'll be back in a minute."

Turner took a seat and watched as Mia walked down a short hallway and entered a room on the right. He leaned over and grabbed a magazine off the table and mindlessly thumbed through the pages while he waited.

A few minutes later, Mia reappeared, followed by a man dressed in business casual attire. Turner stood as the man approached with an outstretched hand. "Mr. Turner," he said. "I'm Jake Seeley. What can I do for you today?"

Turner shook the man's hand and said, "I appreciate you seeing me without an appointment. I'm investigating the death of a man by the name of Ronnie Spatch, Senior, who we believe was murdered because of a possible land fraud incident. His son said that your company performed a survey of their property a month or so ago and I'm hoping you would be so kind as to show me that survey."

Seeley furrowed his brows. "So, you're with the police?"

"Private," replied Turner. "I was hired by the son of the man who was murdered. But I am working alongside of Sergeant Palmer Kraus, who is with the police and assigned to this investigation."

Seeley nodded for a moment before responding. "Well, this is highly unusual," he said. "We file all our surveys with the county deeds office. They are all registered there and available for research during their office hours. However, keep in mind that a land survey is not necessarily considered a public record. So they could deny your request."

This time, Turner nodded before speaking. "I wasn't aware of that. I assumed the records were filed there and available under the Freedom of Information Act."

"A common misconception," replied Seeley. "Of course, if you're working with the police, they should be able to obtain a copy of the survey for you. I'm sorry I'm not able to help you."

"But in this case," Turner pushed back, "your company hasn't filed the survey with the county yet. I know because we've already been there and checked. Is there any possibility of you helping me out?"

"Have you asked the son? If our company performed a land survey for their farm, he should probably have a copy. Perhaps he could show it to you."

"Unfortunately, he doesn't have a copy. We believe whoever killed his father broke into their safe and took the document."

"Well, that is unfortunate," said Seeley. "I would need a warrant from the police before I could show any survey we've performed. I'm sorry but I cannot help you. Now, if you'll excuse me, I think we're finished here." He turned and walked back down the hallway and disappeared into the same room Mia had gone to earlier to fetch him.

Turner shook his head, then looked over at the

receptionist. She had her nose buried in her book and paid no attention to him. He nodded again, this time at no one, pushed out a breath, and walked out of Pyramid Land Surveying's office and into the sunshine.

He got back inside his truck and sat there contemplating his next move. It never occurred to him he wouldn't be able to get a look at the Spatch farm land survey from the company that performed the survey.

He was beginning to question its existence. Maybe Ronnie misunderstood about his father having a survey done. Ronnie is a nice guy, but not exactly the brightest bulb in the box. Of course, if Ronnie was wrong and his father never had the land survey performed, that would mean he'd been wasting a lot of time chasing the wrong lead.

He replayed his conversation with Jake Seeley in his head. Seeley had said *if* they performed the survey. He never actually confirmed or denied that they did the survey.

Turner thought about going back inside and directly asking Seeley if they'd performed a land survey at the Spatch farm. No, based on the way the first conversation had gone, he'd probably be difficult and wouldn't answer the question without demanding a court ordered warrant, anyway.

He fired up his pickup, put it in gear, and drove out of the parking lot.

Since he didn't expect to hear from Kraus about the feed store video until later, he figured he'd head back to Joyce's place, pick up Max, and go over to his cabin. He hadn't been there in a few days and wanted to make sure everything was good.

His phone rang when he was about halfway there. He

smiled. "Hey, beautiful," he said. "I'm on my way back over to the house now."

"Good. As it turns out, I've got the rest of the day off. The Richardsons called this morning—that's the nice couple I showed the condo to—and they decided to make an offer. But they need to talk to their banker before they do and get a few things straightened out first. They asked to see me tomorrow, and since I have nothing else pending at the moment, I thought maybe we could go over to the cabin and get it ready for Ronnie. What do you think?"

"I think that's a great idea. I figured you were working today, so I was going to pick up Max and head to my place since I hadn't been home for the last few days. Your idea is much better, because it means I get to spend time with you. I should be pulling into your driveway in about ten minutes."

"Perfect. I'll have Max ready, and we'll meet you in the driveway."

"Sounds good," he said. "Hey, why don't you see if Jason wants to join us?"

"He's not here. Since I'm not at work, he asked to borrow my car. You missed him by about thirty minutes."

"Let me guess, he went out to Hank and Ann's farm to see Camila?"

"How did you ever guess?" she said with a giggle. "She called him a little while ago and asked if he wanted to go horseback riding. He couldn't get ready fast enough."

"Ha. Just as long as they don't elope and get married," he said, laughing.

"Not before me, he doesn't," she said, still giggling.

Well, that response certainly took him by surprise. He wasn't sure how to reply, so he simply stayed quiet.

"Brandon? Are you still there?"

"Uh, yeah. I'm still here," he said. "Um… sorry. I had to concentrate for a minute. Some guy just pulled out right in front of me."

"Brandon," she said. "It was just a joke."

"Huh? Oh, yeah," he said. "Of course it was. I knew that. Listen, I'll be there soon. You better go get Max ready. I'll see you in a few."

"Okay… we'll be ready," she said. "I love you."

"I love you, too," he said, using an upbeat voice. "More than you know."

He clicked the end call button on his steering wheel and took in a deep breath. "I'm an idiot," he said out loud to no one.

CHAPTER THIRTY

By the time Joyce and Turner finished cleaning the cabin, it was after three o'clock in the afternoon.

"Have you heard from Jason this afternoon?"

"Yes," said Joyce. "He texted me a little while ago. Hank and Ann are cooking a low country boil tonight, and they asked Jason if he wanted to stay for dinner. I told him as long as he can be home by nine, I was good with him staying."

Turner raised an eyebrow. "Has he ever had a low country boil before? Doesn't exactly scream Texas."

"Oh, that's where you're wrong," she said. "A lot of folks in the Texas Hill Country do a low country boil. Jason's dad and I cooked a few when we were together. I mean, what's not to like? Shrimp, potatoes, corn, sausage, Cajun seasoning... an explosion of flavor." She gave him the side eye. "What about you, Mr. New York City? Have you ever eaten a low country boil?"

Turner shook his head and grinned. "If a street vendor didn't sell it on a food cart in the middle of Manhattan, I'd have to say no."

"Well, we're gonna have to change that," she said. "You don't know what you're missing. We'll do one before summer ends."

"Sounds good. Maybe we can do a bigger one and invite Hank and Ann, along with Camila. They've been so good to Jason. It would be a nice thank you from us to them."

Joyce smiled. "That's a great idea. Let's definitely

make that happen."

"And here's another great idea," he said, embracing Joyce in a hug. "How about if we run over to the hospital and tell Ronnie our thoughts about him rehabbing at my cabin until we have the killer locked up? I'm thinking he's probably getting released in a couple days and we still need to talk to him about staying here. And after that, I'll buy you dinner over at the Silver Spoon."

"You're just full of great ideas, aren't you?" she said, as she kissed his chest, then his chin, and finally landing on his lips.

The sudden ringing of Turner's phone interrupted them. He pulled away and fished the device from his pocket. He glanced at Joyce. "It's Palmer," he said, then clicked the green answer button and said into the phone, "Do you have the video?"

"I'll have it when I get back from Lampasas," Replied Kraus.

"Get back?" Turner said, his voice two octaves higher than normal. "Why are you going there? I thought Detective Clark was emailing a link to access the video to you?"

"Donna called me a little while ago. She said she could email me the file or if I wanted to drive up there, she would hand me the recording on a flash drive in person. So, long story short, she's cooking for me tonight, and I'll have the flash drive when I get back."

"You're killing me," Turner said. He sighed, then added, "But I guess I can't blame you for taking her up on the invitation. What time will you be back?"

There was a pause before Kraus answered. "Let's just say I'll meet you in the chief's office at ten tomorrow morning."

Turner shook his head in frustration. Then he took a deep breath, closed his eyes and pinched the bridge of his nose. "Ten o'clock," he replied in a sharp tone. "Did you let Tommy know?"

"He's aware," said Kraus. "You know as well as I that the video's a long shot. Whether we watch it today or in the morning won't change that."

Turner paused, then, in a softer tone, said, "I know that. I'm just getting eager to close this case. Have a good time. I'll see you in the morning."

Joyce gently stroked Turner's shoulder. "Not the news you were hoping for?"

"Not exactly what I wanted to hear," he said. "But it's hard to hold it against him. The email Palmer was supposed to get with a link to the video showing the feed store robbery turned into a dinner date. He's meeting Detective Clark up in Lampasas County tonight. She's cooking for him over at her place."

She hugged him. "Be happy for him. Sounds like this might be the start of something good for Palmer. He just wants what we're lucky enough to have already found." She gave him a kiss. "Is there really that big of a difference if you see the video tomorrow morning instead of tonight?"

"No," he admitted, "you're right. There really isn't."

"Okay then. How about we go talk to Ronnie and then you can buy me that dinner you promised?"

Turner nodded. "Sounds good. I think Max is out back lounging on the grass somewhere. Do me a favor and put down a bowl of food for him and refill his water dish while I go rustle him up."

"Got it," she said and walked into the kitchen.

Turner went outside into his backyard and called out

for the black Lab. A few seconds later, he saw Max come running up the hill from the dock. "Hanging out by the water, huh?"

The dog ran right into him and knocked him over. "You're all wet," he said, laughing as Max began kissing his face. He took a few minutes to rub his buddy's back before they went inside.

Joyce smiled as they walked into the kitchen. "You two looked like you were having fun."

"Yeah," he said, "I love that big, goofy black ball of fur. He watched Max attack his food, then turned back to Joyce. "But I have been feeling a little guilty lately. I haven't spent as much time with him as I usually do."

"Well, to be fair," said Joyce, "you've been a little busy fighting crime over these past few days."

"Still, I wish I could carve out some more quality time for him."

"You will," she said. "As soon as you catch the person who took Ronnie's daddy's life."

Turner nodded. "Once he's finished eating, let's drop him off over at your place before heading over to the hospital. Then, after dinner, we can go back to your house for the night."

"You wanna spend the night at my house again?" she joked. "You think you're gonna get lucky or something?"

He grinned and pulled her in close. "Well, we could stay here, but we just cleaned and all, so…" He leaned in and kissed her lips.

"We could," she said, kissing him back. "But Jason would be home by himself all night."

"He wouldn't be alone. He'd have Max there," he said, while softly running his fingers up and down her back.

"Brandon?"

"Yes, my love?"

"He's sixteen years old. I don't feel comfortable leaving in the house all alone overnight. Not yet anyway. What if he needs me?"

He leaned in, brushing her ear with his lips, and said, "I need you."

She shuddered slightly and then gave him a long, deep, passionate kiss. Then she pulled back and offered him a devilish grin. "I'm getting hungry. Let's go talk to Ronnie so we can eat soon. Then, if you play your cards right, you can join me back at my place after dinner and maybe we can finish what we started."

A slight frown appeared on Turner's face. "Really?" he said. "You're gonna rev up my engine like that and then just leave the car in the garage?" He offered a devilish grin of his own. "You're a cruel woman, Joyce Blackstone. But I accept your terms."

CHAPTER THIRTY-ONE

Turner pulled his pickup into Joyce's driveway and put it in park. He got out and opened the rear driver's side door and watched Max leap out and lumber over into the grass.

Joyce stepped from her side of the truck while she tapped a code into an app on her phone that opened her garage door. When it was about halfway up, she ducked under and went inside.

After inspecting the front lawn for a couple of minutes, Max wandered into the garage, where Joyce waited to let him into the house.

Turner got back inside his truck and waited for her to return. A minute later, she walked out from the garage, tapped her phone again, which triggered the door to go down, and then hopped up into the truck.

"Is he settled?" asked Turner.

"He's settled. He marched right down the hallway to Jason's room and jumped up onto the bed."

Turner nodded, backed his truck out of the driveway, and headed over to the Burnet Medical Center.

"Do you think Ronnie will be okay with us wanting to have him stay at your cabin for a while?"

"I don't see why he'd have an issue with it," replied Turner. "Besides, I don't plan on giving him any choice in the matter. My cabin is the safest option for him until we catch the person who murdered his father and almost killed him."

"I agree. Especially if Tommy has an officer there for

protection."

Turner guided the truck into the visitors lot and found a space that was close to the hospital entrance. "Hmm," he said. "First time that happened. Usually we're hiking from the far regions of the parking lot to the front door."

Joyce agreed. "True. Maybe the time of day has something to do with that. We're kind of in that oddball timeframe between late afternoon and early evening when people are getting home from work and are not quite ready to leave their house again. I saw it all the time when I worked a retail job years ago. Things just died and the parking lot at the mall cleared out before the evening crowd arrived. Hospitals probably experience that same lull with people visiting their loved ones."

"Maybe," said Turner. "I don't care why it happened. I'm just glad I don't have to walk as far this time." He smiled at her. "Come on, let's go."

They got out of the pickup and took the short walk hand-in-hand over to the entrance. Once they were inside, they walked over to the lobby area just as one of the elevator doors swooshed open. They rode up to the third floor and walked down to Ronnie's room.

Officer Hans Winkler was sitting on a folding chair outside the door. He stood as they walked up to him. "Hello, Joyce," he said with a smile. He offered his hand to Turner. "Hey, Brandon. Haven't seen you in a while."

Turner nodded as he shook Winkler's hand. "Yeah, well, I haven't been around the station as much since that new captain of yours came on board."

Hans smiled knowingly. "I understand. He's something, alright. I'd stay away from him myself if I could, but I don't have that luxury."

"I heard he wanted to put you on the overnight shift, but Tommy nixed it. Briggs didn't take that out on you, did he?"

"No, he didn't," said Hans. "He's a pain in the ass, but he's not stupid." He shrugged. "I told the chief I didn't have any problem working the overnights, but he told the captain that he wanted to keep me on first shift until Sergeant Sovern and Georgia Jean got back from their special assignment." He grinned. "Briggs wasn't too happy about his decision being overridden by the chief. Couldn't see the sense in it. To be honest, neither did I. Between you and me, I think the chief made that stuff up about why he wanted me to stay first shift just to mess with the captain. I heard a rumor that the chief thought Briggs might've been getting too big for his britches and wanted to remind him who was really in charge. Know what I mean?"

Turner laughed. "Yup. I know exactly what you mean."

Hans scratched his head. "I'm sorry, guys," he said. "I'm yappin' away, and I'm sure you're eager to go in and see how Ronnie's doing."

Joyce smiled at the officer. "That's okay, Hans," she said. "It's always good to see you."

Winkler nodded and waved them into the room.

Joyce walked in while Turner hung back for a second. He patted Winkler on the shoulder and said, "Good to see you, Hans. I'm sure you've heard I'm working as a PI now. I hope we get to see more of each other in the future. Although the case we worked on together a couple of years ago wasn't fun, I enjoyed getting to know you and hope we get the chance to work together again."

"Thanks, Brandon. I appreciate that." He pushed the

door open and said, "Go on inside. I'll see you later."

Turner nodded and went through the doorway.

Ronnie was sitting up in a chair next to his bed when they walked in. He smiled and gave them a little wave. "Hi Ms. Blackstone... Mr. Turner," he said, with a slight nod of his head.

Joyce walked up and took his hand in hers. "Hi, Ronnie. How are you doing?"

His smile widened and illuminated his face. "I'm feeling like I'm ready to go home."

Turner stepped up next to Joyce. "Good to hear," he said. "Actually, that's why we're here."

Ronnie's smile faded as a worried expression shone in his eyes. "The doctor changed her mind, didn't she?" he said, lowering his head. "She's not lettin' me go home this week. I knew it was too good to be true."

"No, no," Joyce assured him as she squeezed his hand. "We didn't speak to your doctor." She glanced over at Turner. "We have good news for you."

"That's right," said Turner, offering a positive smile. "We want you to move into my cabin for a while when you're released. It'll be safer and easier for you to continue your rehab."

Ronnie had a surprised look on his face. "I... I appreciate the offer, but, but I can't put y'all out like that. B'sides, I ain't gonna be nobody's charity case."

Joyce leaned in closer. Her eyes bore into his. "Now you listen here, Ronnie Spatch," she said, her voice stern yet with a mother's gentleness, "you are *not* a charity case. Brandon and I care about you. We care about your safety. We want you to be able to get healed up without the fear of someone trying to harm you again. You will stay at Brandon's cabin, and I don't want to hear another word about it." She smiled at the young man and patted the back of his hand. "Is that understood?"

Ronnie nodded, and a heartfelt smile appeared. "Yes, ma'am," he said, choking back tears. "I'm appreciative for yer offer and I'll... I'll gladly accept." He glanced up at Turner. "Thank you."

Turner smiled. "You're welcome. And like I said, it'll be temporary. Just until we've got the person who hurt you and took your father from you behind bars. Chief Jager has agreed to assign an officer to be at my place when I'm not there, so you won't be alone. You can simply concentrate on getting your health and your strength back."

"Yes, sir," replied a grateful Ronnie.

"Well," said Joyce. "I'm glad that's settled. Now, have they told you what day they're letting you out of here?"

"Dr. Pope said maybe Thursday as long as nothin' changes 'fore then."

"Okay," she replied. "Thursday it is. We'll stop by the nurses' station on the way out and I'll let them know to call me when your release has been finalized and we'll pick you up." She leaned over and kissed his cheek. "We'll see you soon."

Ronnie smiled. "Hopefully Thursday." He looked over at Turner. "Thank you. I really appreciate what yer doing for me... and for my daddy."

Turner smiled back. "Don't thank me yet," he said. "You might want to wait until I solve your father's murder. It's been more of a challenge than Sergeant Kraus and I believed it would be."

"I have faith in you, Mr. Turner. It's why I came to you in the first place."

Turner nodded. "I won't let you down. I promise. Get

some rest and we'll see you on Thursday."

"Yes, sir," the young man replied. "Thursday."

Turner held the door open for Joyce. She paused, gave Ronnie one last wave, and then left the room. Turner gave the boy a quick nod, then followed her out the door.

They both wished Officer Winkler a nice evening and then walked down to the nurses' station.

CHAPTER THIRTY-TWO

Ten minutes after giving the nurse on duty the information needed for Thursday, they were on their way over to the Silver Spoon for dinner.

"Ronnie's reaction surprised me when you told him you wanted him to stay at your cabin."

"Yeah," said Turner. "That surprised me too." He glanced over at Joyce. "But I was impressed at how quickly you straightened him out on the idea. Nice job."

"It was no biggie," she said with a slight shrug. "He just needed a little hard love that only a mother figure could give."

There was a parking spot across the road from the Silver Spoon when they arrived. Turner guided his truck into the space and turned off the engine.

Lorraine Dillard, the owner of the cafe, looked up when they walked in. She smiled and gave them a wink, then waved at one of her waitresses. She turned the couple she'd been speaking with over and watched them saunter off behind the waitress to a table.

"Well, hello, Brandon... Joyce," she said with a friendly nod as they walked up to her. "It's good to see you. Do you guys have a reservation?"

Turner glanced at Joyce, then back and Lorraine. "Reservations?" he said, his voice showing hesitation. "I didn't know we needed a reservation. When did that change?"

Lorraine slapped her knee and laughed. "I'm just joshin' with ya," she said. "We ain't that fancy around here. Follow me and I'll get ya'll seated."

Turner breathed out a sigh of relief and laughed. "You had me worried there for a minute. Thought I might have to go home and put on a suit and tie."

"Good one, Lorraine," Joyce giggled. "I did not want to have to cook tonight."

They followed her over to a booth over in the corner. After they sat down and got situated, Lorraine handed them a menu, then looked at Turner and said, "Word around town is you're working as a gumshoe nowadays."

He nodded. "The small town rumor mill strikes again," he said, grinning.

"So, it's not true?" Lorraine asked. "It's just a rumor?"

"No, it's true," he said. "I'm just still amazed at how quickly word gets around this town, that's all. What else have you heard?"

Lorraine lowered her head a bit and leaned forward. "I heard you're helping that poor young man, Ronnie Spatch, find the person responsible for killin' his daddy," she said low enough so people eating at the other tables wouldn't hear what she was saying.

Joyce spoke up. "Yes, he is. As a matter of fact, we just came from seeing Ronnie Junior. He's in the hospital. Someone tried to kill him, too."

Lorraine leaned back up and straightened herself. She placed her hand on her chest. "My word," she said. "I wasn't aware of that. Is he going to be okay?"

Joyce nodded. "Yes," she said. "Thankfully, he is being discharged this week and expected to make a full recovery."

"That's good news. With his mama dying at such a young age, and now his daddy's gone…" She paused and gathered herself before continuing. "That boy's been through a lot of traumas in his life, and at such an early age." She looked over at Turner. "I'm glad to hear you're helping him. He's lucky to have a man like you in his corner. Heck, this whole town is lucky that you're in our corner. I, for one, am glad to see you hang your PI shingle out. God knows, the people and the police in this town could sure use your help."

"Thank you," replied Turner. "If only all of Magnolia Bluff's finest felt that way."

"Don't tell me that damn Tommy Jager is givin' you a hard time?" Lorraine said. "He should be grateful. You've helped that man and his officers out of quite a few jams in the last few years. Helped keep the people of this town safer." She grinned. "You want me to straighten him out for ya?"

Turner laughed. "That won't be necessary," he said. "And it's not the chief. It's that new captain he hired. Briggs is not fond of civilians sticking their nose in what he considers police business. And besides, I'm convinced the man outright hates me."

"Never mind him. Davis Briggs is nothing but a big blowhard," replied Lorraine. "If you're working as a private investigator, you're not really considered a civilian anyway, are you?"

Turner nodded. "That's right," he said. "Doesn't seem to matter to Briggs. I could solve the case for my paying client and hand him the guilty party on a silver platter, and he'd try to have me arrested on the spot for interfering in a police investigation."

Lorraine smiled at Joyce. "I heard you put him in his place over at the Really Good awhile back."

"I sure did. He came out of nowhere screaming at that nice new investigator, Palmer Kraus. And just for having coffee with us."

Turner laughed. "You should've seen him. He didn't know what hit him."

Lorraine laughed and looked at Joyce. "Good for you," she said. "Bet he won't try that again."

"He'd better not," said Joyce. She grinned and waved a fist. "I'll have to punch him right in the nose if he ever comes at us in public like that again."

"Well, enough of this," said Lorraine. "I'm keeping you guys from gettin' dinner. I'll be right back with some iced tea and to take your orders."

"Sounds good," replied Turner. "Thanks."

After the cafe owner walked away, Joyce said, "She's right, you know. You are a blessing to the people of this town; they're lucky to have you here, helping to keep them safe." She gave him a warm smile. "I know I feel blessed you're in my life."

Turner reached across the booth and took her hand. "I'm the one who's blessed," he said.

Lorraine arrived with two tall glasses of iced tea. She set them on the table in front of each of them. She looked at the menus, still sitting in the same spot where she'd put them on the table. "You guys haven't even looked at the menus yet," she said. "I'll give y'all some more time."

Turner glanced over at Joyce, and she nodded. He looked up at Lorraine. "That won't be necessary," he said. "We're ready."

Lorraine smiled at Joyce. "Okay then. Shoot."

"I'll have the chicken-fried steak with all the fixin's."

"Make that two," said Turner. He gathered up the menus and handed them back to Lorraine.

"You got it," she replied, then hurried off to place their orders.

"This is nice," said Turner.

Joyce smiled. "It is," she said. "Spending time, just the two of us, having a nice dinner."

Turner nodded. "Yeah, but I can't help feeling it's kind of like the calm before the storm."

"I know what you mean," she said. She gave him a seductive grin and winked. "Let's not think of all that tonight. Let's enjoy this dinner and have this one night for us. No shop talk. I won't talk about any clients who are looking at houses. You say nothing about the investigation. Nothing about death or dying. Let's just talk about us. Deal?"

"Deal," he said, taking her hand again in his. He grinned. "Can I talk about how I'm looking forward to getting lucky later?"

"You are such a bad boy," she giggled.

Lorraine arrived with a serving platter filled with plates holding chicken-fried steak, mashed potatoes, all smothered in country gravy, and several smaller dishes filled with green beans, cornbread, honey and butter.

Turner and Joyce both sat back and watched as she spread the feast out in front of them. Once she had everything in place, along with an enormous pile of napkins, she said, "You guys need anything else?"

Turner and Joyce looked up at her wide-eyed and smiled. They shook their heads in unison and Joyce said, "No, Lorraine. I think you just about covered it. Although we might need a couple of doggie bags later."

"Speak for yourself," said Turner, as he dug into his mashed potatoes.

Lorraine laughed. "You two enjoy," she said, then wandered off to see how the folks at another table were doing.

They stayed quiet for a bit while they eat some of their meal. After a few minutes, Joyce laid down her fork, picked a napkin off the pile, and wiped the corners of her mouth. "Wow, that's good," she said. "I didn't realize how hungry I was until I smelled the wonderful aroma of all this food." She threw the napkin down on the table. "I'm stuffed."

Turner looked across the table and smiled. "You ate like… three bites."

"That's not true," she said. "I ate five bites. And I had some cornbread."

"You nibbled on the corner of a piece of cornbread. I don't think that counts."

She smiled. "Well, I don't want to be too full for our nocturnal activity time."

Turner was about to speak when his phone rang. He pulled it from his pants pocket and looked at the screen. "It's Tommy."

"You'd better answer it," replied Joyce.

"Okay," he said. He swiped the green bar across the screen and put the phone to his ear. "What's up, Tommy?"

"I'm at the hospital," replied the chief. "Someone got inside Ronnie's room and tried to finish the job."

"What? You mean someone tried to kill him?"

"That's exactly what I mean," said Tommy. "Luckily, a nurse walked in, and the person bolted from the room before he could succeed."

Joyce looked up and whispered, "What's going on? Who tried to kill who?"

Turner lifted his finger up to hold her off. He spoke into the phone. "I'm with Joyce at the Silver Spoon. We're leaving now. You can give me the details when we get there.

"I called Sergeant Kraus before calling you," said Tommy. "He should be here any moment. Apparently, he was still up in Lampasas County. I'll have him meet you at the Emergency entrance."

"Okay, we're on our way," said Turner. He clicked the END button and looked over at Joyce. "Someone broke into Ronnie's room and tried to kill him."

Joyce slid across the booth and stood up. "What're we waiting for? Let's go."

CHAPTER THIRTY-THREE

Turner and Joyce arrived at the Burnet Medical Center in record time. They parked and went in through the Emergency entrance where a disheveled Sergeant Kraus was waiting to meet them.

"What the hell happened?" asked Turner as they marched through the hospital corridors on their way to the elevators.

"The evening nurse was making her patient rounds. When she walked into Ronnie's room, there was a man standing over him. Ronnie was asleep. The man must have panicked. He dropped a syringe on the floor and fled the room. He knocked the nurse to the ground as he pushed past her on his way out the door. By the time she stood up and left the room, the man was nowhere to be found."

One of the elevator doors opened. They got on and Joyce pushed number three.

"Where was Officer Winkler during all this?" said Turner, after the doors closed. "How did this guy get past him and into the room in the first place. And why didn't he stop him when he came running from the room?" He shook his head. "Total incompetence. I expected more from Hans."

"It wasn't Office Winkler," replied Kraus. "There was a shift change before the man entered the room."

"Who was it?" asked Joyce.

"Officer Ytzen," replied Kraus.

"I know Logan," she said. "It doesn't sound like him.

Something must've happened that allowed him to let the man pass."

Turner huffed. "Probably fell asleep on the job."

The doors opened on the third floor. They got out and walked toward Ronnie's room.

"That's not fair, Brandon," said Joyce. "We don't know what happened yet."

"Yeah," added Kraus. "Let's wait until we get the full story."

"Whatever," said Turner. "I can't wait to hear his story."

They walked into the room. Ronnie was still lying in bed, but he was awake. There was a nurse attending to him. Tommy was over in the corner speaking to an officer who Turner was not familiar with.

Tommy walked over to where they were standing. Turner nodded toward the officer. "That Officer Ytzen?"

Joyce excused herself and went over to talk to Ronnie.

The chief nodded. "Yes. How about we all go outside the room so we can speak?"

Turner followed Tommy and Kraus out into the hallway. He held the door for Ytzen, who was still over in the corner. "Are you coming?"

"I'll be out when Chief Jager calls me."

Turner started to go back inside. He wanted to speak with Ytzen right then. Kraus grabbed him by the arm. "Come on, Brandon," he said, coaxing him back into the hallway. "Let's hear what the chief has to say. He'll bring Officer Ytzen out in a minute."

Turner nodded and reluctantly let Kraus lead him outside the room. He looked Tommy dead in the eyes and said, "How did this guy get past your officer? If it wasn't for the nurse, Ronnie could be laying on a slab in the hospital morgue right now."

"I understand you're upset," began Tommy. "According to Officer Ytzen, the man was dressed in hospital scrubs. He told him he was the nurse on duty. This was Logan's first shift watching the door. He had no reason to disbelieve the man was who he said he was. He had a Burnet Medical Center name tag on his shirt, and he was carrying a chart."

Turner shook his head. "So, didn't seem odd to him when the second nurse wanted to go in, claiming she was the nurse on duty?"

"Of course it did," replied Tommy. "He questioned the second nurse being there since there was already a nurse in the room. That's when the actual nurse went through the door to see who was in the room. And that's when the man realized he was caught and fled the scene."

"Okay, then explain why Officer Ytzen didn't apprehend the man as he ran from the room."

"He tried," said Tommy. "He was walking in behind the nurse since she marched past him into the room. The man knocked the nurse to the ground and pushed officer Ytzen into the hallway, catching him off guard and knocking him down. By the time he was able to get up and give chase, the man was gone."

Turner was furious. "Gone? What do you mean, gone? How far could he have gone before Ytzen was back on his feet?"

"Normally you'd be correct," said Tommy. "But when the man fled and pushed him, his ankle twisted and gave out on him. It's the reason he fell to the floor. When he tried to stand, he said it was hard because of the pain. He wasn't able to follow the man in pursuit."

Turner frowned. "Hmm... he looked like he was

standing just fine when I saw him in the room."

"How about if we give Officer Ytzen a break?" said Kraus. "In all fairness, you only saw him for a minute before we all came out here in the hallway."

"You're right," Turner replied. "How about we get him out here? I'd like to hear what he has to say."

Tommy nodded. He opened the door to Ronnie's room and waved. "Officer Ytzen please come out here."

As soon as Ytzen came through the doorway, Turner noticed he was walking with a limp. He nodded at the officer's leg. "How's your ankle?"

"Hurts," replied Ytzen. "Look, I'm sorry, but everything happened so fast. The guy appeared to be legit. I had no reason to doubt him until the actual nurse showed up. When he ran toward the door, the nurse was between him and me. He knocked her into me, and she fell to the ground. Then he barreled into me before I had the chance to recover. I fell back, felt my ankle go sideways, and I was on the floor. He continued down the hallway and into the stairwell." He paused. "Not my finest moment. My watch, my responsibility for the outcome."

Turner didn't say it out loud, but he admired Ytzen's straightforward account of what happened. No excuses. No timid attitude. And he held himself accountable for letting the man into the room. "Did you get a look at his face? Maybe his height, weight? Anything that could describe him?"

"He wore green scrubs and was of average height and weight. Clean shaven. Dark hair. Didn't see his face long enough to tell you his eye color, but I would put him a little older than me. Maybe in his mid-thirties. Didn't notice a tattoo or anything, but like I said, it all happened pretty fast."

Turner nodded. "Thanks," he said. "Not sure if it'll help. It's kind of a generic description of half the men in Magnolia Bluff."

"You're right," said Ytzen. "And even so, I'm confident I would recognize him if I saw him again."

Turner looked at the chief, then back at Ytzen. "Confident enough to pick him out of a lineup?"

Officer Ytzen nodded. "Yes, sir."

"Okay," said Turner. "I hope we can take you up on that."

"Officer Ytzen is there anything else you want to share?" asked Tommy.

Ytzen shook his head. "Nothing, chief. But I would like to get back to my post. I will make sure no one other than the *real* nurse on duty or the doctor gets into this room for the rest of the night."

"Not necessary, Logan," said Tommy. "Officer Schreiber is on his way. I want you to go home and rest that ankle. I'll see you tomorrow at the station."

"Yes, sir," replied Ytzen. "I'll stay until Schreiber gets here."

"I've got it," said Tommy. "Now get outta here. Put some ice on your ankle before it swells up like a balloon."

"I agree with the chief," said Kraus. "We'll catch up later if we need anything else."

Ytzen nodded, gave the chief a sharp nod, and hobbled down the hallway toward the elevator.

Tommy used his hand to brush off the folding chair outside the door and sat down. He looked at Turner. "There's nothing more you can do here tonight," he said. "You and Joyce might as well go home."

Turner nodded. "Okay," he said. He glanced over at Kraus. "Did you get the flash drive from Detective Clark?"

"I'll have it first thing in the morning," said Kraus. "We can all still meet in the chief's office tomorrow at ten?" He looked at Tommy. "Is that good with you, Chief?"

"Let's do it," replied Tommy. "And Palmer, you can go too. I've got this until Officer Schreiber arrives."

Kraus nodded at the chief. "I'll walk you and Joyce out," he said to Turner.

"Okay. Give me a few minutes to check in on Ronnie and get Joyce," he said, then walked back into the room.

"Hey, Ronnie," said Turner. "You doing okay?"

"Yes, sir." Ronnie looked up at Joyce. "Me and Ms. Blackstone was just talkin' about how nice it's gonna be once I'm released on Thursday." A worried look appeared on his face. "Sounds like I had a pretty close call tonight. You think he might try again?"

"You have nothing to worry about," Turner assured him. "Chief Jager is standing guard right outside your door. Another officer will be here shortly, and he'll be here watching out all night long. All you need to do is concentrate on getting a good night's sleep."

Ronnie opened his mouth to say something and an enormous yawn came out instead. He shook his head. "Speakin' of sleep, I'm about ready to pass out from bein' so tired. I can't hardly keep my eyes open."

Turner looked over at Joyce. "I think that's our cue to leave."

Joyce nodded and stood up from the chair she'd been sitting in near the bed. She took Ronnie by the hand and smiled. "I'll come by tomorrow and spend some time with you."

"That would be nice," said Ronnie. "I would like that, Ms. Blackstone."

She squeezed his hand, then let go. "You get some

sleep. I'll see you tomorrow." She walked over to where Turner was standing.

"Goodnight," Turner said with a wave. "Don't you worry about anything. We're gonna get this guy. You have my word."

Ronnie nodded. "I know ya will," he said, then closed his eyes and began softly snoring.

Turner pulled the door and held it open while Joyce walked past him. He followed her out and let it close behind him.

He and Joyce met up with Kraus by the elevator. They rode down to the main level and walked back through the Emergency room waiting area, and out the door to Turner's pickup.

Before getting in his truck, Turner asked, "So, is Detective Clark going to email the video link since you don't have the flash drive?"

Kraus smiled. "Actually, I'm headed back up to Lampasas County tonight. Donna texted me earlier and invited me back to her place... that is, if I want to go. Of course, I said yes. She'll have the video copied onto the flash drive by the time I get there."

"Oh, Palmer," said Joyce. "I am so happy for you."

"Thank you, Joyce. I can only hope that Donna and I can find even half the happiness you and Brandon have found in your lives."

"Brandon's a good man," she said. "And so are you. Donna would be crazy to let you get away. You'll find your happiness. I'm sure of it. I can't wait to meet her."

"I appreciate that," he replied. "You'll get the chance to meet her soon. Not sure if Brandon told you, but the four of us are going to do a double date once we've got this investigation wrapped up."

She gave Turner the side-eye. "No, I don't seem to remember him mentioning that."

Turner shrugged. "I've been a little busy," he said, then added, "All right already... enough of this mushy stuff. Palmer, I'll see you in the chief's office tomorrow morning. You enjoy your evening."

Kraus shook Turner's hand. "Thanks, I will. You guys enjoy yours too."

Turner glanced over at Joyce and grinned. "Oh, you can count on it."

Joyce gave him a playful slap on the arm then turned toward the sergeant. "Bye, Palmer."

Kraus grinned, nodded at them both, and walked off to find his vehicle.

After Turner and Joyce got in the truck, she looked at him and said, "Why would you say that the way you did?"

Turner grinned at her. "What?"

"Now he probably thinks we're going home to fool around."

"And he'd be correct," he said, wiggling his eyebrows at her.

Joyce slowly shook her head and gave him a seductive look. "You really are a bad boy."

CHAPTER THIRTY-FOUR

Turner walked into the Magnolia Bluff police department a few minutes before ten AM.

He was still wearing his smile from the night before. All he could think about was what a great time he and Joyce had after getting home from the hospital yesterday.

He reluctantly shook the happy memory from his head. It was time to get back to business.

He walked over to the reception desk to say hello to Gloria just as Captain Briggs came around the corner.

They stood there face-to-face for a second or two before a scowl formed on Briggs' face. "What the hell are you doing here, Turner?"

"Not that it's any of your business, Briggs, but I'm here to see Chief Jager."

"What do you need to see the chief about?"

"Did you not hear me the first time? It's none of your business. Want me to write it on your forehead so you can remember what I said?"

"Are you calling me dumb?"

Turner shrugged. "Well, if the shoe fits…"

Briggs grabbed Turner's arm, pushed him against the wall, and twisted both his arms behind his back. "I've had enough of you," he said, while snapping cuffs on Turner's wrists.

"Have you lost your mind, Briggs?" screamed Turner. "What the hell are you doing?"

"You're under arrest for insulting a police officer."

"You can't be serious," said Turner. "You can't do this."

"Who says, tough guy?"

"The first amendment of the U.S. Constitution, that's who," said Turner. "Take these cuffs off of me."

Gloria slid out from behind her desk and ran down the hallway toward the chief's office. A minute later, Tommy came marching around the corner. "Stand down, Captain," he said. "Now."

Briggs let go of Turner and put his hands on his hips. "But, Chief," he said. "I'm sick of this guy interfering in police business. He doesn't need to be here, and he sure doesn't need to be throwing insults at me."

"For your information, Captain," Tommy said in a stern voice, "I asked Brandon to be here this morning. Not to mention, you can't arrest someone because you don't like them."

"He insulted me."

"And I'm sure you insulted him. If not this time, I am certain you've had choice words for him before. Seems to me you're both guilty of throwing around the insults. Take the cuffs off him."

Briggs reluctantly removed the handcuffs and slipped them into his back pocket.

Turner rubbed his hands around his wrists and glared at the captain. "You're lucky I don't sue you for false arrest."

Briggs' jaw dropped, and he looked over at Tommy. "See what I mean? He has no respect for me or my position."

"I don't have to respect you or your position," said Turner. "I don't work for you."

Tommy stepped between Briggs and Turner, his steely gaze focused on the captain. "You're dismissed. Walk away, Davis," he said. "We'll talk later."

"But Chief…"

"I said, you're dismissed Captain."

Briggs kicked his heels together and gave Tommy a salute. "Yes, sir," he said. He stared down Turner as he stormed off.

"Thanks, Tommy. You need to keep that maniac away from me."

The chief lowered his brows and said, "Davis Briggs is a good cop. A dedicated cop. But he's old school. Maybe you should try to see where he's coming from instead of antagonizing him as your first line of defense."

"Yeah, well, he started it," mumbled Turner.

"Very mature," said Kraus, a smile draped across his face.

Turner's head spun around. "When did you get here?"

Kraus rubbed his chin and looked up at the ceiling. "Oh, somewhere between 'he insulted me,' and 'you're lucky I don't sue you,'" he said.

Turner shook his head. "The man's an ass. What can I tell you?"

"Never said he wasn't," replied Kraus, still smiling.

"All right," said Tommy, "that's enough." He looked at his sergeant. "Do you have the flash drive?"

Kraus reached into his pocket. "Right here," he said, tossing it up and down in his hand.

"Good," he replied. "Let's go see what's on it." He marched off down the hallway to his office. Kraus and Turner followed behind.

Once they were settled, the chief gestured to Kraus with his hand. "Okay, let's have it."

Kraus slid the small metal device across the desktop. Tommy picked it up and inserted it into the slot on the side of his laptop. After a few keystrokes, he turned the computer around and angled it so they could all watch the video of the feed store robbery.

Static filled the screen, causing the picture to jump and distort. The video showed a man wearing a full face mask, and a woman cautiously enter the store, their eyes scanning the surroundings. The woman, with her movements and mannerisms, seemed to be in charge, while the man appeared nervous. She was not wearing any kind of mask.

Turner sat forward, his eyes focused on the screen. "Can you rewind and run this again? It's impossible to get a look at the guy in the mask. And it's hard to make out her face with the picture jumping."

Tommy clicked a couple of keys, and the video started again.

"Stop right there," said Turner. He looked in closer. "Damn, I missed it." He glanced up at Tommy. "Rewind it again and try playing it in slow motion. But be ready to hit pause when I say."

Kraus looked over at Turner. "What are you seeing?"

Turner slowly shook his head. "I'm not quite sure yet. I need to see it again."

The chief ran the video again in slow motion.

"It doesn't jump as much in slow motion," said Turner. "Okay... pause it right there." He leaned in close to the screen and scanned it up and down. "Can you clean it up a little?"

"Maybe," said Tommy. "Give me a second." He turned the laptop around and tapped some keys. "I downloaded one of those video editing apps not too long ago just for things like this. Not sure how good it'll work, since it's not exactly official law enforcement approved or anything, but here goes..."

He moved the mouse around on the desk, tapped a few more keys, and then swung the laptop around so Turner and Kraus could also see the screen. Then he hit play again. "Is this any better?"

Turner leaned in again and stared at the video. "Pause it here," he said after a few seconds. "Play it back one more time."

Tommy obliged.

"Pause here," said Turner. he studied the picture of the two people on the screen for a full sixty-seconds. He shook his head and then sat back in his chair. He smiled, then looked over at Kraus and then at the chief. "Gentlemen, I know who did it."

"Did what?" said Kraus. "You know who killed the Price's son?"

Turner nodded. "I do," he said. "Not only do I know who killed Jason Price during the feed store robbery, I know without a doubt who killed Ronnie's father." He looked across the desk at the chief and gave a chin nod toward the screen. "Take a closer look, Tommy. You know who did it, too."

Tommy spun the laptop around and stared at the video. He hit the rewind button, then play, then pause. His brows scrunched as he moved closer to the screen. He sat back, exhaled, and looked at Turner. "Son-of-a-bitch."

"Yeah," said Turner. "Son-of-a-bitch."

Kraus darted his eyes back and forth between Tommy and Turner. "Is someone gonna let me in on this or what?"

Turner gave Kraus a toothy grin. "Absolutely," he said. "We need to go for a ride."

CHAPTER THIRTY-FIVE

Kraus got into the passenger side of Turner's pickup as he slid into the driver's seat and fired up the truck. They followed Tommy, who was in his police SUV, the half mile or so to the courthouse.

They pulled into the parking lot in front of the building. Turner and Kraus got out of the truck and hopped into the chief's vehicle.

Kraus leaned over the front seat. His head swiveled between the chief in the front and Turner, who was sitting beside him in the back. "Are you trying to tell me that the person who murdered the young man up in Lampasas and Ronnie Senior works inside the courthouse? Who is it? One of the lawyers? A judge?"

"Not even close," said Turner. "It's the clerk working in the County Register of Deeds office."

Kraus sat back and looked at Turner. "That woman who you complained about? The one who you said was not very helpful?"

"Yes. Her name's Celia," he said with a fair amount of disdain.

Tommy had turned himself around so he could see Turner and Kraus in the backseat. He shook his head. "I still can't believe it. Celia Roberts," he said. "I never would've guessed. She's only been working for the county for around six months or so. Seemed like a nice woman."

Turner huffed. "Nice woman, my ass," he said. "More like a knife wielding, cold hearted killer. I'll bet Celia Roberts isn't even her real name."

"Damn," said Kraus.

"Well, let's go get her," said the chief as he opened the door of his SUV.

Turner reached over and put his hand on Tommy's shoulder. "Hold on," he said. "That's her right there. She just walked out of the building."

"Everybody duck down," said Tommy.

"Why?" asked Turner. "We're sitting in a big police vehicle. Might not matter if we duck down at this point."

"Duck," he said. "It does matter. A police vehicle parked at the courthouse is commonplace. She won't think anything about it if she doesn't see all of us inside."

They all ducked as she walked across the lot to where her car was parked. They watched her get into a light blue Honda Civic and drive out onto Main Street.

"Hurry," said Turner. "Everyone in my truck. We'll follow her and see where she's going. She's more likely to spot us if we're in your SUV than my truck."

The three of them all piled into the pickup and fell in behind her, staying far enough back so as not to cause any suspicion.

They followed her up State Highway 28 north. After a few minutes, Kraus said, "Where the hell is she going?"

Turner lowered his head. "I think I know," he said, his voice resigned to a truth he didn't see coming.

They continued tailing the Honda until it turned on to Sunrise Chapel Road. Turner remained on 28, pulling into a gas station a little past the turn.

"Why didn't you follow her onto Sunrise?" asked Tommy. "We're gonna lose her."

"We're not gonna lose her," he said. "I know where she's going."

"Care to share?" said Kraus.

"Pyramid Land Surveying is on Sunrise Chapel Road," he said.

"Well, that can't be a coincidence," said Kraus.

Turner nodded. "Exactly. The masked guy in the video must be Jake Seeley."

"Let's not jump to any conclusions," said Tommy. "She works for the register of deeds office. It could be a coincidence. She might be there on some kind of business for the county."

"You're right," said Turner. "She could be, but I'll bet you a dollar she's not. Think about it. The deeds office has no record of the Spatch farm survey. When I visited Pyramid the other day, Jake Seeley stonewalled me on seeing a copy of the survey his company did for the farm. As a matter of fact, he wouldn't even confirm they did one. Now, Celia Roberts just happens to show up at his place of business in the middle of a workday? I don't believe in that much of a coincidence."

"I have an idea," offered Kraus. "How about we go ask them?"

"Yes, let's," said Turner.

Tommy nodded in agreement. "Brandon," he said. "Have you got a gun in your truck?"

"Yes, I do. My Glock 9 is in the glove box."

"Good," replied Tommy. "Bring it in with you for backup... just in case things go bad. Otherwise, I want you to fall back and let me and Sergeant Kraus handle the questions once we're inside. If they're guilty, this needs to be a clean bust. Understood?"

Turner pushed out a frustrated breath and nodded. "Understood." He put the truck in gear, made a U-turn out of the gas station, and turned down Sunset Chapel Road.

A couple of minutes later, he pulled in and parked in

front of the Pyramid Land Surveying building.

"Okay," said Tommy. "We still don't know for sure that Jake Seeley is the man in the video. We do, however, have Brandon's ID of Celia Roberts inside the feed store stabbing Jason Price. Regardless of whatever happens with Mr. Seeley, we need to walk out with Ms. Roberts in handcuffs." He looked them both in the eye. "I will take the lead with Palmer. Brandon, stay behind us, but be ready."

Turner and Kraus nodded. Then Turner leaned over, opened the glove box, and retrieved his gun. He slid it under his shirt, securing it in his pants at the small of his back.

"Okay, let's go," said Tommy.

They got out of the truck and walked up to the entrance. Turner opened the door. He let Tommy and Kraus walk past and then followed them inside.

They marched over to where the receptionist was sitting. It was the same woman behind the desk who'd helped Turner before. He noticed she was nose deep in the same book she was reading the last time he was there.

She looked up when the chief cleared his voice. "May I help you?" she said, putting a bookmark between the pages of her book. She laid it down on the desk next to a box of tissues near the phone.

"There was a woman who came in here a while ago. Is she in with Mr. Seeley?"

"Yes, sir," she replied. "They're in his office."

"Where is his office?"

She pointed at the hallway around the corner from her desk. "Down there. First door on the right." She let her eyes bounce over to Kraus, then Turner, then back to the chief. "Is there a problem?"

"Not necessarily," said Tommy. "But I do need you to exit the building."

She gave him a strange look. "What? Why?"

"Just do it, ma'am," said Tommy. "Mr. Turner will escort you to the door. Get in your car and drive away. Maybe take an early lunch." He nodded over at Turner. "Make sure she leaves the property. We'll wait for you to return."

Turner led the receptionist outside. Before she got into her vehicle, she looked at him and said, "What is going on?"

Turner smiled. "Nothing for you to worry about, Mia," he said, trying to reassure her.

She nodded, got into her car, and drove off. Once Turner saw her make the left turn onto 28, he went back inside.

He walked over to where Tommy and Kraus were standing. Kraus was speaking on his two-way radio. "That's right, Officer Ytzen, Sunrise Chapel Road. Get here asap," he said. He clicked off the radio and looked at Turner. "I called for backup."

"Is Ytzen the right person to call? Considering how things went at the hospital…"

"That's why he's exactly the right person. He's eager to make up for what happened. He deserves the opportunity to do that, don't you think?"

Turner nodded. "I guess you're right. And I did like the way he presented himself when he told me how the guy got away. He stepped up and owned it." A grin formed on his lips. "Besides, it would be hard for him to screw this up. All he has to do is show up with a patrol car and stuff an already handcuffed Celia Roberts in the back."

Kraus laughed. "And we certainly don't want to arrest

her and stuff her into the back of your pickup truck. That would be unprofessional."

Turner nodded again. "Not to mention if we take down Jake Seeley. I don't have that kind of room in my truck," he said, the grin still plastered on his face.

Tommy shook his head. "Glad you two can find the humor in the situation," he said, obviously displeased.

"Sorry, Chief," said Kraus.

Tommy shook his head and walked down the hallway the receptionist had pointed them to. Kraus followed, with Turner bringing up the rear. When he reached the office door, he pulled his gun and stepped off to the right side of the door. He motioned for Kraus to move to the other side, then he pointed at Turner to fall in behind Kraus.

The chief looked at Kraus, silently counting to three with his fingers before using his gun's barrel to knock on the door. "Celia Roberts, Jake Seeley," he shouted. "This is Chief Tommy Jager. I'm with the Magnolia Bluff police. I need you to open the door and come out slowly with your hands in the air."

Silence swallowed the air in the room.

Tommy took in a deep breath, and shouted again, "I'm only going to ask you one more time, then we're coming in."

The door stayed shut.

Turner's head swung around as he heard the front door to the building open. He watched as Officer Ytzen walked through the entrance. The red and blue lights from his police cruiser danced off his uniform as they shined through the windows and bounced off the interior walls.

Ytzen nodded at Turner and positioned himself

behind the chief.

Tommy glanced over at Kraus and said, "On my count, one, two—"

Gunfire erupted from behind the office door as a barrage of bullets blew through the frame, tearing the door off its hinges.

"TAKE COVER!" yelled Tommy.

They retreated up the hallway as another round of bullets pinged off the surrounding walls. The chief returned fire, unloading his gun across the threshold of the swinging door.

Turner, Kraus, and Ytzen moved around the corner and out of the line of fire.

Kraus reached around the corner and blasted four shots from his Walther P99 semi-automatic. "Chief, move now," he called out. "I've got you covered."

Turner peered around the corner and waved. "Over here," he said as Tommy came running up the hall.

The air was eerily quiet as the echo from the gunfire died.

"There's nowhere to run and nowhere to hide," Tommy shouted at the damaged office door. "Drop your weapons and come out with your hands in the air."

Turner pointed. "Look, someone's coming out."

They watched as Celia Roberts stepped through the broken door frame, her hands high above her head.

The chief nodded at Ytzen. "Search her then cuff her."

Officer Ytzen quickly moved to where she was standing. "Keep your hands above your head." He patted her down for weapons. "Got a knife," he said as he pulled a four-inch dagger from a leather sheath strapped beneath the cuff of her pants.

He handed the knife over to Tommy then pulled her

hands down and around her back. He fastened the carbon steel handcuffs on her wrists and read her Miranda rights to her. Then he pushed her forward to where Tommy, Kraus, and Turner were waiting.

Turner scowled at her. "Where's Jake Seeley?" he said. "Why didn't he come out of the office with you?"

She stood there in silence. Her eyes were unfocused yet seemed to stare right through him. The look on her face was that of someone who didn't care anymore.

Turner grabbed her arms and shook her. "Are you and Jake Seeley working together? Why did you put a knife in Ronnie Spatch and leave him to die in the grass outside his home? What about his son? Why did you try to kill him?"

Kraus stepped over to where Turner was and put a hand on his shoulder. "Brandon, enough. There will be time for questions once we get her back to the station."

Turner stopped shaking Celia Roberts. He took a step back and shook his head. "A senseless murder," he said, almost in a whisper. He looked up at Kraus, his jawline rigid. "Ronnie Senior was an old man. He shouldn't have had to die like that."

"I know," said Kraus. "And she'll pay."

Kraus nodded at Officer Ytzen and instructed him to secure her in the car. "Don't leave yet," he said.

Ytzen gave him a curt nod and walked Celia Roberts out of the building.

Chief Jager had been watching the office door for any signs of movement. "Sergeant Kraus, see if you can entice Mr. Seeley into joining us," he said, then added, "and be careful. He might still be armed."

Kraus drew his weapon back out from his shoulder harness and cautiously walked toward the office. He stepped through the doorway and disappeared inside.

Turner and Chief Jager anxiously waited for Kraus to reappear.

"Cuff that son-of-a-bitch and bring him out here," yelled Turner.

Another few seconds went by before Kraus popped his head outside of the office and said, "Not necessary. He's lying on the floor in a pool of blood. Dead."

CHAPTER THIRTY-SIX

Tommy rode back to the station with Ytzen to process Celia Roberts while Kraus and Turner waited at Pyramid for Wylie Garrison to arrive and pronounce Jake Seeley dead.

The Justice of the Peace and part time coroner showed up about five minutes after Ytzen and Chief Jager rolled out of the parking lot.

Wylie looked around at the bullet hole damaged walls as he made his way to the crime scene area. He examined the busted-up office door swinging on one hinge while stepping across the threshold.

He looked up at Turner and Kraus and shook his head. "Looks like you boys reenacted the shootout at the O.K. Corral."

"Felt that way too," said Kraus. He finished bagging two Ruger 9mm Luger pistols and put them on the desk.

Turner was busy gathering four spent clips off the floor. He stuffed them into a plastic bag and sealed it. He looked over at Wylie, who was kneeling over the body, checking it for any signs of life. "So, what's the verdict? Still as dead as he was when you walked in here?"

"And then some," said Wylie. "You need me for anything else?

Kraus shook his head. "No. I've already called for a forensics team. They're on their way from Austin."

"Thanks, Wylie," said Turner.

The older man nodded, packed up his stuff, and walked out.

Kraus glanced over at Turner. "Well, partner," he said. "We solved two murders today. We've got Celia Roberts behind bars where she will most likely spend the rest of her life. And Jake Seeley here," he said, nudging the body with his foot, "is taking a dirt nap. All in all, a good day."

Turner had a sour look on his face. "Yeah, but we still don't know the 'why' behind the crime. And Celia Roberts doesn't appear to have any interest in telling us what that is."

"Take the win, Brandon," Kraus said, leveling his eyes at Turner.

"I guess you're right," he said. "Still... it bugs me not knowing. I feel like if I could've just got my hands on that damn survey, I would've had the answer."

Kraus smiled. "You know," he said, "we're literally standing inside the company that performed the survey. What's stopping us from digging out the Spatch file right now and taking a look?"

Turner's eyes lit up. "There's nothing stopping us," he said, then glanced down at a very dead Jake Seeley. "Certainly not him. Not anymore."

They stepped around the body and walked out of the office. There was a team of forensics people walking toward them as they made their way down the hallway.

Kraus waved at the men and women, then looked at Turner. "You go find the records room and look for the Spatch file. I'll handle the forensics team and meet you in a few minutes."

Turner nodded, then walked over to the receptionist desk to see if there was some sort of directory. He didn't want to waste time searching rooms unnecessarily.

He looked up when he heard the front entrance door open and saw Mia walking in. When she reached the desk, he said, "I told you to stay away from here."

"You told me to take an early lunch," she rebutted. "I did that." She glanced over at the group of people who were moving around up and down the adjacent hallway. "What is going on? I have a right to know."

Turner took a moment to think about what he should say to her. Finally, he said, "How long have you worked here?"

Mia gave him a strange look. "Why does that matter? I want to know what's happening. Where's Mr. Seeley?"

Turner took in a breath. "Mr. Seeley passed away earlier."

Mia gasped. "He *what?!*"

He knew he would have to explain. "Your boss and the woman that was in his office with him when we arrived earlier are responsible for the murders of at least two people. We were here to arrest them. Mr. Seeley and Ms. Roberts chose to resist. They shot at us, and we returned fire, killing him." He paused. "I'm sorry."

She stood there, speechless.

Turner stepped around the desk and helped walk her over to the waiting area where they both sat down. "Are you going to be okay?" he asked.

His words brought her out of her trance. "I... I'm not sure," she said. I had no idea they were murderers.

"Did Celia come by here often?"

Mia nodded. "Almost daily. They were together." She paused and rubbed her eyes. "Why did you ask me how long I'd been working here? I can assure you, I had nothing to do with... with whatever the reason was they murdered those people."

"I know that," said Turner. "I was hoping you could help me find a file."

She was quiet for a few seconds, then said, "Does the file have something to do with all this?"

"Yes, it does," nodded Turner.

Mia sighed and rubbed her eyes again.

Turner got up and went over to the desk and grabbed the box of tissues sitting next to the phone. "Here," he said, offering her the box.

She took the tissues and pulled one out. "Of course I'll help," she said. "What file are you looking for?"

"I would like to see the survey that was done on the property owned by Ronnie Spatch, Senior."

She gave him a slight nod and said, "Wait here."

Kraus walked up as Mia went to locate the file. "What's she doing back here?" he asked. He sat down in the same chair Mia was in earlier.

"She came in right as I was beginning to search her desk for some kind of directory. I ended up having to tell her what happened after we told her to leave."

"I guess there wasn't any way to hide it from her," said Kraus. "How did she take it?"

"Better than I thought she would. I asked her if she would find the Spatch survey. That's where she was going when you walked up."

"That works for me."

"Yes," said Turner. "Maybe now we can really put this investigation to bed."

"What are you going to do if there's nothing out of the ordinary on the survey?" asked Kraus. "Are you gonna let it go and just accept that we may never know the truth?"

"I don't know," he said. "But I can't shake the feeling that this whole thing has something to do with the land. And Ronnie deserves the truth."

Kraus nodded. "And so do we."

Mia appeared from around a corner and walked over to where Turner and Kraus were seated. She was empty-handed.

Turner jumped up from the chair. "Where's the file? Please don't tell me you couldn't find it." There was no hiding his disappointment.

Kraus glanced over at Turner and then looked up at the young lady and smiled. "It's okay if you weren't able to locate the survey."

"No," she said, her chin pointed upward. "I found it. It's in the file room. I rolled it out flat on the table. I figured that would be easier than you trying to hold it up and read it at the same time."

"That's a great idea," said Kraus. He glanced over at Turner, then back to Mia. "You did good. Thank you."

"Yes… thank you," said Turner. "That will definitely make it easier to read. I'm sorry I jumped at you."

Mia shrugged off his last comment. "You're welcome. Now, if you gentlemen will follow me." She turned around and walked off.

Turner and Kraus fell in line behind Mia and followed her through a doorway behind her desk. They walked about twenty feet down a corridor. She stopped in front of another door, took out a set of keys, and unlocked it. She pushed the door open, and they went inside.

Turner put his hands on the table and leaned over the document. It reminded him of a blueprint for a house. Only this was sectioned off by lot numbers, and a line drawing of the perimeter of the house, the barn, and the surrounding property lines. Ronnie Spatch's property was on *Lot 16*. Everything was labeled, which made it somewhat easy to follow.

Kraus was standing over the document from the

other side of the table. He was scanning it from one side to the other.

"You see anything strange?" asked Turner.

"No. You?"

"Not yet, but I don't know what we're looking for, either." He looked over to where Mia was standing. "How familiar are you with reading these land documents?"

She gave him a sour grin. "I'm familiar enough with this to know it's called a survey plat map, not a land document."

Turner and Kraus looked at each other and shrugged.

"Does that really matter?" asked Turner.

She rolled her eyes. "Probably not." She moved closer to the table. "What are you trying to find out?"

"If there's anything that looks out of the ordinary on this... survey plat map."

Mia leaned over the table and took a few minutes to scour the map. When she was through, she looked at Turner. "See this?" she said, pointing a finger at a circle that was drawn on the far end of the property, away from the house and barn.

"That's the well, isn't it?" he said. "At least that's what I assumed. It's hard to make out what's written beneath it."

"Look closer," said Mia. She picked up a magnifying glass from a counter across from where they were standing. "Here, use this."

Turner held the magnifying glass over the area of the map where the circle was and peered through it. After a solid minute of staring at the words, he stood up and said, "I'll be damned." A wide grin spread across his face. He handed the magnifying glass over to Kraus. "Take a look at this. You're not gonna believe it."

Kraus focused the lens over the same spot that Turner was looking at. He stood up and smiled at Turner. "Son of a bitch," he said. "We need to pay Ronnie Junior a visit."

Turner nodded. "You can say that again."

CHAPTER THIRTY-SEVEN

After thanking Mia for her help, and checking in with the forensics team, Turner and Kraus headed over to the Burnet Medical Center.

While Turner drove, Kraus called Tommy and filled him in on what they'd learned after the chief and Officer Ytzen left to take Celia Roberts in for processing.

After hanging up, he looked over at Turner and smiled. "Jager said that Ronnie may finally get the break he deserves."

"He's right. That boy's had a lifetime of bad luck. It's about time something went his way. I'm happy for him. But you know what I'm extremely happy about? That I was right. I knew there must've been a powerful reason for someone wanting that old man dead. Ronnie Senior was the nicest person you'd ever wanna meet. He wouldn't have hurt a fly."

Kraus nodded. "Jager also told me that Celia Roberts' prints popped in AFIS. She'd been arrested before for fraud but never murder. And you called it—that's not her real name. She's actually Margaret Ann Phillips, and she's wanted for murder and home title identity fraud in Cottonwood, Arizona for killing an elderly woman. She's also wanted in Dune Acres, Indiana, for title theft and murdering an older couple. A hunting knife was her weapon of choice both times, and she used a different alias in each place. And get this—in both Arizona and Indiana, she took a job as a county clerk in the register of deeds office, giving her direct access to home and property titles, deeds, and land surveys." Kraus paused and shook his head. "Talk about being the kid in a candy store."

"So, it seems our Ms. Roberts… or should I say, Ms. Phillips, has an established modus operandi."

"It would seem so," agreed Kraus. "And she's obviously upped her game by adding murder to her resume since those early fraud arrests."

"So, how does Jake Seeley fit in?"

"They hooked up in Arizona. Seeley was out there working for a land survey company and met her through dealings with the county deeds office. He followed her to Indiana. He's been on the FBI's radar for a while, but he's not wanted for anything. They could never put him at the scene of the crimes."

"That makes sense," said Turner. "Lily's known him for years. He grew up in Magnolia Bluff. She said he was in and out of trouble all the time, right up until he moved away. I guess he was a thief, just not a killer."

"He didn't have to be," said Kraus. "Not when he had a girlfriend who enjoyed playing with knives. By the way, Jager notified the FBI that we had her in custody. They're sending a couple of agents to Magnolia Bluff to pick her up."

"How's the chief feel about that? He has an airtight case right here."

"According to what he said, he's happy to wash his hands of her and let the feds handle it."

Turner shook his head. "Knowing the chief and his team's track record with less than competent police work, it's probably for the best." He glanced over at Kraus and grinned. "Present company excepted."

"Geez, thanks for the clarification," Kraus said with a

chuckle. "By the way, aren't you going to call Joyce and tell her we caught the bad guys? She might also be interested in what we found on the survey."

Turner shook his head. "She's at the hospital with Ronnie. I'll tell her when I see her there."

"Before we tell Ronnie, or at the same time we're telling Ronnie?" Kraus turned his head to look out his window. "Because I know what I would do if I were you."

Turner looked over at Kraus and could see the smile he wore through the passenger window's reflection. "Before," he said.

Kraus swiveled his head so he could see Turner. "Good man."

Turner pulled into the Burnet Medical Center's visitor's parking lot across from the main entrance. He and Kraus crossed the lot, went inside, and walked down to the elevators. They rode up to the third floor and walked down to Ronnie's room.

Dick Schreiber was guarding the door this time. He stood as they approached. "Sergeant Kraus, good to see you. You too, Brandon."

"Officer Schreiber," said Kraus with a quick tip of his head.

"Hey, Dick," said Turner. "How're things going here?"

"Quiet. No visitors except for the misses," he said, winking at Turner.

"You know we're not married, right?"

"I know," Dick said with a smile. "When you gonna fix that?"

"Officer Schreiber," said Kraus. "We're here on police business, so can we cut the chit-chat?"

"Yes, Sergeant." He waved at the door. "Go right in," he said, stepping aside.

When they were on the other side of the door, Turner glanced over at Kraus.

"I figured you could use the help," he said with a shrug, then he smiled. "Unless you wanted to answer his question?"

Turner smiled but kept quiet. He walked over to where Joyce and Ronnie were seated. He leaned over and gave Joyce a peck on the cheek and then shook Ronnie's hand. "What're you guys talking about?"

"Since Ronnie's leaving here in a couple of days," Joyce said, "we were working on a rehabilitation schedule that would be easy for him to follow."

"Ms. Blackstone's been a big hep to me," Ronnie said. "She also hep't me to remember what my daddy tole me. He took pictures with his camera of all the important papers in the safe, in case we was ever robbed and stashed 'em under the mattress in his room."

Joyce smiled at the boy. She reached over and gave his hand a squeeze. "Happy to help," she said.

Turner thought about the old Polaroid he'd found at Ronnie's house. "So those photos are still under the mattress? That's great news. When you're ready, I'll help you sort though them. Oh, and I've got some news to share with you. But first, would you mind if I stole Ms. Blackstone away for a few minutes?"

A grin washed across the young man's face. "I hope it's good news."

"It is. I think you'll be pleased to hear what I have to say." He glanced over at Joyce and grinned. Then he took her by the hand and gently pulled her to her feet. "Come with me, my dear."

Her eyes narrowed, as he led her out into the hallway. "What's this all about?"

He didn't answer until they were in the waiting area down the hallway. "We arrested the killer. It was the woman who works at the Register of Deeds office in the courthouse."

Her eyes grew as big as saucers. "Oh my God, I can't believe it. You mean a woman is responsible for murdering Ronnie Senior and leaving him lying in his own blood by his tractor?"

"Yes. And she's also the one who stabbed Junior and left him for dead. Turns out she's wanted in two other states for similar crimes."

Joyce shook her head. "But why? Why did she kill that sweet old man?"

"Property title theft. She's been killing the landowners and committing identity fraud."

She let out a sigh. "So, you were right all along."

Turner nodded. "I was right. But she didn't act alone. She had help."

He filled her in on what they'd learned about Celia Roberts and her relationship with Jake Seeley. He also told her about the gunfight at the survey company and how Jake Seeley didn't come out on the winning end of that battle.

"So what is it about Ronnie's farm that made them target him?"

"Blue topaz."

"You mean there's a possibility that Ronnie's property has blue topaz on it?"

"Not just blue topaz, imperial blue topaz worth up to a thousand dollars per caret," smiled Turner. "Ronnie's father never farmed all thirty acres. There's an area that looks like someone had mined it in the past. Maybe by one of their long-ago relatives. Who knows? But that area shows up clearly on the land survey. Jake Seeley likely discovered some of the topaz while on their property doing the survey. And where there's some, there could be more. Lots more."

"I'm confused," said Joyce. "Imperial blue topaz is only found in one place in the Texas Hill Country, and it's not Magnolia Bluff. Mason County lays claim to that find. They pride themselves on being the only town in the Hill Country where imperial blue topaz can be found.

"Just because no one's discovered it in Magnolia Bluff in the past doesn't mean it's impossible. Maybe Mason County should get used to sharing that claim."

Joyce smiled. "You know, if this is true, and there really is imperial blue topaz on the land, this could really change things for Ronnie."

Turner had a giddy look on his face. "I know. Let's go tell him."

CHAPTER THIRTY-EIGHT

One Month Later...

Turner stood on his back patio watching the steam rise from the sixteen-quart pot sitting on the side burner of his Blackstone griddle. It was an add-on he bought just for this occasion.

He leaned over and inhaled the aroma of freshly steamed shrimp, crab legs, sausage, corn, and potatoes. "This smells delicious," he said. "How have I been missing out on this my whole life?"

Tommy laughed. "That's what happens when you grow up in a big city up north. You miss out on the sweet smells of a low country boil... with a kiss of Texas love."

"Have you got that paper spread out on the table, Joyce? Cause this is ready to eat."

"Bring it over. We're ready to go."

Turner grabbed one handle on the pot, and Tommy took hold of the other handle. They poured everything into a large strainer to drain the water, then carefully made their way over to the table where Joyce and Lily were standing and dumped the contents of the strainer across the table.

"Come and get it everybody," yelled Lily.

Jason, Camila, and Max came running up the hill from the dock. He had asked Turner earlier if he could throw a ball out into the water so Max could retrieve it.

Turner saw his dog crest the top of the lawn first, with Jason and Camila running a close second and third behind him. "Did you guys have fun playing toss with

Max?" he asked when they reached the patio.

"Eh, not really. It's such a sunny day I thought Max would love chasing the ball out into the lake."

"That's too bad," said Turner. "He usually loves going in the water when it's hot."

"Oh, he did," said Jason as he grabbed a paper plate and piled on some food. "He jumped in and splashed around and had a good old time. He just wasn't interested in playing catch."

Turner laughed. "Sorry about that. Maybe next time."

"No issues," replied the boy. He grinned. "I should've known it was too hot to expect him to work for his swim time."

Camila smiled at Turner and said, "Thank you for inviting me. I love a low country boil, especially the little pieces of sausage and the potatoes."

"You're welcome," Turner said, returning her smile. "It's too bad Hank and Ann couldn't make it."

"I know," she said. "They would've enjoyed this." She grabbed a plate and made her way down the table behind Jason while she gathered shrimp, potatoes, some of the sausage, and an ear of corn.

Turner watched the kids take their plates over to the Adirondack chairs where they sat and began eating.

Joyce pulled a couple of soft drinks from the cooler and brought them to the kids. "You guys forgot to grab a soda," she said, handing them each one of the chilled cans.

"Thanks, mom," Jason called out as his mother walked off and made her way over to where Turner was standing.

She put her arm around the small of his back and moved it up and down, giving him a light massage.

"They're good kids," said Turner.

Joyce nodded. "And they really make a cute couple."

Turner's eyes darted around his yard. "Speaking of couples," he said. "Have you seen Palmer and Donna anywhere?"

"I think I saw them sneak around the side of the cabin a little while ago."

"I'm gonna go find them. They're missing all this great food."

"Oh, leave them alone, Brandon. I think they were looking for a little privacy."

"It's their loss if they don't get to eat," he said.

Joyce giggled. "It's a brand-new relationship," she said. "I doubt they're even thinking about food."

"Oh, well," he said with a shrug. "I'm gonna grab some of this grub before Tommy eats it all." He took a plate off the stack and piled a cluster of crab legs, sausage, and potatoes onto it, then went off to find an empty chair.

Lily waved him over to where she was sitting. "Park it over here, Brandon," she said. "Plenty of room with me and Tommy."

They were sitting on his outdoor sofa with their plates balancing on their laps. Lily scooched over to the middle so she would be sitting between Turner and Tommy.

He made a pitstop over at the cooler and pulled out three Lone Stars and then went to join them on the sofa. He passed each a beer and then sat down next to Lily.

"The chief was just tellin' me about Ronnie's good fortune," she said. "'Bout time that young man caught a break."

Turner's mouth was full of crab meat, so he nodded. Once he'd swallowed, he said, "I agree. That boy's been through it, that's for sure."

"How long did he stay at yer place?"

"Not a real long time. No need since we caught the people who killed his father. He rehabbed here for the first two weeks, then he went home. It's gonna take him a while to adjust to life without his father, but we're helping him build a strong team of people he can rely on."

Lily nodded. "Speakin' of that, I hear Stanton Lauderbach offered his lawyerin' services pro bono to help him get through some of the legal stuff on that nice blue topaz find of his. I know Stanton and he don't do nothin' for free. How'd you manage to get him to do *pro bono* work for Ronnie? I'm surprised he didn't want a little taste."

"Oh, that wasn't me," said Turner. He glanced over at the chief. "That was all Tommy. I had nothing to do with that."

Lily twisted herself around so she could face Tommy. "Well, Chief... how'd you get a highfalutin lawyer like Stanton Mirabeau Lauderbach to offer his help for free?"

"I explained what Ronnie'd been through recently and what a hard life he'd had ever since his mama died. And how we were all trying to help him now that his daddy's gone too. I told him it was the right thing to do and how good it would make him feel helpin' the poor boy out."

Lily gave him a skeptical look. "And when that didn't work?"

Tommy smiled. "I reminded him about a few secrets I'd had on him and how it would be terrible if those secrets got out somehow."

"So ya blackmailed him," Lily said with a snicker.

"We're not calling it that," said Tommy. "That would be against the law. Let's just say we have an understanding."

Turner grinned. "Well played, Chief."

Lily smiled at Tommy, then said to Turner, "So where *is* Ronnie? I thought he'd be here."

"We invited him," he said. "Told us no. he wanted to tackle the dirt and dust in his house. He admits he'd let things go pretty badly. Said his father wouldn't appreciate the mess."

Lily nodded. "I knew his daddy, and he's right about that."

"He said making things look the way they did before his father died was the only way he had left to make sure his father would've been proud of him."

The three sat silently for a minute, then Tommy nodded and stood up. "There's Palmer and Detective Clark," he said. "You know, I still can't believe those two got together." He paused. "But I'm happy for them. I gonna go over and chat."

Turner looked over at Kraus and Donna. They were making their way down the table, loading up plates with an assortment of what was left of the food.

Joyce walked over to the sofa. She glanced over her shoulder at Kraus and Donna. They were laughing and having fun feeding each other pieces of shrimp. "I told you they wouldn't care about eating. They don't seem to mind that the food got cold."

"You were right," conceded Turner. he smiled at her. "And that's why I love you."

"Geez," she said, smiling back at him. "I hope there are more reasons than that." She leaned over and gave him a kiss. "I'm going to go visit with Palmer and Donna."

As soon as Joyce walked away, he turned toward Lily. "There's something I want to show you," he said.

He glanced over at Joyce to make sure she wasn't paying attention to them, then reached into the front pocket of his shorts and pulled out a small box. It had a hinged top and was covered in gray velvet. The box was old and had seen better days. He handed it to Lily.

She lifted the top and quickly snapped it shut. She glanced around to make sure no one was looking their way. "Does this mean what I think it does?"

Turner nodded. "It was my mother's engagement ring."

"It's beautiful. When are you going to ask her?"

"I was thinking of doing it here, now. In front of all my friends."

Lily took in a deep breath. When she blew it out, she said, "This is a big decision. Are you sure?"

"I've never been more sure of anything in my entire life."

She reached over and cupped her hand over his and smiled. "Then what are you waiting for?"

He stood and walked over to where Joyce was talking to Kraus and Donna. "I need to borrow her for a minute," he said. He took her by the hand and led her over to the grass.

"That was kind of rude," she said.

"They'll understand in a minute." He raised his arms up and waved. "Can I get everyone to join us over here, please?"

Joyce gave him a puzzled look. "What are you doing?"

"You'll see."

He waited until everyone had circled around him and Joyce. "I wanted to thank you all for coming out to share in my first ever low country boil experience."

"Texas style," shouted Tommy.

Everyone laughed and cheered.

"That's right," grinned Turner. "Texas style."

He waited until everyone quieted down, then said, "There's something I need to say to Joyce, and I want you all to hear it."

"What're you up to?" she asked, giving him the side-eye.

He took the small velvet box from his pocket and got down on one knee. He lifted it up in his extended hands and cracked open the top, allowing for the sun to gleam off the sparkling diamond inside.

He watched the woman he loved begin to tremble. "Joyce Blackstone," he said. "Will you marry me?"

Joyce gasped as her hand flew to her chest, and her eyes widened.

Everyone was silent while they waited for her answer.

Turner stood, his eyes twinkling, and gently wiped away a tear that was rolling down her cheek. He smiled at her. "So, what do you say? Ya wanna get hitched?"

Jason yelled out, "She says yes!"

At the sound of his voice, Max began barking and doing zoomies in circles around everyone.

Joyce wrapped her arms around Turner and through cries of joy and laughter, said, "Yes! Yes! I say... yes, I will marry you!"

Turner lifted her off the lawn and spun her around in a circle before putting her back down on the grass.

There was laughter everywhere as Max yipped and sprinted around the happy couple, knocking them both to the ground. The big Labrador jumped on top of them and began kissing them all over.

Turner wiped the wet dog kisses from his face and looked at his fiancé. "Is this what it's gonna be like for the rest of our lives?"

Joyce gazed into his eyes. "I certainly hope so," she said, then pressed her lips against his.

WHAT'S UP NEXT IN THE WORLD OF MAGNOLIA BLUFF?

Enjoy this excerpt from

Flight Enigma

By Breakfield and Burkey

Available August 2025

CHAPTER 1 – THE AMBUSH – CURRENT DAY

Mike completed his pre-flight check and then topped off the Cessna's fuel tanks. It took extra time, but he had learned the criticality of safety and never scrimped when flying. He recalled Juan Senior's training: "If the plane breaks down in the air, you can't just get out and walk."

He climbed into the cockpit, took another hearty swig of his special coffee brew, and complained, "Rats, cold already. I'll nuke it at Burnet Muni. It's too good to waste."

Mike fitted the headset and fastened his seat belt. He pressed the brakes firmly and started the engine. He wanted it to warm up before taxiing to the runway's north end. He spoke about his takeoff intentions to the chief, who was monitoring the radio of the private airstrip, and received a thumbs-up. Scanning the field, he decided it was clear that no one was approaching. He pushed the throttle forward, positioning for takeoff. Seconds later, the plane roared down the runway and easily climbed to his desired altitude, heading on course to Magnolia Bluff, Texas.

Forty minutes into the short flight, Mike's eyes couldn't distinguish the blurred numbers on the instruments. He blinked, wiping his eyes with the handkerchief, yet still unable to focus. Sweat beaded up on his brow, rushing down his face to his chin, and then pooling in his lap. He took a calming breath and concentrated on staying on the correct heading. A few minutes later, he noticed the yoke not responding despite his physical efforts to steer.

Mike felt a wave of dizziness. His gut tightened as stomach contents rose in the back of his throat. He swallowed several times, then held his breath for a long minute while focusing on the horizon. Praying to get the lightheadedness under control, he muttered, "Ash, honey, I won't crash because I got sick. I'm ... what the hell?" He checked gauges, sensing the loss in altitude. "What the hell! The plane is set for landing. I've never seen this overgrown terrain on my approach to Burnet before." Panicking, he pulled back on the stick, but the aircraft continued its descent. "Why is nothing working?"

The plane barely cleared the tree line before it bounced hard on the field. The engine whine decreased to landing speed. Mike's right hand grabbed the handle of his briefcase. His body jerked behind the seatbelt the moment the front wheel fell into a deep depression. The Cessna dropped its nose into the soil, upending the plane. The abrupt stop caused Mike's head to hit the window, further dazing him. Stunned, he tried to comprehend the landing, but his throbbing head made him want to close his eyes and rest. Fighting to stay awake, he saw the ground from the front window and felt the straps of the restraints press painfully into his shoulders. He unexpectedly saw or imagined the passenger door open, followed by dark hands groping for something under the dashboard. The angles of everything looked wrong. Unable to move, he squinted, trying to identify the object the hands held before they disappeared. Noises of a struggle or fight outside flooded his brain, making his head ache further. Mike fought to release his door. It abruptly released, but sounded wrong. His brain screamed to rest.

Then he imagined a familiar voice shouting.

"Mike, Mike, are you alright? Can you talk? It's JJ."

"JJ, hide my briefcase," he insisted before darkness overcame his last thoughts.

CHAPTER 2 – A NEW ASSIGNMENT – THREE WEEKS EARLIER

JJ grinned, seeing the caller ID. He quickly answered, "Hey Mike, how's it going?"

"Work's crazy busy. I'm finalizing the specs for the radar sensing redirect we discussed for my F-35. I keep hitting a wall with the combined distance and direction variables needed to meet my safety specifications. I've added a new SOW for you to help verify the software and increase security on access to the program."

JJ enjoyed his work with Lockheed Martin, making this call a pleasant surprise. "Let me escalate this call to a meeting with video so you can show me." When the video engaged, he noticed deeper worry lines on his friend's face compared to the last time they had spoken. "There we are. You look a bit tired, buddy. Is this problem keeping you up at night?"

Pressing his fingers to his temple, Mike sighed. "Ashley's fed up with me and looking for a new place to live. She says I don't give her enough attention. She put her wedding ring on the counter in the kitchen with a terse note. Almost five years. I can't believe she's calling it quits. She's my one and only."

"Wow. I'm shocked. Jo and I both like her. Your home in the Pecan Plantation area reflects elements of you both." He arched an eyebrow and questioned, "Did you forget an important date like the anniversary of your meeting, your first kiss, or something like that? Women keep track of those types of details." JJ tapped his chin and looked Mike square in the eye. "You didn't stand her up at a restaurant again, did you?"

Mike laughed. "No. I've been working late nights to get this improvement ready for testing. She's angry at me for not being around." He took a sip from the disposable cup and sighed. "I recall we discussed all my faults before we agreed to build our home in Pecan. I'm fine with giving her the house, I don't want to live in it without her. She's made a lot of friends in the area. I'll find another place to hang my clothes. A simple apartment will suffice. I don't need much."

"You need a life, man." JJ's mind wandered back to their college days. He recalled the two of them, roughly the same age and height, when they exited the Fort Worth testing facility into the May afternoon sun. They sauntered to the parking lot, wiggling their fingers, then twisted their bodies to unkink after two-plus hours of sitting.

JJ sensed the relief coursing through his body fifteen years ago after finishing the exam with his best friend.

Then he said, "Whew! I'm glad the test is over. It was killer comprehensive. How do you think you did?"

He watched as Mike shoved his longish blonde hair behind his ear and rolled his eyes. "I'm not sure. Some of the questions seemed ambiguous. I thought your dad was reviewing the smallest details to annoy us, but now I'm so glad he did."

"Mike, what did you think about those extra credit questions? They were tough."

"JJ, I figured it was worth the effort. I chose the one with the red telephone on the desk. Make a call to start World War III and report the socio-political effects."

"Yeah, I saw that one. What was your answer?"

Mike kept a straight face as he deadpanned. "I stated I

would call my wife and tell her to go on a diet because her derriere was getting way too wide. I added, Honey, when I watched you walk away in your vacuum-packed workout pants, I thought your bottom looked like two Volkswagens trying to pass each other on a hill."

Laughing uproariously, JJ finally snorted a response. "I could see that observation starting a major war."

Mike punched his friend in the shoulder. "I added a few other gently finessed issues to round out the socio-political effects of relationships. Which one did you do?"

"I chose the one about the five hundred riot-crazed aborigines storming the room, whom I needed to calm down using any ancient language besides Latin or Greek. I created a meme library as a language tool mimicking Egyptian Hieroglyphics to help calm them down. The pictographs I built looked like they would do the trick." He pulled a piece of note paper used for scribbling during the test and showed it to Mike. "I made an extra copy with the proctor's permission. I can use them in my intern position with the computer sciences department at ETH Zürich."

"Good thinking, man. You're always repurposing stuff. I'm glad you got into their computer science program. It's supposed to be the best in the world."

"Mister socio-political details guy. Geez. Have you decided to accept your MIT or Georgia Tech scholarship yet?" he asked, finger-combing his untamed raven-black hair.

"I haven't. I prefer Georgia Tech because I'd also like to play ball. However, my dad wants me to focus on my studies, not sports. Massachusetts gets too much snow for this Texas boy. How about you? When do you return to Europe for your higher education?"

"Not for a couple of weeks. Dad wants to do some motorcycle riding and camping. Mom and my twin Gracie are doing a girls' shopping spree, so Dad voted for the male bonding thing."

Mike checked his watch. "We need to move it, buddy. Our check rides at the field are scheduled soon. We'll push it to make it on time, going the speed limit."

JJ jumped into the driver's side because the top was down on his gray Porsche 911. When he turned the key, the engine purred to life. Mike methodically opened the door and sat on the other side, tightening his seatbelt.

"Our dads said they'd meet us at the field to take us for a celebration dinner. What if we don't pass everything?"

JJ laughed as he shifted and spun out of the parking lot, leaving a bit of rubber on the way to the airfield. "Mr. Hayes, when have you ever failed a test? Two full-ride college offers, and you're worried?"

"Yep. That's my middle name to make me try harder."

"Ah, finally. I've discovered the chink in your armor."

Skidding into the private airfield parking lot, JJ parked beside the men, eyeing his maneuver.

Juan, an older version of JJ with strands of white sparkling in his mane, checked his watch. "Three minutes to spare. I was unsure if this car was the best idea, but it does help you stay on time. Gordon, what sort of car did you get, Mike?"

"A practical pick-up truck. After all, we are Texans, my friend." The older man adjusted his Stetson, tilting it back, revealing close-cropped, graying blonde hair."

Juan gestured toward the two planes with a man standing by each. "Complete your check rides, then we can go eat. I'm famished. I should have the other test results by then, too."

Gordon grinned, wiggling the fingers of his right hand for emphasis. "Get it done, boys. You've spent a year of hard *study and practice. I know you will both pass at the top of the class."*

The memory receded. JJ felt lucky to have maintained a relationship with his best friend. He worried about how the possible breakup would impact Mike's productivity. "Heck, you don't drink often, never gamble, or do drugs, and you routinely work out. Why don't I ask Jo to talk to Ashley to see if she can find some way for you two to patch things up? She has a knack for helping folks and being empathetic."

Mike pursed his lips and nodded. "That would be great. I love Ashley, but I'm clueless on the romance side. I wish I were as good with Ashley as you are with Jo. You both seem to have a secret wordless language." He glanced at his watch. "Enough on me for now. Let's get back to the new work order I sent you to leverage the parameters I want included in the radar-masking capabilities of the F-35. We incorporated its viability with your former contract. I need this change to call it complete. It's critical to the pilots' lives."

JJ opened the new assignment and quickly scanned it. "I see where you're going, and it makes sense. Please send the analytics to date to our shared Dropbox. I can begin work on it after I sign the contract and receive confirmation. Your projects go to the top of the queue every time. Is there anything else?"

Faced with the image on the screen, JJ saw the seriousness reflected in his friend's expression.

"Actually, yes, but I can't prove it yet." He frowned. "It'll have to wait because I have another meeting. Do you have time in the morning for another call?"

"Certainly. Pick your time and send me a bridge. Looking forward to it."

CHAPTER 3 – I WANT TO STAY AND PLAY

Mike was about to launch his conference call with JJ when he spotted his IT technician, Kamal, leaning into his office. Appreciating the man's ability to move like a cat with his wiry build, he said, "You're practicing your ninja moves today. What's up?"

"Hey, Mike. I've had to shut down your network access. Your email account appears hacked. Our policy states we must disable your login ID until a review is completed. The secure Dropbox was also disabled. Someone or something has you in their sights. Our alpha-numeric phrased user IDs are not keeping you cloaked. Whatever you're working on, someone wants to see. Sorry, man. We're running forensics on the accounts to verify nothing was taken."

Tired and frustrated, Mike wiped his face with his hands. "Without a valid login, Kamal, I can't use our corporate communications system to join a conference bridge I created. What am I supposed to do?"

Kamal grinned, his white teeth shining through, as his expresso-colored eyes tried to convey empathy. "Call the attendees from your cell phone and instruct them to stand down until you send a new meeting request. Don't forget you may not use your mobile device to hold or join a conference call about defense contractor business, because it's not secure."

"Yeah, I know. I follow the rules so I don't have to wear an orange jumpsuit in a maximum-security prison. How long before I get a new user ID and password?"

"Mike, forensics will need to clear the old stuff before issuing you a new credential. Right now, you're off the clock."

"Kamal, did I tell you that I don't like this? I've got deadlines to meet. Will my corporate PC be impounded too?"

Hanging his head, his long ponytail cascading over his right shoulder, Kamal quietly offered, "I've already locked it down with a remote kill program. At this point, it's nothing more than a square paperweight with no USB port."

Mike sarcastically stated, "That's right. Guilty until proven innocent. I might as well go home since this place is depressing to be in with nothing to do. Mind if I take my PC with me so when everyone gets over their cranial-rectal inversion problem under control, I can get back to work without coming to the office?"

"Mike, I don't make the rules here. I also don't see anything wrong with you taking a dead PC home in anticipation of them reenabling your work account." He turned away from the doorway, then slapped his head with his hand. Looking over his shoulder, he said, "I almost forgot. Your hyper-charged mocha coffee latte infused with dandelion extract is at the front desk in the reception area."

"Humph." Mike picked up personal items and his corporate laptop, stuffing them into his briefcase. "At least there's one thing going right. You do someone a good turn, and it's paid back tenfold. Thanks. I'll get it on the way out."

0101010101100101

Mike's call went to voicemail, which deepened his frustration. "JJ, this is Mike. My circumstances changed.

We won't be having that call I asked for. Don't bother to call me back. I've been excommunicated from work for an unknown period. According to the security team, it will take some time to resume. Ciao for now."

A few minutes later, Mike's phone chirped with a text message from JJ:

Cool. A timely vacation. Take Ashley away for a few days to patch things up. Fly to Magnolia Bluff and spend a few days with us. The girls will have fun.

Mike flinched. JJ meant well. He returned a text.

Great idea. I'll see if I can talk her into it. We had a big bruhaha last night.

Mike laughed as he read the response.

Bring your laptop. We'll talk through some ideas rattling around in my head.

ACKNOWLEDGEMENTS

Thank you, Dave Murray, for your suggestions and editorial help. Your willingness to get on the phone practically anytime with me several times a year during the writing of this book (all of my books and writing projects, actually) helped me shape a pile of poo into something worth reading. You've made me a better writer more times than you'll ever know.

I'd also like to acknowledge three amazing people I get to share ideas and suggestions with in a monthly critique group. Thank you to my fellow Underground Authors: CW Hawes, Linda Pirtle, and April Nunn Coker. All three are terrific writers in their own right, and their ability to see the things I am blind to on my manuscript has helped make this a better book.

And last, but certainly not least, a big thank you to Jim McClenthan. Jim has been a good friend of mine for many years, and he'd be the first to tell you he's not an avid reader. And even though he will probably never be one of my beta readers, he is one of my biggest supporters. He has a copy of all my books (but will never read them... lol) and proudly tells everyone he knows, and anyone else who is in earshot, that I am an author who they need to be reading, and for that, I am forever grateful.

ABOUT THE AUTHOR

Joe Congel grew up in Central New York. After thirty-five years of braving long winters enhanced by lake effect snow, and ridiculously brief summers, he made his way below the Mason-Dixon Line to beautiful Charlotte, NC.

He spent twenty-five plus years helping to raise two wonderful kids into adulthood and now spends his time enjoying his grandson, two granddaughters, baseball, playing guitar, reading, and, of course, writing stories he hopes people will want to read.

If you enjoyed **Blood is Thicker than Money**, the author asks that you please take a moment to leave a review.

You can reach Joe at **jc.razzman@gmail.com**

Follow Joe on:
Instagram: Joe Congel (@joecongelauthor) | Instagram
Twitter: Joe Congel (@JoeCongelAuthor) / Twitter
FaceBook: Joe Congel Author | Facebook

Visit Joe's
Amazon Page: Amazon.com: Joe Congel: Books, Biography, Blog, Audiobooks, Kindle
Webpage: Books by Joe Congel – Indie Book Source
Blog: Joe Congel Fiction Stories

BOOKS BY JOE CONGEL

The Razzman Mystery Crime Files

- Dead is Forever: A Tony Razzolito PI Story – Book 1
- Deadly Passion: A Tony Razzolito PI Story – Book 2
- Dirty Air: A Tony Razzolito PI Story – Book 3
- Best Served Cold: A Tony Razzolito PI Story – Book 4

Short Stories

- The Razzman Chronicles: A Trio of Tony Razzolito PI Short Stories
- Leftovers: *A mix of six unrelated short stories*

Magnolia Bluff Crime Chronicles

- Second Chances – Book 17
- Catch a Tiger by the Toe – Book 26
- Blood is Thicker than Money – Book 38

Made in the USA
Middletown, DE
01 August 2025